ABRAHAM C_____ most influential Jewish Americans of the twentieth century. Born in Lithuania, he and his family fled from Tsarist pogroms and starvation, arriving in New York City in 1881—only to face poverty in the notorious tenements and sweatshops of the Lower East Side. His experiences working in a cigar factory led him to join a growing circle of Jewish union organizers and socialist workers and their families. Cahan cofounded *The Jewish Daily Forward,* a Yiddish-language newspaper that became the primary political, cultural, and educational influence on Jews in America. He was its editor and hugely popular advice columnist for over fifty years. In addition to short stories, novellas, and reams of journalism, Cahan is the author of a classical novel of immigration and assimilation, *The Rise of David Levinsky* (1917).

GORDON HUTNER is Associate Professor of English at the University of Wisconsin and editor of the journal *American Literary History*.

The Imported Bridegroom

and Other Stories of the New York Ghetto

Abraham Cahan

Introduction by Gordon Hutner

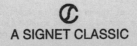

A SIGNET CLASSIC

SIGNET CLASSIC
Published by the Penguin Group
Penguin Books USA Inc., 375 Hudson Street,
New York, New York 10014, U.S.A.
Penguin Books Ltd, 27 Wrights Lane,
London W8 5TZ, England
Penguin Books Australia Ltd, Ringwood,
Victoria, Australia
Penguin Books Canada Ltd, 10 Alcorn Avenue,
Toronto, Ontario, Canada M4V 3B2
Penguin Books (N.Z.) Ltd, 182–190 Wairau Road,
Auckland 10, New Zealand

Penguin Books Ltd, Registered Offices:
Harmondsworth, Middlesex, England

Published by Signet Classic, an imprint of Dutton Signet,
a division of Penguin Books USA Inc.

First Signet Classic Printing, March, 1996
10 9 8 7 6 5 4 3 2 1

Introduction copyright © Gordon Hutner, 1996
All rights reserved

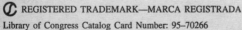 REGISTERED TRADEMARK—MARCA REGISTRADA

Library of Congress Catalog Card Number: 95–70266

Printed in the United States of America

Contents

Introduction

Abraham Cahan's short fiction has long been overshadowed by his masterpiece, the novel *The Rise of David Levinsky* (1917). Published during the last few years of the nineteenth century, the stories in this volume—"The Imported Bridegroom," "Providential Match," "A Sweatshop Romance," "Circumstances," "A Ghetto Wedding," and *Yekl*—help us to recover the time when American society was about to become modern. For Cahan, that time was experienced through the lives of Jewish immigrants. His short stories record the social and spiritual anxieties of a million new Americans, most of whom escaped state-sponsored anti-Semitism in Russia and Eastern Europe by fleeing to the U.S., where they again found social prejudice, but where they also met disorienting possibilities of assimilation. Like *David Levinsky*, which concerns the material rise and spiritual decline of an immigrant Jewish clothing manufacturer, Cahan's stories were written, in part, to explain the clash between the potential for alienation and success in the meeting of the two cultures. They suggest that the conflict between the Old World and the New was enacted as a struggle to balance the freedom of individualism with the social as well as religious requirements of Jewish life. This radical synthesizing of the immigrant and host culture experience would eventually be understood as the quintessential American tale.

Yekl, A Tale of the New York Ghetto (1896) and *The Imported Bridegroom and Other Stories of the New York Ghetto* (1898) mark his emergence as a fiction writer, but for much of the twentieth century, he was better known as the politically committed editor and cultural commentator whose vision of America had helped to make the transition from greenhorn to Yankee more manageable for a generation of Jewish immigrants. "It is hard to be a Jew in America," one of Levinsky's friends in Russia prophesies; Cahan's writings were largely devoted to describing why this was so, and what it meant to surrender one way of identifying oneself and the society to which one belonged for the reward of becoming a "Yankee." Cahan began writing some six months after he arrived in the U.S., to protest a renewal of the Russian state policy of Jewish persecution. In 1882, he worked as a free-lance journalist for socialist newspapers and some of the less prestigious mainstream papers too, publishing sketches and news stories. He rose to the editorship of *Arbeiter Zeitung,* a socialist paper, but he would eventually make his name during his fifty-year tenure as editor-in-chief of the *Jewish Daily Forward,* which he had earlier helped to establish.

As the editor of the Yiddish-language *Jewish Daily Forward,* he helped to establish a readership of a quarter-million subscribers and thus came into close contact with the Jewish working class. Cahan's point of view was central to this generation's shared cultural biography. He shaped their opinions daily: in the editorials and sketches he published, in the letters to the editor he chose to reply to, and in the social and political criticism he endorsed and circulated. His constant focus was interpreting the imperatives and nuances of American life for new, would-be Americans. He tried to help them make their way through the maze of strange manners and customs; but he never forgot that while this new world might offer financial reward to a few, at its worst, America would despise their religion and hate their racial difference.

Perhaps the broadest question these immigrants faced concerned the extent to which they could pursue happiness and still maintain their collective identities as Jews. How could they reconcile their embracing of the individualism they found in America—an orthodoxy underlying their hopes for economic advancement—with their religious principles and communal loyalties? That issue manifested itself in several ways, and particularly in exploring how intimate life in America might be conducted. Indeed, Cahan's first story, a tale of love and marriage called "A Providential Match" (1895), makes the question of the relation between love and money central, but it also establishes how this concern characterizes immigrant experience. In doing so, Cahan evokes the tone that would later resonate throughout his magnum opus.

Written ten years after he himself settled in the U.S., "A Providential Match" tells of an immigrant who, upon returning to his native village, arranges to marry the daughter of his old boss. In former days, the poor, unprepossessing Rouvke could never have hoped to wed the lovely Hanele; but now, her father (having suffered financial reverses) insists that Hanele accept Rouvke's offer. The story unfolds according to a familiar pattern in which the young man hopes that his new wealth will be given meaning by his attaining the object of his desire, and also recalls his early, humiliating sense of deprivation. Seeking revenge against the past, the young man wants to rewrite his history and authenticate his new identity, a self that America has enabled him to create. In this way, the tale belongs to the genre of American success literature that recounts how important people got where they were, a tradition that goes back at least as far as Benjamin Franklin. Yet Cahan resists sentimental or formulaic conventions in this tradition. At the story's end, Hanele disturbs Rouvke's plans by having met a "collegian" (named Levinsky) en route, a shipboard romance that she sees as her own "providential match." When the lovers arrive in New York, Rouvke's hopes are devastated, and his new self disintegrates.

There is an especially powerful cultural meaning in the ending of Cahan's tale, for the last words belong not to Rouvke or Hanele or even the "collegian." They are uttered by a runner for an "immigrant hotel" who meets new arrivals: "Git out, or I'll punch your pock-marked nose, ye monkey," he taunts Rouvke, and the young man's dream crashes, while even the "young peddlers bandied whispered jokes." America, land of aspirations and fantasies, is also the country of cruel disappointments. Rouvke demands that his money be returned, but ultimately his dignity cannot be retrieved. Business triumphs in America may help to prop up his identity, but they cannot secure the self-validation he wants so desperately. His money cannot provide him with the means to connect his present to his past, either by rewriting his youth or by giving Old World substance to his New World self. (It will remain for Anzia Yezierska, writing a few years later, to explore how gender shapes ideals of intimacy in immigrant culture.)

As in his journalism, Cahan had truly found his subject for fiction—the moral history of the Russian and Eastern European Jews as they made their way in the U.S., especially the lower East Side slums into which so many of them were crammed. Their saga is now so familiar that it seems part of our general cultural heritage, one of the happiest chapters in the nation's history: A million Jews, most of them impoverished, committed to a vision of justice and a fair chance at prosperity, changed the shape of modern America. They did so through their support for organized labor, their demand for business opportunity, their defense of the rights of the downtrodden, their conviction of social mobility through education, and their talent for creating popular entertainment. Cahan's short stories, like his novel, give us a glimpse into the life of feelings and desires underlying that larger history, but unlike the *Rise of David Levinsky,* Cahan's perspective in the stories is infused with the immigrants' conviction of possibility.

On reading Cahan's stories, William Dean Howells, the great realist author and critic, wrote encouragingly to the author and urged him to continue his efforts. Howells had sought out Cahan a few years earlier when the eminent writer approached the editor of *Arbeiter Zeitung* during Howells's research into union politics for *A Traveler from Altruria* (1894), a fictive study of contemporary social and economic problems. The meeting had been important to Cahan, who deeply admired Howells's writings. Howells convinced the Russian to develop a more ambitious tale of the challenges facing Jewish immigrants, a novella that Cahan called *Yekl, A Tale of the New York Ghetto* (1896). It was made into a film, *Hester Street,* in 1974.

Howells urged Cahan to give up the Jewish quarter as his milieu, convinced that if he wrote only "ethnic" fiction, he would never be taken as seriously as he deserved. Still, Howells's patronage proved instrumental in getting Cahan launched, as it had for Stephen Crane and Hamlin Garland, among many others. He promoted Cahan as a Russian realist who might bring a cosmopolitan influence to American writing, following the model of the expatriate Turgenev in Paris. Cahan shared Howells's favor with another journalist-turned-fiction writer: Crane, whose works, like *Maggie: A Girl of the Streets* (1893) and "George's Mother" (1896), also gave scale and density to the New York slums, especially those of the Irish immigrants. Howells reviewed them together as new writers who boldly rendered New York's grim aspect without falling into the sensationalism that characterized so much urban fiction. Not only were they part of this new generation of city writers, but they were also regionalists, who as surely as Mary Wilkins Freeman or Sarah Orne Jewett for New England, Edward Eggleston for Indiana, George Washington Cable or Kate Chopin for Louisiana, or Garland for the rural Midwest, were able to render the folkways and defining milieu of specific places, a popular variant of literary realism in the last quarter of the nineteenth century.

When Cahan tried to sell his new novella, *Yekl,* he

was dismayed to find that publishers were less sanguine about the market for stories of Jewish peasants. No contract was forthcoming until, finally, Howells exerted his influence with his own publishers and the book was brought out in 1896. The reviews were generally positive, although one hundred years later they do not seem very enlightened about the author's minority status. They make no effort to see Cahan as anything other than a Jew, and certainly not an American writer. If some critics in Cahan's day did appreciate that he was virtually inventing a new subject—the tensions and rewards of immigrant experience—they stopped short of the kind of admiration necessary to herald his emergence as a major new literary figure. As much as a few reviewers prized the grittiness of Cahan's story of a young man who has assimilated so much that he wants to renege on his promise to bring over his Old World wife, *Yekl* lacked broad appeal and, as the publishers expected, sold poorly.

What did American readers buy in 1896? Perhaps the biggest of the bestsellers was a historical romance of Rome under Nero and the early Christians, *Quo Vadis* by Henryk Sienkiewicz, a Polish author. Surprisingly, Harold Frederic's tale of an alienated minister, *The Damnation of Theron Ware,* was a critical as well as commercial success. While the erotic intensity in Frederic's book— mild as we might find it now—helped to stoke sales, we should also remember that pervading the 1890s was a vigorous controversy over the place of Christianity in American life: These debates comprised the culture wars, the divisions in the country that led to the ascendancy of William Jennings Bryan, the evangelical populist who won the Democratic nomination for president in the same year that saw Billy Sunday—the baseball player-turned-preacher—convert to evangelism and begin a ministry that helped make him one of the best-known Americans of his time. Also in 1896, Charles Sheldon was gathering his sermons for publication in the following year of one of the most widely purchased books in American history, *In His Steps,* a guide for perplexed

Christians in which Jesus provides the model for solving modern moral dilemmas.

Cahan had formed hopes that his "tale of the New York Ghetto" might reach a larger audience than the immigrants whose struggles the novella chronicles. Before he accepted Howells's suggestion to call it *Yekl,* he preferred Yankel the Yankee, hoping that this title would capture the interest of readers who had made such successes out of works like Jacob Riis's *How the Other Half Lives* (1890) and later, *The Spirit of the Ghetto* (1902) by Hutchins Hapgood (a friend and colleague from the *Advertiser* whom Cahan led through the lower East Side). As much as *Yekl* Jake enjoys a connection to the kind of urban travel literature that uncovers New York City's dimmest corners, the story's originality derives from the moral drift that Yekl/Jake experiences. Dreams of personal freedom are seen to distort human values, so that the basis for love and commitment is disturbed, even overturned. Yekl does not find happiness in divorcing Gitl and in relinquishing his son, Yossele, nor does he find it, we are led to anticipate, with his new wife, the more thoroughly Americanized Mamie, who provides him with the means to finance his divorce. In the U.S., Jake has forsaken Old World modesty, especially in his enthusiasm for dancing academies, where he assiduously applies himself to an ideal of assimilation. Out of his desire to erase his immigrant past and see himself as a Yankee, he comes to despise his wife, who looks so out of place in the New World with her old-fashioned clothes and manners. Jake imagines that he is completing what Levinsky calls a "magical transformation," wherein he loses the shameful, incriminating signs of racial identity. Or so he hopes that his conversation, aping current slang and filled with allusions to baseball, will attest.

The surprising turn that Cahan provides is neither to vilify nor to trivialize Yekl. We see him living out the contradictory logic of his illusions, compelled by a fantasy of social success that only brings defeat and fear. He even knows that his repudiation of being a good Jew in favor of the glitzy Americanized ideal he finds in

Mamie will not sustain him. At the close, "painfully reluctant" to part with his dearly bought freedom, Yekl
wonders whether he should return to Gitl even while he
speeds along to City Hall to marry Mamie. Then, Cahan
complicates the story yet again. Gitl finds happiness in
marrying Bernstein, the lodger and former rabbinical
student, with whom she opens a grocery store. Yekl, on
the other hand, entangles himself anew, and in a way
that predicts more suffocation to come.

A small mainstream market did exist for Cahan's stories, and he had several more tales solicited or accepted
by magazines like the *Atlantic* and *Cosmopolitan*. Two
years after *Yekl,* he published *The Imported Bridegroom
and Other Stories of the New York Ghetto* (1898), in
which he collected—along with "A Providential
Match"—several affecting stories of love and marriage,
which summarize the social tensions that intimacy and
courtship multiply in the process of assimilation. In
"The Ghetto Wedding," when bad times reduce Nathan's fortunes as a peddler and discourage his fonder
hopes for a "basis" on which to marry his beloved
Goldy, she devises a plan by which they expend their
dwindling capital on a "respectable wedding," one that
is sumptuous enough, relatively speaking, to encourage
their friends and associates to offer substantial gifts. But
the bad times apply to everyone, and so many guests
beg off that the "grand wedding" they expected to yield
a bounty turns out to be a "miserable failure." So disconsolate is Nathan that when anti-Semitic street toughs
taunt his new wife on the couple's lonely walk home,
Goldy must restrain him from a "desperate attack"
against these antagonists. For Goldy, such annoyances
have become trifles, left as she is with only poverty and
a sense of love that surpasses the travails that immigrants face.

In "A Sweatshop Romance," Cahan similarly discov-
ers love to be emboldening, even sustaining, in a world
that so little accommodates the needs and desires of the
peasant class of immigrants. Here the brutally exploitive
working conditions of the sweatshop and the bosses' casual disregard of workers' humanity are made to stand

for a host culture which welcomes and despises Jews as cheap labor. The scene is a small shop in the lower East Side, presided over by a "cock-roach," a contract tailor for a large Broadway firm, who supervises a desperate team of "hands" who are paid by the piece. Even in such dehumanizing conditions, love may be said to flourish; at least until the one female worker, Beile, is insulted and dismissed by the boss's wife, who is showing off the power she imagines her wealth to confer. It is not Beile's presumptive fiancé, but another youth who tries to preserve her dignity by challenging the wife's impulse to degrade Beile. Not surprisingly, the bold youth replaces the timid suitor in Beile's affections.

Why do Cahan's tales of immigrant experience concentrate on the general question of marriage and its mixed promise of a happy life? Little is known about Cahan's domestic arrangements, but there is evidence to suggest that his own personal life does not support any vision of marriage as particularly tranquil or redeeming. It may be, of course, that he tried to create in his fiction a sense of conjugality that his own reality did not afford. Later, in *The Rise of David Levinsky,* such compensatory views of marriage are developed as the tragic snare of self-aggrandizement that Cahan associated with American individualism. Levinsky cannot find an appropriate object of his affections even as he grows richer, for the more he makes, the more he imagines that his self-worth and his bankroll are the same. He yearns for something in the New World to take the place of the spiritual intensity he has sacrificed in dedicating himself to making money. Love seems to him to give luster to his riches, purpose to his soullessness. "... dreams of family life became my religion," he says. Levinsky invents the consolations of intimacy as a way of restoring the heart to Jewish identity, which he has relinquished as the cost of assimilation, the price of identifying too much with America.

Among the poorer immigrants, the idealizing of love also signals a sense of well-being and freedom that seem so improbable under the Czarist suppression that drove so many, including Cahan, to the U.S. during the quarter century between 1880 and 1905. Now, in America, the chance to follow out the logic of love seems available to any and all. A father may want to insist on his daughter marrying a rabbinical student, as Asriel Stroon wants Flora to do, but the lesson of "The Imported Bridegroom" is that while love may survive the Old World style of matchmaking, the U.S. offers the chance to choose freely. Shaya, the prodigy of Jewish learning whom Stroon brings to America, demonstrates this when he gives up his Talmud study in favor of the pleasure of free-thinking, a tendency that soon surpasses his interest in Flora. So disgusted is Stroon by this repudiation of his values that he takes his new wife to live in Palestine, where they might escape the corruptions of Old World Jewish values that life in the U.S. occasions.

While the stature of *The Rise of David Levinsky* ensures that Americans will always read Abraham Cahan, the novel's magnitude also has the result of returning readers to his short fiction. When we read these stories, we find ourselves reminded, a hundred years later, of something nearly forgotten about the America to which many new citizens came: the identity-forging challenges of immigrants becoming Americans. Thus these stories of intimate lives are not exclusively concerned with transplanted Russian Jews. To think so misunderstands a crucial chapter in our national history. Not only do these tales illuminate something eternal in the lives and loves of immigrants, but they also tell the story of how twentieth-century America came into being.

—Gordon Hutner
Madison, Wisconsin, 1995

I

The Imported Bridegroom

*and Other Stories of the
New York Ghetto*

1898

The Imported Bridegroom

I

Flora was alone in the back parlor, which she had appropriated for a sort of boudoir. She sat in her rocker, in front of the parlor stove, absorbed in *Little Dorrit*. Her well-groomed girlish form was enveloped in a kindly warmth whose tender embrace tinged her interest in the narrative with a triumphant consciousness of the snowstorm outside.

Little by little the rigid afternoon light began to fade into a melancholy gray. Dusk was creeping into the room in almost visible waves. Flora let the book rest on her lap and fixed her gaze on the twinkling scarlet of the stove-glass. The thickening twilight, the warmth of the apartment, and the atmosphere of the novel blended together, and for some moments Flora felt far away from herself.

She was the only girl of her circle who would read Dickens, Scott, or Thackeray in addition to the *Family Story Paper* and the *Fireside Companion,* which were the exclusive literary purveyors to her former classmates at the Chrystie Street Grammar School. There were a piano and a neat little library in her room.

She was rather tall and well formed. Her oblong ivory face, accentuated by a mass of unruly hair of a lusterless black, was never deserted by a faint glimmer of a smile, at once pensive and arch. When she broke into one of her hearty, good-natured laughs, her deep,

dark, appealing eyes would seem filled with grief. Her
nose, a trifle too precipitous, gave an unexpected tone
to the extreme picturesqueness of the whole effect,
and, when she walked, partook of the dignity of her
gait.

A month or two before we make Flora's acquaintance she had celebrated her twentieth birthday, having
been born in this little private house on Mott Street,
which was her father's property.

A matchmaker had recently called, and he had
launched into a eulogy of a young Jewish physician;
but old Stroon had cut him short, in his blunt way: his
only child was to marry a God-fearing business man,
and no fellow deep in Gentile lore and shaving his
beard need apply. As to Flora, she was burning to be a
doctor's wife. A rising young merchant, a few years in
the country, was the staple matrimonial commodity in
her set. Most of her married girl friends, American-
born themselves, like Flora, had husbands of this
class—queer fellows, whose broken English had kept
their own sweethearts chuckling. Flora hated the notion of marrying as the other Mott or Bayard Street
girls did. She was accustomed to use her surroundings
for a background, throwing her own personality into
high relief. But apart from this, she craved a more refined atmosphere than her own, and the vague ideal
she had was an educated American gentleman, like
those who lived uptown.

Accordingly, when the word "doctor" had left the
matchmaker's lips, she seized upon it as a great discovery. In those days—the early eighties—a match of
this kind was an uncommon occurrence in the New
York Ghetto.

Flora pictured a clean-shaven, high-hatted, specta-
cled gentleman jumping out of a buggy, and the image
became a fixture in her mind. "I won't marry anybody
except a doctor," she would declare, with conscious
avoidance of bad grammar, as it behooved a doctor's
wife.

But what was to be done with father's opposition?
Asriel Stroon had never been the man to yield, and

now that he grew more devout every day, her case seemed hopeless. But then Flora was her father's daughter, and when she took a resolve she could not imagine herself otherwise than carrying it out, sooner or later.

Flora's thoughts were flowing in this direction when her father's gruff voice made itself heard from the dining room below. It was the anniversary of his father's death. In former years he would have contented himself with obit services, at the synagogue; this time, however, he had passed the day in fasting and chanting psalms at home, in addition to lighting his own candle in front of the cantor's desk and reciting *Kaddish* for the departed soul, at the house of prayer. It touched Flora's heart to think of him fasting and praying all day, and, with her book in her hand, she ran down to meet him.

"Just comin' from the synagogue, papa?" she greeted him affectionately, in English. "This settles your fast, don't it?"

"It is not so easy to settle with Him, my daughter," he returned, in Yiddish, pointing to the ceiling. "You can never be through serving the Uppermost. Hurry up, Tamara!" he added, in the direction of the adjoining kitchen.

"You ain' goin' to say more Thilim* tonight, are you, pa?"

"Why, does it cost you too much?" he snarled good humoredly.

"Yes it does—your health. I won't let you sing again. You are weak and you got enough."

"Hush! It is not potato soup; you can never have enough of it." He fell to tugging nervously at his white beard, which grew in a pair of tiny imperials. "Tamara! It's time to break the fast, isn't it?"

"You can wash your hands. Supper is ready," came the housekeeper's pleasant voice.

He took off his brown derby, and covered his steel-gray hair with a velvet skullcap; and as he carried his

*Psalms.

robust, middle-sized body into the kitchen, to perform his ablutions, his ruddy, gnarled face took on an air of piety.

When supper was over and Asriel and Tamara were about to say grace, Flora resumed the reading of her novel.

"Off with that lump of Gentile nastiness while holy words are being said!" the old man growled.

Flora obeyed, in amazement. Only a few months before she had seldom seen him intone grace at all. She was getting used to his new habits, but such rigor as he now displayed was unintelligible to her, and she thought it unbearable.

"You can read your book a little after. The wisdom of it will not run away," chimed in Tamara, with good-natured irony. She was a poor widow of forty. Asriel had engaged her for her piety and for the rabbinical learning of her late husband, as much as for her culinary fame in the Ghetto.

Asriel intoned grace in indistinct droning accents. By degrees, however, as he warmed up to the Hebrew prayer, whose words were a conglomeration of incomprehensible sounds to him, he fell to swaying to and fro, and his voice broke into an exalted, heart-rending singsong, Tamara accompanying him in whispers, and dolefully nodding her bewigged head all the while.

Flora was moved. The scene was novel to her, and she looked on with the sympathetic reverence of a Christian visiting a Jewish synagogue on the Day of Atonement.

At last the fervent tones died away in a solemn murmur. Silence fell over the cozy little room. Asriel sat tugging at his scanty beard as if in an effort to draw it into a more venerable growth.

"Flora!" he presently growled. "I am going to Europe."

When Asriel Stroon thought he spoke, and when he spoke he acted.

"Goin' to Europe! Are you crazy, papa? What are you talkin' about?"

"Just what you hear. After Passover I am going to Europe. I must take a look at Pravly."

"But you ain't been there over thirty-five years. You don't remember not'in' at all."

"I don't remember Pravly? Better than Mott Street; better than my nose. I was born there, my daughter," he added, as he drew closer to her and began to stroke her glossless black hair. This he did so seldom that the girl felt her heart swelling in her throat. She was yearning after him in advance.

Tamara stared in beaming amazement at the grandeur of the enterprise. "Are you really going?" she queried, with a touch of envy.

"What will you do there?—It's so far away!" Flora resumed, for want of a weightier argument at hand.

"Never mind, my child; I won't have to walk all the way."

"But the Russian police will arrest you for stayin' away so long. Didn't you say they would?"

"The kernel of a hollow nut!" he replied, extemporizing an equivalent of "fiddlesticks!" Flora was used to his metaphors, although they were at times rather vague, and set one wondering how they came into his head at all. "The kernel of a hollow nut! Show a *treif** gendarme a *kosher*† coin, and he will be shivering with ague. Long live the American dollar!"

She gave him a prolonged, far-away look, and said, peremptorily: "Mister, you ain' goin' nowheres."

"Tamara, hand me my Psalter, will you?" the old man grumbled.

When the girl was gone, the housekeeper inquired: "And Flora—will you take her along?"

"What for? That she might make fun of our ways there, or that the pious people should point their fingers at her and call her Gentile girl, hey? She will stay with you and collect rent. I did not have her in Pravly, and I want to be there as I used to. I feel like taking a peep at the graves of my folks. It is pulling me by the

---

*Food not prepared according to the laws of Moses; impure.
†The opposite of *treif*.

heart, Tamara," he added, in a grave undertone, as he fell to turning over the leaves of his Psalter.

II

When Asriel Stroon had retired from business, he suddenly grew fearful of death. Previously he had had no time for that. What with his flour store, two bakeries, and some real estate, he had been too busy to live, much less to think of death. He had never been seen at the synagogue on weekdays; and on the Sabbath, when, enveloped in his praying-shawl, he occupied a seat at the East Wall, he would pass the time drowsing serenely and nodding unconscious approval of the cantor's florid improvisations, or struggling to keep flour out of his mind, where it clung as pertinaciously as it did to his long Sabbath coat.

The first sermon that failed to lull him to sleep was delivered by a newly landed preacher, just after Asriel had found it more profitable to convert his entire property into real estate. The newcomer dwelt, among other things, upon the fate of the wicked after death and upon their forfeited share in the World to Come. As Asriel listened to the fiery exhortation it suddenly burst upon him that he was very old and very wicked. "I am as full of sins as a watermelon is of seeds," he said to himself, on coming out of the synagogue. "You may receive notice to move at any time, Asriel. And where is your baggage? Got anything to take along to the other world, as the preacher said, hey?"

Alas! he had been so taken up with earthly title deeds that he had given but little thought to such deeds as would entitle him to a "share in the World-to-Come"; and while his valuable papers lay secure between the fireproof walls of his iron safe, his soul was left utterly exposed to the flames of Sheol.

Then it was that he grew a pair of bushy sidelocks, ceased trimming his twin goatees, and, with his heart divided between yearning after the business he had sold and worrying over his sins, spent a considerable part of his unlimited leisure reading psalms.

What a delight it was to wind off chapter after chapter! And how smoothly it now came off, in his father's (peace upon him!) singsong, of which he had not even thought for more than thirty years, but which suddenly came pouring out of his throat, together with the first verse he chanted! Not that Asriel Stroon could have told you the meaning of what he was so zestfully intoning, for in his boyhood he had scarcely gone through the Pentateuch when he was set to work by his father's side, at flax heckling. But then the very sounds of the words and the hereditary intonation, added to the consciousness that it was psalms he was reciting, "made every line melt like sugar in his mouth," as he once described it to the devout housekeeper.

He grew more pious and exalted every day, and by degrees fell prey to a feeling to which he had been a stranger for more than three decades.

Asriel Stroon grew homesick.

It was thirty-five years since he had left his birthplace; thirty years or more since, in the whirl of his American successes, he had lost all interest in it. Yet now, in the fifty-eighth year of his life, he suddenly began to yearn and pine for it.

Was it the fervor of his religious awakening which resoldered the long-broken link? At all events, numerous as were the examples of piety within the range of his American acquaintance, his notion of genuine Judaism was somehow inseparably associated with Pravly. During all the years of his life in New York he had retained a vague but deep-rooted feeling that American piety was as tasteless an article as American cucumbers and American fish—the only things in which his ecstasy over the adopted country admitted its hopeless inferiority to his native town.

III

On a serene afternoon in May, Asriel drove up to Pravly in a peasant's wagon. He sat listlessly gazing at the unbroken line of wattle-fences and running an

imaginary stick along the endless zigzag of their tops.
The activity of his senses seemed suspended.

Presently a whiff of May aroma awakened his eye to
a many-colored waving expanse, and his ear to the lan-
guorous whisper of birds. He recognized the plushy
clover knobs in the vast array of placid magnificence,
and the dandelions and the golden buttercups, although
his poor mother tongue could not afford a special name
for each flower, and he now addressed them collectively as *tzatzkes*—a word he had not used for thirty-
five years. He looked at the tzatzkes, as they were
swaying thoughtfully hither and thither, and it somehow seemed to him that it was not the birds but the
clover blossoms which did the chirping. The whole
scene appealed to his soul as a nodding, murmuring
congregation engrossed in the solemnity of worship.
He felt as though there were no such flowers in America, and that he had not seen any since he had left his
native place.

Echoes of many, many years ago called to Asriel
from amid the whispering host. His soul burst into
song. He felt like shutting his eyes and trusting himself
to the caressing breath of the air, that it might waft
him whithersoever it chose. His senses were in confu-
sion: he beheld a sea of fragrance; he inhaled heavenly
music; he listened to a symphony of hues.

"What a treat to breathe! What a paradise!" he exclaimed in his heart. "The cholera take it, how delicious! Do you deserve it, old sinner you? Ten plagues
you do! But hush! the field is praying—"

With a wistful babyish look he became absorbed in
a gigantic well-sweep suspended from the clear sky,
and then in the landscape it overhung. The woody
mass darkling in the distance was at once racing about
and standing still. Fleecy clouds crawled over a hazy
hilltop. And yonder—behold! a long, broad streak of
silver gleaming on the horizon! Is it a lake? Asriel's
eyes are riveted and memories stir in his breast. He recalls not the place itself, but he can remember his reminiscences of it. During his first years in America, at
times when he would surrender himself to the sweet

pangs of homesickness and dwell, among other things, on the view that had seen him off to the unknown land, his mind would conjure up something like the effect now before his eyes. As a dream does it comes back to him now. The very shadows of thirty-five years ago are veiled.

Asriel gazes before him in deep reverence. The sky is letting itself down with benign solemnity, its measureless trough filled with melody, the peasant's wagon creaking an accompaniment to it all—to every speck of color, as well as to every sound of the scene.

At one moment he felt as though he had strayed into the other world; at another, he was seized with doubt as to his own identity. "Who are you?" he almost asked himself, closing and reopening his hand experimentally. "Who or what is that business which you call life? Are you alive, Asriel?" Whereupon he somehow remembered Flora's photograph, and, taking it out of his bosom pocket, fell to contemplating it.

The wagon turned into a side road, and the Polish peasant, leaning forward, cursed and whipped the animal into a peevish trot. Presently something gray hove in sight. Far away, below, hazy blotches came creeping from behind the sky. The wagon rolls downhill. Asriel is in a flurry. He feels like one on the eve of a great event, he knows not exactly what.

The wagon dashes on. Asriel's heart is all of a flutter. Suddenly—O Lord of the Universe! Why, there glistens the brook—what do you call it? " 'Repka?' " he asks the driver.

"Repka!" the other replies, without facing about.

"Repka, a disease into her heart! Repka, dear, may she live long! Who could beat Asriel in swimming?" Over there, on the other side, it was where Asriel's father once chased him for bathing during Nine Days. He bumped his head against the angle of a rock, did the little scamp, and got up with a deep, streaming gash in his lower lip. The mark is still there, and Asriel delights to feel it with his finger now. As he does so the faces of some of his playmates rise before him. Pshaw! he could whip every one of them! Was he not a dare-

devil of a loafer! But how many of those fellow truants
of his will he find alive? he asks himself, and the question wrings his heart.

Asriel strains his eyes at the far distance till, behold!
smoke is spinning upward against the blue sky. He can
make out the chimney pots. His soul overflows. Sobs
choke his breath. "Say!" he begins, addressing himself
to the driver. But "say" is English. *"Sloukhai!"* he
shouts, with delight in the Polish word. He utters the
names of the surrounding places, and the dull peasant's
nods of assent thrill him to the core. He turns this way
and that, and in his paroxysm of impatience all but
leaps out of the wagon.

The rambling groups of houses define their outlines.
Asriel recognizes the Catholic church. His heart
bounds with joy. "Hush, wicked thing! It's a church
of Gentiles." But the wicked thing surreptitiously re-
sumes its greeting. And over there, whitening at some
distance from the other dwellings—what is it? "The
nobleman's palace, as sure as I am a Jew!" He had forgotten all about it, as sure as he was a Jew! But what
is the nobleman's name? Is he alive?—And there is the
mill—the same mill! "I'll swoon away!" he says to
himself audibly.

Asriel regains some composure.

Half an hour later he made his entry into his native
town. Here he had expected his agitation to pass the
bounds of his physical strength; but it did not. At this
moment he was solemnly serene.

The town had changed little, and he recognized it at
once. Every spot greeted him, and his return of the sal-
utation was a speechless devotional pathos. He found
several things which had faded out of his enshrined
picture of the place, and the sight of these moved his
soul even more powerfully than those he had looked
forward to. Only in one instance was he taken aback.
Sure enough, this is Synagogue Lane, as full of pud-
dles as ever; but what has come over him? He well remembers that little alley in the rear; and yet it runs
quite the other way. Length has turned into width.

And here is Leizer Poisner's inn. "But how rickety it

has become!" Asriel's heart exclaims with a pang, as
though at sight of a friend prematurely aged and run to
seed. He can almost smell the stable occupying the entire length of the little building, and he remembers every room—Hello! The same market place, the same
church with the bailiff's office by its side! The sparse
row of huts on the river bank, the raft bridge, the
tannery—everything was the same as he had left it;
and yet it all had an odd, mysterious, far-away air—
like things seen in a cyclorama. It was Pravly and at
the same time it was not; or, rather, it certainly was the
same dear old Pravly, but added to it was something
else, through which it now gazed at Asriel. Thirty-five
years lay wrapped about the town.

Still, Stroon feels like Asrielke Thirteen Hairs, as his
nickname had been here. Then he relapses into the
Mott Street landlord, and for a moment he is an utter
stranger in his birthplace. Why, he could buy it all up
now! He could discount all the rich men in town put
together; and yet there was a time when he was of the
meanest hereabout. An overpowering sense of triumph
surged into his breast. Hey, there! Where are your
bigbugs—Zorach Latozky, Reb Lippe, Reb Nochum?
Are they alive? Thirty-five years ago Asrielke considered it an honor to shake their palm branch on
the Feast of Tabernacles, while now—out with your
purses, you proud magnates, measure fortunes with
Asrielke the heckler, if you dare! His heart swells with
exultation. And yet—the black year take it!—it yearns
and aches, does Asriel's heart. He looks at Pravly, and
his soul is pining for Pravly—for the one of thirty-five
years ago, of which this is only a reflection—for the
one in which he was known as a crack-brained rowdy
of a mechanic, a poor devil living an oatmeal and her-
ring.

With the townspeople of his time Asriel's experience
was somewhat different from what he felt in the case
of inanimate Pravly. As he confronted them some faces
lighted up with their identity at once; and there were
even some younger people in whom he instantly recognized the transcribed images of their deceased parents.

But many a countenance was slow to catch the reflection of the past which shone out of his eyes; and in a few instances it was not until the name was revealed to Asriel that the retrospective likeness would begin to struggle through the unfamiliar features before him.

"Shmulke!" he shrieked, the moment he caught sight of an old crony, as though they had been parted for no more than a month. Shmulke is not the blooming, sprightly young fellow of yore. He has a white beard and looks somewhat decrepit. Asriel, however, feels as if the beard were only glued to the smooth face he had known. But how Asriel's heart does shrink in his bosom! The fever of activity in which he had passed the thirty-five years had kept him deaf to the departing footsteps of Time. Not until recently had he realized that the words "old man" applied to him; but even then the fact never came home to him with such convincing, with such terrible force, as it did now that he stood face to face with Shmulke. Shmulke was his mirror.

"Shmulke, Angel of Death, an inflammation into your bones!" he shouted, as he suddenly remembered his playmate's byname and fell on his shoulder.

Shmulke feels awkward. He is ashamed of the long-forgotten nickname, and is struggling to free himself from the unwelcome embrace; but Asriel is much the stronger of the two, and he continues to squeeze him and pat him, grunting and puffing for emotion as he does so.

Aunt Sarah-Rachel, whom Asriel had left an elderly but exceedingly active and clever tradeswoman, he found a bag of bones and in her dotage.

"Don't you know me, auntie?" he implored her. She made no reply, and went on munching her lips. "Can it be that you don't know Asrielke, who used to steal raisins from your grocery?"

"She does not understand anything!" Asriel whispered, in consternation.

IV

Asriel's first Sabbath in the native place he was revisiting was destined to be a memorable day in the annals of that peaceful little town.

At the synagogue, during the morning service, he was not the only object of interest. So far as the furtive glances that came through the peepholes of the women's compartment were concerned, a much younger guest, from a hamlet near by, had even greater magnetism than he. Reb* Lippe, for forty years the "finest householder" of the community, expected to marry his youngest daughter to an *Illoui* (a prodigy of Talmudic lore), and he now came to flaunt him, and the five-thousand rouble dowry he represented, before the congregation.

Only nineteen and a poor orphan, the fame of the prospective bridegroom, as a marvel of acumen and memory, reached far and wide. Few of the subtlest rabbinical minds in the district were accounted his match in debate, and he was said to have some two thousand Talmudical folios literally at his fingers' ends. This means that if you had placed the tip of your finger on some word of a volume, he could have told you the word which came under your pressure on any other page you might name. As we shall have to cultivate the young man's acquaintance, let it be added that he was quite boyish of figure, and that had it not been for an excess of smiling frankness, his pale, blue-eyed face would have formed the nearest Semitic approach to the current portraits of Lord Byron. His admirers deplored his lack of staidness. While visiting at Pravly, in a manner, as the guest of the town, he was detected giving snuff to a pig, and then participating with much younger boys in a race over the bridge.

His betrothment to Reb Lippe's daughter was still the subject of negotiation, and there were said to be serious obstacles in the way. The prodigy's relatives were pleased with Reb Lippe's pedigree and social rank, but

*Abbreviation of Rabbi, and used as the equivalent of Mister.

thought that the boy could marry into a wealthier family and get a prettier girl into the bargain. Nevertheless Reb Lippe's manner at the synagogue was as though the engagement were an accomplished fact, and he kept the young man by his side, his own seat being next the rabbi's, which was by the Holy Ark.

Asriel, as a newcomer, and out of respect for his fabulous wealth, was also accorded a seat of honor on the other side of the Ark. Before he had expatriated himself his place used to be near the door—a circumstance which was fresh in the mind of Reb Lippe, who chafed to see him divert attention from the prodigy and his purchaser. Now Reb Lippe was a proud old gentleman, too jealous of the memory of his rabbinical ancestry and of his own time-honored dignity to give way to a mere boor of a heckler, no matter how much American gold he had to atone for his antecedents. Accordingly, when his fellow trustee suggested that the American ought to be summoned to the reading of the Third Section in the week's portion of the Pentateuch—the highest honor connected with the reading of the Law, and one for which the visiting nabob was sure to pay a liberal donation—the venerable countenance turned crimson.

"Let the sections be auctioned off!" he jerked out.

The proceeding was seldom practiced on an ordinary Sabbath; but Rep Lippe's will was law, as peremptory and irresistible as the Law of Moses, with which it was now concerned. And so the worshippers presently found themselves converted into so many eyewitnesses of a battle of purses.

"Five gildens for the Third!" called out the weazen-faced little sexton from the reading platform, in the traditional singsong that became his draggling black beard so well. As a bona-fide business transaction is not allowed on the holy day, even though the house of God be the sole gainer by it, the sexton's figures were fictitious—in so far, at least, as they were understood to represent double the actual amount to be paid to the synagogue by the purchaser of the good deed.

"Six gildens for the Third!" he went on in interpretation of a frowning nod from Reb Lippe.

A contemptuous toss of Asriel's head threw another gilden on top of the sum. Two other members signaled to the auctioneer, and, warming up to his task, he sang out with gusto, "Eight gildens for the Third!"

Then came in rapid succession: "Nine gildens for the Third! Ten gildens for the Third! Eleven gildens, twelve, thirteen, fourteen gildens for the Third!"

The other bidders, one by one, dropped out of the race, and when the sum reached sixty gildens the field was left to Reb Lippe and Asriel.

The congregation was spellbound. Some with gaping mouths, others with absorbed simpers on their faces, but all with sportsman-like fire in their eyes, the worshipers craned their necks in the direction of the two contestants alternately.

The prodigy had edged away from his seat to a coign of vantage. He was repeatedly called back by winks from his uncle, but was too deeply interested in the progress of the auction to heed them.

"Seventy gildens for the Third! Seventy-one, seventy-two, three, four, five, seventy-six, seventy-seven, eight, nine, eighty gildens for the Third!"

The skirmish waxed so hot, shots flew so thick and so fast, that the perspiring sexton, and with him some of the spectators, was swiveling his head from right to left and from left to right with the swift regularity of gymnastic exercise.

It must be owned that so far as mute partisanship was concerned, Asriel had the advantage of his adversary, for even some of Reb Lippe's stanchest friends and admirers had a lurking relish for seeing it brought home to their leading citizen that there were wealthier people than he in the world.

The women, too, shared in the excitement of the morning. Their windows were glistening with eyes, and the reports of their lucky occupants to the anxious knots in the rear evoked hubbubs of conflicting interjections which came near involving the matronly assemblage in civil war.

The Third Section brought some twenty-eight rubles, net. Asriel was certain that the last bid had been made by him, and that the honor and the good deed were accordingly his. When it came to the reading, however, and the Third Section was reached, the reader called out Reb Lippe's name.

Asriel was stupefied.

"Hold on! That won't do!" he thundered, suddenly feeling himself an American citizen. "I have bought it and I mean to have it." His face was fire; his eyes looked havoc.

A wave of deprecation swept over the room. Dozens of reading desks were slapped for order. Reb Lippe strode up to the platform, pompous, devout, resplendent in the gold lace of his praying-shawl and the flowing silver of his beard, as though the outburst of indignation against Asriel were only an ovation to himself. He had the cunning of a fox, the vanity of a peacock, and the sentimentality of a woman during the Ten Days of Penance. There were many skeptics as to the fairness of the transaction, but these were too deeply impressed by the grandeur of his triumphal march to whisper an opinion. The prodigy alone spoke his mind.

"Why, I do think the other man was the last to nod—may I be ill if he was not," the *enfant terrible* said quite audibly, and was hushed by his uncle.

"Is he really going to get it?" Asriel resumed, drowning all opposition with his voice. "Milk a billy goat! You can't play that trick on me! Mine was the last bid. Twenty-eight scurvy rubles! Pshaw! I am willing to pay a hundred, two hundred, five hundred. I can buy up all Pravly, Reb Lippe, his gold lace and all, and sell him at a loss, too!" He made a dash at the reading platform, as if to take the Third Section by force, but the bedlam which his sally called forth checked him.

"Is this a market place?" cried the second trustee, with conscious indignation.

"Shut the mouth of that boor!" screamed a member, in sincere disgust.

"Put him out!" yelled another, with relish in the scene.

"If he can't behave in a holy place let him go back to his America!" exclaimed a third, merely to be in the running. But his words had the best effect: they reminded Asriel that he was a stranger and that the noise might attract the police.

At the same moment he saw the peaked face of the aged rabbi by his side. Taking him by the arm, the old man begged him not to disturb the Sabbath.

Whether the mistake was on Asriel's side or on the sexton's, or whether there was any foul play in the matter, is not known; but Asriel relented and settled down at his desk to follow the remainder of the reading in his Pentateuch, although the storm of revenge which was raging in his breast soon carried off his attention, and he lost track.

The easy success of his first exhortation brought the rabbi to Asriel's side once again.

"I knew your father—peace upon him! He was a righteous Jew," he addressed him in a voice trembling and funereal with old age. "Obey me, my son, ascend the platform, and offer the congregation a public apology. The Holy One—blessed be He—will help you."

The rabbi's appeal moved Asriel to tears, and tingling with devout humility he was presently on the platform, speaking in his blunt, gruff way.

"Do not take it hard, my rabbis! I meant no offense to any one, though there was a trick—as big as a fat bull. Still, I donate two hundred rubles, and let the cantor recite 'God full of Mercy' for the souls of my father and mother—peace upon them."

It was quite a novel way of announcing one's contribution, and the manner of his apology, too, had at once an amusing and a scandalizing effect upon the worshipers, but the sum took their breath away and silenced all hostile sentiment.

The reading over, and the scrolls restored, amid a tumultuous acclaim, to the Holy Ark, the cantor resumed his place at the Omud, chanting a hurried *Half-Kaddish*. "And say ye Amen!" he concluded abruptly, as if startled, together with his listeners, into sudden silence.

Nodding or shaking their heads, or swaying their forms to and fro, some, perhaps mechanically, others with composed reverence, still others in a convulsion of religious fervor, the two or three hundred men were joined in whispering chorus, offering the solemn prayer of *Mussaff*. Here and there a sigh made itself heard amid the monotony of speechless, gesticulating ardor; a pair of fingers snapped in an outburst of ecstasy, a sob broke from some corner, or a lugubrious murmur from the women's room. The prodigy, his eyes shut, and his countenance stern with unfeigned rapture, was violently working his lips as if to make up for the sounds of the words which they dared not utter. Asriel was shaking and tossing about. His face was distorted with the piteous, reproachful mien of a neglected child about to burst into tears, his twin imperials dancing plaintively to his whispered intonations. He knew not what his lips said, but he did know that his soul was pouring itself forth before Heaven, and that his heart might break unless he gave way to his restrained sobs.

At last the silent devotions were at an end. One after another the worshipers retreated, each three paces from his post. Only three men were still absorbed in the sanctity of the great prayer: the rabbi, for whom the cantor was respectfully waiting with the next chant, Reb Lippe, who would not "retreat" sooner than the rabbi, and Asriel, who, in his frenzy of zeal, was repeating the same benediction for the fifth time.

When Asriel issued forth from the synagogue he found Pravly completely changed. It was as if, while he was praying and battling, the little town had undergone a trivializing process. All the poetry of thirty-five years' separation had fled from it, leaving a heap of beggarly squalor. He felt as though he had never been away from the place, and were tired to death of it, and at the same time his heart was contracted with homesickness for America. The only interest the town now had for him was that of a medium to be filled with the rays of his financial triumph. "I'll show them who they are and who Asriel is," he comforted himself.

The afternoon service was preceded by a sermon. The "town preacher" took his text, as usual, from the passage in the "Five Books" which had been read in the morning. But he contrived to make it the basis of an allusion to the all-absorbing topic of gossip. Citing the Talmud and the commentaries with ostentatious profuseness, he laid particular stress on the good deed of procuring a scholar of sacred lore for one's son-in-law.

"It is a well-known saying in tractate *Psohim*." he said, "that 'one should be ready to sell his all in order to marry his daughter to a scholar.' On the other hand, 'to give your daughter in marriage to a boor is like giving her to a lion.' Again, in tractate *Berochath* we learn that 'to give shelter to a scholar bent upon sacred studies, and to sustain him from your estates, is like offering sacrifices to God'; and 'to give wine to such a student is,' according to a passage in tractate *Sota*, 'tantamount to pouring it out on an altar.' "

Glances converged on Reb Lippe and the prodigy by his side.

Proceeding with his argument, the learned preacher, by an ingenious chain of quotations and arithmetical operations upon the numerical value of letters, arrived at the inference that compliance with the above teachings was one of the necessary conditions of securing a place in the Garden of Eden.

All of which filled Asriel's heart with a new dread of the world to come and with a rankling grudge against Reb Lippe. He came away from the synagogue utterly crushed, and when he reached his inn the prodigy was the prevailing subject of his chat with the landlord.

v

In the evening of the same day, at the conclusion of the Sabbath, the auction of another good deed took place, and once more the purses of Reb Lippe and Asriel clashed in desperate combat.

This time the good deed assumed the form of a prodigy of Talmudic learning in the character of a prospective son-in-law.

The room (at the residence of one of the young man's uncles) was full of bearded Jews, tobacco smoke, and noise. There were Shaya, the prodigy himself, his two uncles, Reb Lippe, his eldest son, and two of his lieutenants, Asriel, his landlord, and a matchmaker. A live broad-shouldered samovar, its air-holes like so many glowing eyes, stood in the center of the table. Near it lay Flora's photograph, representing her in all the splendor of Grand Street millinery.

The youthful hero of the day eyed the portrait with undisguised, open-mouthed curiosity, till, looked out of countenance by the young lady's doleful, penetrating eyes, he turned from it, but went on viewing it with furtive interest.

His own formula of a bride was a hatless image. The notion, therefore, of this princess becoming his wife both awed him and staggered his sense of decorum. Then the smiling melancholy of the Semitic face upset his image of himself in his mind and set it afloat in a haze of phantasy. "I say you need not look at me like that," he seemed to say to the picture. "Pshaw! you are a Jewish girl after all, and I am not afraid of you a bit. But what makes you so sad? Can I do anything for you? Why don't you answer? Do take off that hat, will you?"

Reb Lippe's daughter did not wear a hat, but she was not to his liking, and he now became aware of it. On the other hand, the word "America" had a fascinating ring, and the picture it conjured was a blend of Talmudic and modern glory.

Reb Lippe's venerable beard was rippled with a nervous smile.

"Yes, I am only a boor!" roared Asriel, with a touch of Bounderby ostentation. "But you know it is not myself I want the boy to marry. Twenty thousand rubles, spot cash, then, and when the old boor takes himself off, Shaya will inherit ten times as much. She is my only child, and when I die—may I be choked if I take any of my houses into the grave. Worms don't eat houses, you know."

The quality of his unhackneyed phrase vexed the sedate old talmudists, and one of them remarked, as he pointed a sarcastic finger at the photograph: "Your girl looks like the daughter of some titled Gentile. Shaya is a Jewish boy."

"You don't like my girl, don't you?" Asriel darted back. "And why, pray? Is it because she is not a lump of ugliness and wears a hat? The grand rabbi of Wilna is as pious as any of you, isn't he? Well, when I was there, on my way here, I saw his daughter, and she also wore a hat and was also pretty. Twenty thousand rubles!"

By this time the prodigy was so absorbed in the proceedings that he forgot the American photograph, as well as the bearing which the auction in progress had upon himself. Leaning over the table as far as the samovar would allow, and propping up his face with both arms, he watched the scene with thrilling but absolutely disinterested relish.

After a great deal of whispering and suppressed excitement in the camp of Asriel's foe, Reb Lippe's son announced: "Ten thousand rubles and five years' board." This, added to Reb Lippe's advantages over his opponent by virtue of his birth, social station, and learning, as well as of his residing in Russia, was supposed to exceed the figure named by Asriel. In point of fact, everybody in the room knew that the old talmudist's bid was much beyond his depth; but the assemblage had no time to be surprised by his sum, for no sooner had it been uttered than Asriel yelled out, with impatient sarcasm: "Thirty thousand rubles, and lifelong board, and lodging, and bath money, and stocking darning, and cigarettes, and matches, and mustard, and soap—and what else?"

The prodigy burst into a chuckle, and was forthwith pulled down to his chair. He took a liking to the rough-and-ready straightforwardness of the American.

There was a pause. Shaya and his uncles were obviously leaning toward the "boor." Asriel was clearly the master of the situation.

At last Reb Lippe and his suite rose from their seats.

"You can keep the bargain!" he said to Asriel, with a sardonic smile.

"And be choked with it!" added his son.

"What is your hurry, Reb Lippe?" said one of the uncles, rushing to the old man's side with obsequious solicitude. "Why, the thing is not settled yet. We don't know whether—"

"*You* don't, but I do. I won't take that boy if *he* brings twenty thousand rubles to *his* marriage portion. Good-night!"

"Good-night and good-year!" Asriel returned. "Why does the cat hate the cream? Because it is locked up."

An hour afterward the remainder of the gathering were touching glasses and interchanging *mazol-tovs* (congratulations) upon the engagement of Flora Stroon to Shaya Golub.

"And now receive my *mazol-tov*!" said Asriel, pouncing upon the prodigy and nearly crushing him in his mighty embrace. "*Mazol-tov* to you, Flora's bridegroom! *Mazol-tov* to you, Flora's predestined one! My child's dear little bridegroom!" he went on, hiding his face on the young man's shoulder. "I am only a boor, but you shall be my son-in-law. I'll dine you and wine you, as the preacher commanded, pearls will I strew on your righteous path, a crown will I place on your head—I am only a boor!"

Sobs rang in the old man's voice. The bystanders looked on in smiling, pathetic silence.

"A boor, but an honest man," some one whispered to the uncles.

"A heart of gold!" put in the innkeeper.

"And what will Flora say?" something whispered to Asriel, from a corner of his overflowing heart. "Do you mean to tell me that the American young lady will marry this old-fashioned, pious fellow?" "Hold your tongue, fool you!" Asriel snarled inwardly. "She will have to marry him, and that settles it, and don't you disturb my joy. It's for her good as well as for mine."

With a sudden movement he disengaged his arms, and, taking off his enormous gold watch and chain, he put it on Shaya, saying: "Wear it in good health, my child. This is your first present from your sweetheart. But wait till we come to America!"

The next morning Asriel visited the cemetery, and was over-awed by its size. While living Pravly had increased by scarcely a dozen houses, the number of dwellings in silent Pravly had nearly doubled.

The headstones, mostly of humble size and weather-worn, were a solemn minority in a forest of plain wooden monuments, from which hung, for identification, all sorts of unceremonious tokens, such as old tin cans, bottomless pots, cast-off hats, shoes, and what not. But all this, far from marring the impressiveness of the place, accentuated and heightened the inarticulate tragedy of its aspect. The discarded utensils or wearing apparel seemed to be brooding upon the days of their own prime, when they had participated in the activities of the living town yonder. They had an effect of mysterious muteness, as of erstwhile animated beings—comrades of the inmates of the overgrown little mounds underneath, come to join them in the eternal rest of the city of death.

"Father! Father!" Asriel began, in a loud synagogue intonation, as he prostrated himself upon an old grave, immediately after the cantor had concluded his prayer and withdrawn from his side. "It is I, Asriel, your son—do you remember? I have come all the way from America to ask you to pray for me and my child. She is a good girl, father, and I am trying to lead her on the path of righteousness. She is about to marry the greatest scholar of God's Law hereabouts. Do pray that the boy may find favor in her eyes, father! You know, father dear, that I am only a boor, and woe is me! I am stuffed full of sins. But now I am trying to make up and to be a good Jew. Will you pray the Uppermost to accept my penance?" he besought, with growing pathos in his voice. "You are near Him, father, so do take pity upon your son and see to it that his sins are for-

given. Will you pray for me? Will you? But, anyhow,
I care more for Flora—Bloome, her Yiddish name is.
What am I? A rusty lump of nothing. But Flora—she
is a flower. Do stand forth before the High Tribunal
and pray that no ill wind blow her away from me, that
no evil eye injure my treasure. She lost her mother
when she was a baby, poor child, and she is the only
consolation I have in the world. But you are her
grandfather—do pray for her!"

Asriel's face shone, his heavy voice rang in a dismal, rapturous, devotional singsong. His eyes were dry,
but his soul was full of tears and poetry, and he poured
it forth in passionate, heart-breaking cadences.

"What is the difference between this grass blade and
myself?" he asked, a little after. "Why should you give
yourself airs, Asriel? Don't kick, be good, be pious,
carry God in your heart, and make no fuss! Be as quiet
as this grass, for hark! the hearse is coming after you,
the contribution boxes are jingling, the Angel of Death
stands ready with his knife—Oh, do pray for your son,
father!" he shrieked, in terror.

He paused. A bee, droning near by, seemed to be
praying like himself, and its company stirred Asriel's
heart.

"Oh, father! I have not seen you for thirty-five
years. Thirty-five years!" he repeated in deliberate
tones and listening to his own voice.

"We are the thirty-five?" some distant tombstones
responded, and Asriel could not help pausing to look
about, and then he again repeated, "Thirty-five years!
Can I never see you again, father? Can't I see your
dear face and talk to you, as of old, and throw myself
into fire or water for you? Can't I? Can't I? Do you remember how you used to keep me on your knees or
say prayers with me at the synagogue, and box my ears
so that the black year took me when you caught me
skipping in the prayer book? Has it all flown away?
Has it really?"

He paused as though for an answer, and then resumed, with a bitter, malicious laugh at his own expense: "Your father is silent, Asriel! Not a word, even

if you tear yourself to pieces. All is gone, Asrielke! All, all, all is lost forever!"

His harsh voice collapsed. His speech died away in a convulsion of subdued sobbing. His soul went on beseeching his father to admit him to the restful sanctity of his company.

When Asriel rose to his feet and his eye fell upon a tombstone precisely like his father's, he frowned upon it, with a sense of jealousy. On his way to his mother's grave, in the older part of the cemetery, he ever and anon turned to look back. His father's tombstone was rapidly becoming merged in a forest of other monuments. His dead father, his poor father, was losing his individuality, till he was a mere speck in this piebald medley of mounds, stones, boards, and all sorts of waste. Asriel felt deeply hurt. He retraced his steps till his father's resting place once more became the center of the world.

Then he went to pay his respects and tears to the graves of his mother, sisters, brothers, uncles. At last, completely exhausted, he took to walking among the other headstones. As he stopped to make out their Hebrew inscriptions, he would now hang his head, in heart-wringing reminiscence, now heave a sigh, or clap his hands, in grievous surprise.

The tombstones and tomb-boards were bathed in the reddish gold of the late afternoon sun. Asriel had not yet broken his fast, but although shattered in body and spirit he felt no hunger and was reluctant to leave the graveyard. He found here more of his contemporaries that he well remembered, more of the Pravly of his time, than in the town a verst or two away. The place asserted a stronger claim upon him and held him by the force of its unearthly fascination.

When he reached town at last, he felt newborn. Pravly was again dear to his heart, although Flora and America drew him to them with more magnetism than ever. He strove to speak in soft accents, and went about the houses of his relatives and the poor of the town, distributing various sums and begging the recipients of his gifts "to have pity and not to thank him," lest it should detract from the value of his good deed.

Then he went to make peace with Reb Lippe.

"You are going to stay here, so you can get another prodigy," he pleaded humbly. "But one cannot get such goods in America. Besides, you can read Talmud yourself, while I am only a boor, and what have I done to make sure of my share in the world to come? Here are three hundred rubles for charity. Do forgive me, Reb Lippe, will you? What will you lose by it?"

There were others in the room, and the unique pathos of the plea touched and amused them at once. Reb Lippe was moved to the point of tears. Moreover, the present situation took the venom out of his defeat.

"I forgive you with all my heart," he said impulsively, patting "the boor" as he would a child. "Be seated. May the Uppermost bring you home in peace and bless the union. There is another young man who is worthy of my daughter; and Shaya—may the Holy One—blessed be He—grant him the will and the power to spread His Law in America. The Jews there want a young man like him, and I am glad he is going with you. You are taking a precious stone with you, Reb Asriel. Hold it dear."

"You bet I will," Asriel replied gleefully.

VI

The nearer Asriel, with the prodigy in tow, came to New York, the deeper did Pravly sink into the golden mist of romance, and the more real did the great American city grow in his mind. Every mile added detail to the picture, and every new bit of detail made it dearer to his heart.

He was going home. He felt it more keenly, more thrillingly every day, every hour, every minute.

Sandy Hook hove in sight.

Can there be anything more beautiful, more sublime, and more uplifting than the view, on a clear summer morning, of New York harbor from an approaching ship? Shaya saw in the enchanting effect of sea, verdure, and sky a new version of his visions of paradise, where, ensconced behind luxuriant foliage, the righteous—venerable old men with silvery beards—were nodding and swaying over gold-bound tomes of the Talmud. Yet, overborne with its looming grandeur, his heart grew heavy with suspense, and he clung close to Asriel.

All was bustle and expectation on board. The little deck engines never ceased rumbling, and the passengers, spruced up as if for church, were busy about their baggage, or promenading with a festive, nervous air.

Asriel twitched and bit his lip in rapture.

"Oh, how blue the water is!" said Shaya wistfully.

"America is a fine country, is it not?" the old man rejoined. "But it can't hold a candle to Flora. Wait till you see her. You just try to be a good boy," he kept murmuring; "stick to your Talmud, and don't give a *peper* for anything else, and all God has given me shall be yours. I have no son to say *Kaddish* for my soul when I am dead. Will you be my Kaddish, Shaya? Will you observe the anniversary of my death?" he queried, in a beseeching tone which the young man had never heard from him.

"Of course I will," Shaya returned, like a dutiful child.

"Will you? May you live long for it. In palaces will I house you, like the eye in my head will I cherish you. I am only a boor, but she is my daughter, my only child, and my whole life in this world."

Asriel kept Flora unadvised as to the name of the steamer or the date of his arrival. Upon landing he did not go directly to his residence, but first took his importation into a large "clothing and gents' furnishing store" on Broadway, from which the *illoui* emerged completely transformed. Instead of his uncouth cap and the draggling coat which had hidden his top boots from view, he was now arrayed in the costliest "Prince Albert," the finest summer derby, and the most elegant button shoes the store contained. This and a starched shirt-front, a turned-down collar, and a gaudy puff-tie set into higher relief the Byronic effect of his intellectual, winsome face.

Asriel snapped his fingers for delight. He thought him easily the handsomest and best-dressed man on Broadway. "It is the Divine Presence shining upon him!" he murmured to himself, dragging the young man by the hand, as if he were a truant schoolboy. Barring the prodigy's sidelocks (badges of divine learning and piety), which were tightly curled into two little cushions in front of his ears, he now thought him thoroughly Americanized.

The prodigy, however, felt tied and fettered in the garb of Gentile civilization, and as he trudged along by his convoy's side, he viewed his transformed self in the store windows, or stared, rabbit-like, at the lumbering stagecoaches and the hurrying noblemen.

Asriel let himself and his charge in noiselessly with the latchkey, which had accompanied him, together with a bunch of other keys, on his tour. They entered the hallway on tiptoe.

The little house rang with the voluminous tones of Flora's piano, through which trickled the doleful tremolo of her subdued contralto. Since her father had left her pining for his return, "Home, Sweet Home" had become her favorite tune.

Flora was alone in the house, and her unconscious welcome was all the sweeter to Asriel's soul for the grieving note which ran through it. His heart throbbed with violence. Shaya's sank in awe. He had never heard a piano except through the window of some nobleman's house.

"Hush! Do you hear?" the old man whispered. "That's your predestined bride." With that he led the way downstairs. There they paused to kiss the divine name on the *Mezuzah* of the doorpost.

"Tamara!" Asriel called, under his breath, looking for the pious housekeeper in the dining room and in the kitchen. "She is not in. Must be out marketing or about her good deeds. A dear soul she! Oh, it's her fast day; she fasts Mondays and Thursdays."

Then he stepped up in front of a tin box that was

nailed to one of the kitchen doors and took out his pocketbook. It was one of the contribution-boxes of the "Meyer-the-Wonder-worker Fund," which is devoted to the support of pious old European Jews who go to end their days in the Land of Israel. Every orthodox Jew in the world keeps a similar box in his house and drops a coin into it whenever he escapes some danger. Asriel had safely crossed the wide ocean, and his offering was a handful of silver.

"Well, you stay here, Shaya, and don't budge till you are called," he said; and leaving the young man to his perplexity he betook himself upstairs, to surprise his daughter.

Flora burst into tears of joy, and hugged him again and again, while he stroked her black hair or stood scowling and grinning for admiration.

"Ah, you dear, cranky papa!" she burst out, for the fourth time realizing that he was actually come back to her, and for the fourth time attacking him.

At last he thought they had had enough. He was dying to protract the scene, but there was that troublesome job to get rid of, and Asriel was not the man to put such things off. Whenever he felt somewhat timid he would grow facetious. This was the case at the present juncture.

"Well, Flora, guess what sort of present your papa has brought you," he said, reddening to his ears. "I'll bet you you won't hit if you keep on guessing till tomorrow. No girl has ever got such a present as long as America is America."

Flora's eyes danced with joyous anticipation. Her mind was ablaze with diamonds, rubies, emeralds, sapphires, pearls.

"I have got a bridegroom for you—a fifteen-thousand-dollar one. Handsomest and smartest fellow on earth. He is an *illoui*."

"A what?" she asked, in amazement.

"Oh, a wonderful chap, you know, deep in the Talmud and the other holy books. He could knock all the rabbis of Europe to smithereens. The biggest bug in

Pravly was after him, but I beat him clean out of his boots. Shaya! Come right up!"

The girl gazed at her father in bewilderment. Was he joking or was he in dead, terrific earnest?

Shaya made his appearance, with his eyes on the floor, and wringing the index finger of his right hand, as he was wont to do whenever he felt ill at ease, which was seldom, however.

Flora's brain was in a whirl.

"This is your predestined bridegroom, my daughter. A fine present, is it not? Did you ever expect such a raisin of a sweetheart, hey? Well, children, I must go around to see about the baggage. Have a chat and be acquainted." With that he advanced to the door.

"Papa! Papa!" Flora frantically called to him. But he never turned his head and went his way.

In her despair she rushed at the young stranger, who was still wringing his finger, as he stood in the middle of the parlor, eyeing the carpet, and snapped out:—

"Mister, you had better go. If you think you are going to be my bridegroom, you are sadly mistaken."

She spoke in Yiddish, but her pronunciation, particularly of the latter "r," was so decidedly American that to Shaya it sounded at once like his native tongue and the language of Gentiles. However, it was Yiddish enough, and the fact of this imposing young lady speaking it gave him the feeling of being in the presence of a Jewish princess of biblical times.

"Where shall I go? I don't know anybody here." He said it with an air of naïve desperation which touched the girl's heart. "Where is my fault?" he added pleadingly.

She gave him a close look, and, taking him by his clean-cut beardless chin, opened her eyes wide at him, and broke into a hearty laugh.

"My father has really brought you over to marry me?" she questioned, for the first time awakening to the humorous side of the situation, and again she burst out laughing.

Shaya blushed and took hold of his finger, but he forthwith released it and also broke into a giggle. Her merriment set him at his ease, and her labored Yiddish struck him as the prattle of a child.

Flora was amused and charmed as with a baby. Shaya felt as if he were playing with another boy.

Of all the immigrants who had married or were engaged to marry some of her girl friends, none had, just after landing, been so presentable, so sweet-faced, and so droll as this scholarly looking fellow. There would have been nothing odd in her marrying him a year or two later, after he had picked up some broken English and some of the customs of the country. But then her mind was firmly made up, and she had boasted to her friends that she was bound to marry a doctor, and here this boy was not even going to be a business man, but an orthodox rabbi or something of the sort. The word "rabbi" was associated in her mind with the image of an unkempt, long-skirted man who knew nothing of the world, took snuff, and made life a nuisance to himself and to others. Is she going to be a *rabbitzen* (a rabbi's wife)? No! No! No! Come what may, none but a refined American gentleman shall lead her under the nuptial canopy! And in her rage she fled from the parlor and went to nurse her misery on the dining room lounge.

Presently, as she lay with her hands clasped under her head, abandoned to her despair and fury, and yet unable to realize that it was all in real earnest, a fretting sensation settled somewhere in her heart. At first it was only like a grain of sand, but it kept growing till it lay a heavy, unbearable lump. She could not stand the idea of that poor, funny dear being left alone and scared out of his wits. Still, she would not stir. Let papa take him away or she will leave the house and go to work in a factory.

"Tamara!" she suddenly raised herself to say, the moment the housekeeper came into the room. "There is a man upstairs. He must be hungry."

"Then why don't *you* give him something to eat?" Tamara responded tartly. "You know it is Monday and I am faint. But who is he and what is he doing upstairs? Let him come down."

"Go and see him for yourself," snapped Flora. "You will find him one of your set—a Talmudical scholar, a pious soul," she added, with a venomous laugh.

Tamara bent upon her a look full of resentment as well as of devout reproach, and betook herself upstairs.

When Asriel came he explained that Shaya was not going to be a rabbi, nor dress otherwise than as an American gentleman, but that he would lead a life of piety and spend his time studying the Talmud, partly at home and partly at some synagogue. "What, then, have I worked all my life for?" he pleaded. "I am only a boor, my daughter, and how long does a fellow live? Don't darken my days, Flora."

Tamara kept nodding pious assent. "In the old country a girl like you would be glad to marry such a child of the Law," she expostulated with the girl. "It is only here that we are sinners and girls marry none but worldly men. May every daughter of Israel be blessed with such a match."

"Mind your own business!" Flora exploded. She understood her father's explanation but vaguely, and it had the opposite of the desired effect upon her.

"Leave her alone. The storm will blow over," Asriel whispered.

When Asriel's baggage arrived it proved to include a huge box full of Hebrew books. They were of various sizes, but twenty-five of them were large, uniform, leather-bound folio volumes, portly and resplendent in a superabundance of gilding and varnish. Of these, twenty contained the whole of the Babylonian Talmud together with the various commentaries, the remaining five comprising the Alphos. After a little a walnut bookcase made its appearance. It was accorded a place of honor in the front parlor, and Asriel, Tamara, and Shaya busied themselves with arranging the sacred books on its shelves.

Flora sat eyeing them sarcastically, till, sobs rising to her throat, she retired to the seclusion of her bedroom, on the top floor, and burst out crying as if her heart would break. The contents of all those books, which her father had imported as accessories of her would-be bridegroom, were Chinese to her. She had never seen so many of them nor given a moment's attention to the occasional talks which she had chanced to overhear concerning such books and the men who spent their lives reading them. They now frightened her, as if they were filled with weird incantations and Shaya were the master of some uncanny art.

The prodigy was busy arranging his library, now and then opening a book to examine its print. Presently, as he was squatting down before a chair upon which he was turning over the leaves of a bulky volume, his attention was arrested by a celebrated passage. Without changing his posture, he proceeded to glance it over, until, completely absorbed, he fell to humming the words, in that peculiar singsong, accompanied by indescribable controversial gesticulations, which seem to be as indispensable in reading Talmud as a pair of eyes.

"Look, look!" Tamara nudged Asriel, whom she was helping to transfer the remaining books to the marble table. Asriel turned his head toward the prodigy, and for a few moments the two stood staring at the odd, inspiring spectacle with gaping admiration. Then the housekeeper and her employer exchanged a glance of intelligence, she nodding her bewigged head piously, as much as to say: "What a find Heaven has placed in your way!"

"The Uppermost has blessed you," she added in whispers.

"May he enjoy long life with us!" Asriel returned, with a sigh.

"Flora does not know what a treasure the Lord of the Universe has sent her."

"She will," he rejoined curtly.

VII

It was at the head of a dozen venerable Talmudists, including the rabbi of the congregation, that Asriel returned from the synagogue next Saturday morning. The learned company was entertained with wine, cold fish, and some of the lemon pie and genuine Yiddish pastry for which Tamara was famous.

"Here is life, Mr. Stroon! Here is life, Shaya!" each of the guests said, raising his glass.

"Life and peace! Life and peace!" was the uniform response.

"God bless the union and let them live a hundred and twenty years," pursued Reb Mendele, a little man with luxuriant red sidelocks, as he reached for a piece of Sabbath cake.

"And grant that they give birth to children and bring them up to the Law, the Bridal Canopy, and deeds of righteousness," chimed in another, whose ear-locks were two sorry corkscrew-like appendages, as he held up a slice of fish on the points of his fork.

"And Shaya continue a child of the Law and study it with never-failing zeal," came from between a dangling pair of tubes.

"That's the point!" emphasized a chorus of munching mouths.

"But where is the bride?" somebody demanded. "She must show herself! she must show herself!"

"That's right," Reb Mendele seconded heartily. "Out with the bride! 'And the daughters of Jerusalem come out dancing,' " he quoted; " 'and what do they say? "Lift thine eyes, young man, and behold the maiden thou choosest. Do not set thine eye on beauty——" ' " He broke off abruptly, reddening. The remainder of the quoted passage runs as follows: "Set thine eye (the maidens say to the young man) on good family connections, as is written in Proverbs: 'False is grace and vain is beauty: a woman that feareth the Lord shall indeed be praised.' " It would have been anything but appropriate to the occasion, and while the Chaldaic and the Hebrew of the citation were Greek to Asriel, there was the prodigy to resent it.

Another hoary-headed child of the Law interposed: " 'Go forth and look, O ye daughters of Zion, on King Solomon, with the crown wherewith his mother hath crowned him on the day of the joy of his espousals, and on the day of the joy of his heart.' Saith the Talmud: 'By "the day of his espousals" is meant the day of the Giving of the Law.' Accordingly, when Shaya's wedding takes place, if God be pleased, it will be an espousal in the literal as well as in the Talmudic sense, for is he not full of Law? It will therefore be the Giving of the Law in marriage to Reb Asriel's daughter, will it not?"

"Never mind blushing, Shaya," said the rabbi, although the prodigy, engrossed with the "paradise taste" of the lemon pie—a viand he had never dreamed of—and keeping a sharp eye on the dwindling contents of the tart-dish, was too busy to blush.

Flora was in her bedroom, the place of her voluntary exile most of the time that her compulsory sweetheart was in the house. Her father was kind and attentive to her, as usual, and never mentioned Shaya's name to her. But she knew that he was irrevocably bent upon the marriage, and her mood often verged on suicide. Could it really be that after all her cherished dreams of afternoon drives in Central Park, in a doctor's buggy and with the doctor himself by her side, she was doomed to be the wife of that clumsy rustic, who did not even know how to shake hands or to bow to a lady, and who could not say a word without performing some grotesque gesture or curling his horrid sidelocks? Oh, what would the girls say! She had twitted them on the broken English of their otherwise worldly and comparatively well-mannered sweethearts, and now she herself was matched with that wretch of a holy soul!

And yet Shaya was never in her mind invested in the image of a "clumsy rustic" nor of a "holy soul." Whenever she saw him she would screw up a frown, but on one occasion, when their eyes met across the supper table, they could not help smiling to each other, like children at church.

"Flora dear, I want to speak to you," Asriel said, knocking at the locked door of her hiding-place.

"Leave me alone, papa, will you? I've got a headache," she responded.

"That's all right, but unlock the door. I won't eat you up."

She was burning to have her father broach the painful subject, so that she might have it out with him. With that end in view, she set her teeth and turned the key. But Asriel came in so unaggressive, so meek, in a pleasing attitude so utterly unlike him, that he took her by surprise, as it were, and she stood completely disarmed.

"I beg you, my daughter, do not shorten my days, and come downstairs," he entreated with heartfelt ardor. "I have so little to live, and the Uppermost has sent me a piece of comfort so that I may die a righteous Jew—will you take it away from me? Will you put me to shame before God and man?"

The words and the pathos with which they were delivered so oddly contrasted with all she knew of her father that she felt as if he were really praying for his life. She was deeply touched and dazed, and before she knew what she was about, found herself in the crowded little dining room below.

"Good Sabbath, Flora, good Sabbath!" the venerable assemblage greeted her.

"Good Sabbath!" she returned, bowing gracefully, and blushing.

"May your guest be pleasing to you," one of the company went on in time-honored phrase; "and, if God be pleased, we shall live to make merry at your wedding."

Flora's face turned a deeper red.

Several of the Talmudists were itching for some banter at the expense of the young pair, but the American girl's dignified bearing and her commanding figure and dress bore down every tendency in that direction, so that the scholarly old gentlemen turned their overflowing spirits in other channels.

"Give us some Law, Shaya!" said Reb Mendele, with a Talmudic wave of both hands.

"That's right," the others concurred. "Your prospective father-in-law is feasting us upon fare of the earth, and it is meet that you should regale us with Words of Law."

Shaya, his face as red as Flora's, was eyeing the tablecloth as he murmured, " 'No conversing during repast.' "

"Words of Law are no converse," Reb Mendele retorted.

"The Commentary adds: 'Not so much as to quote the precept about silence during repast,' " Shaya rejoined reluctantly, without raising his eyes. "Now the precept is Words of the Law, is it not? Which means that the prohibition does extend to Words of Law."

Apart from his embarrassment, the prodigy was somehow loath to engage in a spiritual discussion in the presence of the stylish young lady.

"Why did you quote it then?" Reb Mendele pursued aggressively. He referred to two other passages, in support of his position; and Shaya, with his eyes still on the tablecloth, and refraining from all gesticulation, could not help showing the irrelevance of both. It was a "knock-out blow," but his red-bearded opponent cleverly extricated himself from the ignominy of his defeat by assuming an amused air, as if it had all been mere bait to decoy the prodigy to a display of his erudition and mental powers; and retaining his smile against further emergency, Reb Mendele hazarded another assault. Some of the other Talmudists took a hand. The battle waxed hot, though Shaya, fighting single-handed against half a dozen elders, remained calm, and parried their blows with a shamefaced but contemptuous look, never raising a finger nor his eyes from the tablecloth. Once in the fray, he would not have Flora see him get the worst of it.

She, on her part, could not help a growing interest in the debate, and finally accepted the chair which Tamara had tenderly placed by her side five minutes before. To be sure, she understood not a word of the controversy. To her it was something like a boxing-match, with every exciting element of the sport, but without any of its violence (which alone kept Flora from attending pugilistic performances), though the

arms and fingers of our venerable combatants were
even more active than are the arms and fists of two
athletes in a modern ring. As she watched the progress
of the discussion she became conscious of a decided
partisan feeling in favor of the younger man. "It ain't
fair a bit!" she said to herself. "Six old-timers against
one boy—I declare!"

Asriel and Tamara, to both of whom the contest was
as unintelligible as it was to Flora, were so abandoned
to their admiration of the youthful disputant that they
omitted to notice the girl's undisguised interest in the
scene and to congratulate themselves upon it. The host
followed the controversy with a sheepish look of reverence, as if the company were an assemblage of kings.
The housekeeper looked on with a beaming face, and
every time one of the patriarchs made a bold attack,
she would nod her head as if she understood it all, and
conceded the strength of his contention.

Egged on by Flora's presence as well as by the on-
slaughts of his adversaries, Shaya gradually warmed
up to the debate, until, having listened, with sardonic
patience, to a lengthy and heated argument by a fleshy
child of the Law, he suddenly leaped upon his man.

"Is this the way you understand the passage?" he
shouted, with a vicious chuckle. Then, thrusting his
curly head in his opponent's face, and savagely gesticulating, he poured forth a veritable cataract of the most
intricate syllogisms and quotations.

It was quite a new Shaya. His blue eyes flashed fire,
his whole countenance gleamed, his singsong rang
with tuneful ferocity.

"But it seems to me that Rabbi Yohanon does not
say that," the portly Talmudist objected. "I am afraid
you have misquoted him."

It was the drowning man's straw. Even Flora, who
understood the Yiddish of the retort, could see that;
and her heart bounded with cruel delight.

"Have I? You are sure, are you?" Shaya demanded,
with boyish virulence. "All right. We shall see!" With
which he darted out of the room and upstairs.

"The boy is a *gaon*,"* the corpulent old man re-marked humbly. "What a head! What a memory, what a *chariff*!"†

"Yes, and what a *bokki!*"‡ chimed in the rabbi. "One cannot help wondering when he had time to study up so much."

"He'll just take a peep at a book and then he knows it all by heart," put in Asriel. "He licked all the rabbis around Pravly."

The boorish remark disposed some of the listeners to laugh, but they did not.

"You have got a treasure, Mr. Stroon," said Reb Mendele.

"You bet!" the host answered with a blissful simper, as he took to stroking his daughter's hair.

"You know what the Talmud says, Mr. Stroon?" resumed the rabbi. "That he who supports a scholar of the Law is like unto him who offers sacrifices."

"I know," Asriel returned exultingly. At the Pravly synagogue the preacher had applied the same quotation to Reb Lippe.

Presently Shaya returned with a pile of huge volumes in his arms. His citation proved correct, and meeting with no further opposition, but too far carried away by the subject to quit it so soon, he volunteered an extemporaneous discourse. His face was now wrapped in genial, infantile ecstasy and his intonation was a soft, impassioned melody. The old man followed him with paternal admiration.

When he concluded and leaned back in his chair, he gave Flora a triumphant smile. The color mounted to her cheeks and she dropped her gaze. At the same moment Asriel flung himself upon the young hero.

"Oh, you dear little sparrow!" he exclaimed, lifting Shaya in his arms like a baby, and passionately kissing him.

Tamara wiped her eyes with her apron. Flora had a

*A genius.
†Acute intellect.
‡Man of erudition.

mind to flee for safety, but she forthwith saw herself
out of danger, for her father seemed unmindful of her
presence, and the first thing he did as he let the prodigy down was to invite his guests upstairs to show
them the newly imported library.

As the patriarchal company was filing out of the dining room, Shaya, passing by Flora, said to her gleefully: "I gave it to them, didn't I?"

"Tell me now," said Tamara, when the two women
found themselves alone in the room; "ought you not to
thank God for such a treasure of a sweetheart?"

"He is nothing of the kind to me," Flora burst out,
"and he never will be, either. I don't care how long
papa is going to keep him in the house."

VIII

"Oh, papa!" sobbed Flora; "will you ever put an end
to it? You know I'll never marry him."

"Do I compel you to?" he replied. "What do you
care if he is in the house? He does not take away your
dinner, does he? Imagine that he is your brother and
don't bother your head about him. The boy has become
so dear to me that I feel as if he were my own son.
Will *you* recite Kaddish for my soul? Will you play for
me at the anniversary of my death? God thought I was
not good enough to have a son, but he sent me this
holy child to take the place of one. As I hear him read
his holy books," he went on, with mounting pathos, "it
melts like ice cream in my heart. It pleased the Uppermost to make a boor of your papa. Well, I suppose He
knows his business, and I am not going to poke my
nose in, and ask questions; but He seems to have taken
pity on me after all, and in my old age he has sent me
an angel, so that I may get the credit of supporting
him. Did you hear what the wise men said? That to
support a man who does nothing but study sacred
books is as good as offering sacrifices. Yes, my daughter, God has put this boy in my hands; He sent me all
the way to Pravly for him—all to give me a chance to

make up for my sins. Do you want me to kick him out? Not if New York turned upside down."

"But, father—"

"Hold on! Let me talk the heart out of myself. It's no use asking me to send him away. He is God's gift. He is as holy as a Purity (the scrolls of the Law). You are my daughter, and he is my son. I don't chase you under the bridal canopy with a strap, do I? If God does not wish the match, it won't come off, that's all."

The conversation took place about a fortnight after the great debate. Asriel lived in the hope that when Shaya had learned some English and the ways of Flora's circle, she would get to like him. He could not see how it was possible to withstand the charms of the young man whom he sincerely thought the handsomest fellow in the Jewish colony. He provided him with a teacher, and trusted the rest to time and God.

"Just fix him up in English and a little figuring, and that's all," he instructed the teacher. "But mind you, don't take him too far into those Gentile books of yours. He does not want any of the monkey tricks they teach the children at college. Do you understand?"

Flora was getting used to Shaya's presence in the house, as if he actually were a newly discovered brother of hers, brought up in a queer way which she could not understand, and it was only occasionally and at growing intervals that the situation would burst upon her, and she would plead with her father as she had done.

The two young people frequently found themselves alone. The door between the front parlor, which was now Shaya's study, and Flora's boudoir was most of the time open. They often talked together, and she quizzed him about his manners, and once or twice even went over his English lessons with him, laughing at his mispronunciations, and correcting them in the imposing manner of her former schoolteachers.

"Why do you work your fingers like that?" she once said, with a pained look. "Can't you try and read without them?"

"I am used to it from the Talmud-he-he-he!" he tittered, as if acknowledging a compliment.

Her piano did not disturb him in his studies, for in the synagogues, where he had grown up, he had been used to read in a turmoil of other voices; but he loved the instrument, and he would often pause to listen to Flora's energetic strokes through the door. When the tune was a melancholy one its first chords would make him start, with a thrill; and as he proceeded to listen his heart would contract with a sharp feeling of homesickness, and at the same time he would be longing for still more familiarity in the performer's manner toward him. Sometimes he would cross over to her room and quietly stand behind her while she was playing.

"Ah, it is so nice!" he once said, feeling himself in a paradise on earth.

"What are you doing here?" she exclaimed, facing about toward him, in affected surprise. "Music ain't for a 'holy child' like yourself." She mocked a favorite expression of her father's.

"Don't say that," he reproached her. "You always like to tease me. Why don't I tease you?"

Upon the whole, Shaya took the situation quite recklessly. He studied his Talmud and his English, let Tamara cloy him with all sorts of tidbits, and roamed about the streets and public buildings. In less than six months he knew the city and its suburbs much better than Flora, and could tell the meaning of thousands of printed English words, although he neither knew how to use them himself nor recognized them in the speech of others. Flora was amazed by his rapid progress, and the facility with which he mastered his Arithmetic and English Grammar—in neither of which she had been strong at school—even piqued her ambition. It was as if she had been beaten by the "holy soul" on her own ground.

The novelty of studying things so utterly out of his rut was like a newly discovered delicacy to his mental palate. He knew by heart a considerable part of the English translation in his Hebrew prayer book and Old Testament, and his greatest pleasure, when Asriel was not about, was to do arithmetical problems. But the problems were all child's play to him, and he craved some higher grade of intellectual food in the same Gentile line. This he knew from his Talmud to be contained in the "Wisdom of Measuring," which he had learned of his teacher to call Geometry.

"Bring me a Geometry, please," he whispered to his instructor.

"I will, but don't say a word to Mr. Stroon about it."

The forbidden fruit was furnished, and the prodigy of sacred lore applied himself to it with voracity.

"How cunning!" he said to the teacher, in a transport of enthusiasm. "Of course, it is not as deep as Talmud, but I never dreamed there were such subtle things in the Gentile books at all—may I be ill if I did."

"This is only the beginning of it," the other returned, in whispered exultation. "Wait till you get deeper into it. And then there are other books, far more interesting."

"Say, young fellow!" Asriel said to Shaya's teacher a week or so later; "you need not trouble your righteous legs to bring you here any more. You are getting too thick with the boy."

Shaya now found no difficulty in plodding through the theorems and problems unaided. But he yearned after his teacher and friend, and for several days could relish neither his Talmud nor his contraband Geometry. He grew restless. His soul was languishing with thirst.

"Guess where I have been," he confidentially said to Flora, coming from the street one afternoon. He spoke in Yiddish, and she answered in English, interspersed with the same dialect.

"Not in the synagogue, studying?" she queried.

"No—at the Astor Library," he whispered. "They have such a lot of books there, Flora! Upstairs and downstairs—large rooms like rich synagogues, with shelves all over the walls, and all full of books. Have you ever been there, Flora?"

"N-no!" she owned, with reluctance. The "holy soul" was clearly forging ahead of her in a world which she considered all her own; and she hated the idea of it, and liked it at the same time. "What did you there?"

"I just looked at the books—oh, what a lot!—and then I found out how to get a Geometry—they have everything in the world, I tell you—and I did some problems. Don't tell your father I was there."

"Of course I won't," she said intimately. "Can ladies come in?"

"Certainly; they have a separate place for them, though; will you go there with me?"

"Some day," she rejoined evasively

"Will you? Oh, it's so nice to be sitting and reading there! Only you must sit still. I forgot myself, and as I was figuring out some nice point, I began to reason aloud, so a fine old gentleman stepped up to my side and touched me on the shoulder. Oh, I got so scared, Flora! But he did not do me anything—may I be ill if he did. He only told me to be quiet."

Flora burst out laughing.

"I'll bet you, you was singing in that funny way you have when you are studying the Talmud."

"Yes," he admitted joyfully.

"And working your hands and shaking the life out of yourself," she pursued, mimicking his gestures.

"No, I was not—may I not live till tomorrow if I was," he protested vehemently, with a touch of resentment. "Oh, it is so nice to be there! I never knew there were so many Gentile books in the world at all. I wonder what they are all about. Only I am so troubled about my English." He interrupted himself, with a distressed air. "When I asked them for the book, and how to get it, they could not understand me."

"*I* can understand everything you say when you speak English. You're all right," she comforted him. His troubled, childlike smile and his shining clear blue eyes, as he spoke, went to her heart.

"*You* can, but other people can't. I so wish I could speak it like you, Flora. Do read a page or two with me, will you? I'll get my Reader—shall I?"

"What's your hurry? Can't you wait?"

He could not wait. He was in a fever of impatience

to inhale the whole of the Gentile language—
definitions, spelling, pronunciation, and all—with one
desperate effort. It was the one great impediment that
seemed to stand between him and the enchanted new
world that had revealed itself to him.

"Oh, do hear me read—may you live long, Flora! It
somehow draws me as with a kind of impure force.
Will you?"

"All right," she yielded, with kindly curiosity at the
fervor of his request, and feeling flattered.

He had been reading perhaps a quarter of an hour
when he grew absent-minded.

"You must have skipped a line again," she said, in
an awkward undertone.

"Oh, yes!"

They were seated at a respectful distance, with the
corner of the marble table between them, her full, well-
modeled bust erect and stately against the pier-glass. She
wore a waist of dark-blue silk, trimmed with red, and
there was a red ribbon in her shock of inky hair. Presently she leaned forward to see a mispronounced word
for herself. Their heads found themselves close together.
Her ivory cheek almost touched his.

"Where is it?" she questioned, under her breath.

He made no reply. His glance was riveted to her
raven eyelashes. A dash of scarlet lurking under her
chin dazed his brain. After a slight pause he said, as he
timidly stroked her burning cheek: "It is so smooth!"

She had an impulse to withdraw her face, but felt be-
numbed. He went on patting her, until, meeting with no
resistance, his lips touched her cheek, in a gingerly
kiss. Both lowered their eyes. They were silent, but
their hearts, each conscious of the other's beatings,
throbbed wildly.

"Bad boy!" she then whispered, without raising her
head.

After another silence, as their eyes met, they burst
into a subdued nervous titter.

"You must not do that again," she said. "Is this the
kind of pious man you are?"

"Don't say that, Flora—pray don't. You know it

hurts my feelings when you speak like that," he implored her. And impelled by the embarrassed, affectionate sadess of her mien, he seized her hand and fell
to kissing first her fingers and then her eyes, as though
beseeching them to reveal the meaning of their somber
look. Their lips met and clung together in a trance of
passion. When they parted Shaya felt ten years older,
and as his eye fell upon the bookcase, he wondered
what those glittering, massive tomes were doing there.

"Will you tell your father that you want to be my
sweetheart?" he asked after a while.

His voice and his features appeared to her in a novel
aspect.

"How do you know I do?" she said, with playful defiance, hiding a burst of admiration which was lost
upon the unworldly young man.

"Why—don't you?" he demanded solicitously.

Then, a sudden light of inspiration coming in her
eyes, Flora said, "Hol' on! How would you like to be
a doctor, Shayie?"

"But your father would turn me out if I began to
study for it."

She grew thoughtful. "But suppose he had no objection?" she queried, her bashfulness suddenly returning
to her face.

"Oh, then I should be dying to study doctor books—
any kind of Gentile books you wanted me to, Flora.
But Reb Asriel won't let me."

"Listen! Can you keep a secret?" she asked like a
conspiring little schoolgirl.

"You mean about your being my sweetheart?"

"No!" she rejoined impatiently. "I mean the other
thing—your studyin'. Papa needn't get wind of it till
it's too late—your understand? If you are smart, we
can fix that."

"That's all right. I am awful clever at keeping a secret," he boasted.

"Well, I want you to be a doctor, Shayie," she resumed, with matronly tenderness. "If you are, I'll care
for you, and you'll be my birdie boy, an' all; if not,
you won't. Oh, won't it be lovely when everybody

knows that you go to college and study together with nice, educated up-town fellows! We would go to theaters together and read different books. You'll make a daisy of a college boy, too—you bet. Would you like to wear a high hat, and spec's, and ride in a buggy with a driver? Would you, would you, bad boy, you? Hello, Doctor Golub! How are you?"

She presented her lips, and they kissed again and again.

"You know what, Shayie? When papa comes I'll go out somewheres, so you can tell him—you know what I mean. It'll make it so much easier to fool him. Will you tell him?"

"I am ashamed."

"*I* won't tell him."

"Don't be angry—I will. I shall always do everything you tell me, Flora," he said, looking into her black gleaming eyes—"always, always!" And in the exuberance of his delight he once again felt himself a little boy, and broke out into a masterly imitation of the crow of a cock, jumping up and flapping his arms for a pair of wings.

When Asriel and Shaya were alone in the parlor, the young man said, as he fell to wringing his index finger, "Flora wants me to tell you that she is satisfied."

"Satisfied with what?" the old man demanded, leaping to his feet

"To be my sweetheart."

"Is she? Did she say so? When? Tamara!" he yelled, rushing downstairs and dragging the prodigy along, "Tamara! May you live long! The Uppermost has taken pity upon me after all. Floraly* has come around—blessed be the Uppermost."

"Blessed be the Uppermost!" Tamara echoed, her pleasant, swarthy face beaming with heartfelt delight. "When He wills, walls of iron must give way. It is a divine match—any one can see it is. May they live a hundred and twenty years together. Mazol-tov!"†

*Affectionate diminutive.
†Good luck.

"Mazol-tov to you and to all of us," Asriel responded. "But where is Flora? Fetch some drink, Tamara."

He stepped up to the "Wonder-worker box," and deposited a silver coin for the support of the pilgrims at Palestine, saying as he did so: "I thank and praise thee, O Lord of the Universe, for thy mercy toward me. Mayest Thou grant the children long years, and keep up in Shaya his love for thy sacred Law. You know the match is all of your own making, and you must take care of it. I am only your slave, that's all."

IX

"Is Shayaly in?" inquired old Asriel on entering Flora's room one morning in midsummer. It was four months after his daughter's betrothal to the Talmudist had been celebrated by a solemn ceremony and a sumptuous feast, the wedding having been set for a later date. The crowning glory of his achievement Stroon postponed, like a rare bottle of wine, for some future day. He dreaded to indulge himself in such a rapid succession of This World joys lest he might draw upon his Share in the World-to-come. Will the Uppermost let him live to see his daughter and the "holy child," standing side by side under the Canopy? Asriel was now confident that he would. "Is Shayaly in ?"

"Of course he is—papa," Flora answered, raising her face from her book. Her "papa" was added aloud, and as if upon afterthought.

The parlor door stood ajar. Asriel stationed himself near by and listened to the young man's habitual singsong. The old man's face gradually became radiant with bliss.

"My crown, my Messiah, my Kaddish! My Share in the World-to-come!" he muttered.

"Did you have breakfast, papa?" Flora demanded, speaking still louder than before.

At this moment Shaya's singsong broke out with fresh enthusiasm and his Hebrew words became distinct. Asriel waved her away fiercely. After a little he remarked in a subdued voice, as he pointed to the front parlor, "*This* is my breakfast. This is for the soul, my child; the worms of the grave cannot touch it, and you take it along to the other world. Everything else is a lot of rubbish."

He made to leave, but could not help pausing, in fresh admiration, and then, softly opening the parlor door he entered the sanctum, on tiptoe, in order to feast his eye as well as his ear on the thrilling scene. He found Shaya rapturously swaying and singing over a Talmud volume. Flora watched her father with roguish delight.

"I am afraid I must not be gloating over him like this," Asriel rebuked himself in his heart. "I may give him the evil eye." When he regained the back parlor he said, under his breath: "Floraly, I am afraid your company may disturb him sometimes. A pretty sweetheart is apt to stir a fellow's brains, you know, and take him away from the Law. He had better study more at the synagogues."

The girl blushed to her charcoal hair and dropped her glance. But her father had scarcely gained his room, on the floor above, when she flew into the front parlor with a ringing giggle.

"Now you can go right on, dearie," she said, encircling Shaya's neck with one arm, and producing with the other an English textbook on Natural Philosophy, which had lain open under the huge Hebrew volume.

"You heard me holler, didn't you?'

"Of course I did," Shaya answered beamingly. "He interrupted me in the middle of such a cunning explanation!"

"Did he? What was it about? All about sounds—the same as before?"

"Yes, but it is even more brainy than what I told you."

He proceeded to expound, in Yiddish, what he had been reading on Acoustics, she listening to his enthusiastic popularization with docile, loving inattention.

* * *

The young man made a pretense of spending his afternoons, and sometimes also mornings, at the various synagogues of the Jewish quarter. His proud guardian encouraged this habit, in order that his "daughter's bridegroom" might disseminate his sacred knowledge among other congregations than his own. "Your learning is the gift of God, Shayaly," he would say, "and you needn't be ashamed to peddle it around. Reb Lippe said America wanted a man like you to spread the holy Law here. Go and do it, my son, and the Uppermost will help us all for your sake."

The prodigy and his importer were the talk of the orthodox colony, and nothing was more pleasing to Asriel than to hear the praises of his daughter's fiancé sounded by the Talmudists. There came a time, however, when, in his own synagogue, at least, these encomiums ceased. Asriel missed them keenly and pestered the learned men of the congregation with incessant talks about Shaya, for the purpose of worrying out some acknowledgment of his phenomenal talents. But the concession was mostly made in a half-hearted way, and poor Asriel would be left hungrier than ever. Particularly was his heart longing for the warm eulogies of Reb Tzalel, a poor, sickly old peddler, who was considered one of the most pious and learned men in the neighborhood. Asriel liked the man for his nervous sincerity and uncompromising self-respect. He often asked him to his house, but the tattered, underfed peddler invariably declined the invitation.

"What will I do there, Reb Asriel?" he would say, with the pained sort of smile which would light up his ghastly old face whenever he spoke. "Look at your costly carpet and furniture, and bear in mind that you are a landlord and I a poor peddler! At the synagogue I like you better, for here we are equals. Saith the verse in the Book of Job: 'Whereas He is one that shows no favor to chieftains, and distinguishes not the rich before the indigent, for all of them are the work of his hands.' " Reb Tzalel translated the verse into Yiddish for the benefit of his listener, whereupon Asriel felt a much wealthier man than he was, and at the same time he had a sense of humiliation, as though his money were something to be ashamed of.

This man's unusual reticence on the point of Shaya's merits chagrined Asriel sorely, and his mind even began to be troubled by some vague misgivings on that score.

One evening Asriel sat by Reb Tzalel's side in the study rooms of his synagogue. It was in the latter part of November, and Shaya's wedding was to take place during the Feast of Hanuccah, some few weeks later. The evening services, which on week days were held in these rooms, were over, and the "learners" could now give themselves to their divine studies undisturbed, save for the possible and unwelcome advent of some belated Ten Worshipers. The two spacious, dingy rooms, their connecting doors wide open, were dimly lighted with candles placed upon the plain long deal tables ranged against their discolored walls. The open bookcases were filled with dilapidated old volumes, many more being in use or strewn about, in chaotic heaps, on the tables, benches, or window sills.

In one room, around one of the long tables, were gathered the members of the daily Mishnah class. There were about a dozen of them, mostly poor peddlers or artisans—a humble, seedy, pitiable lot, come after a hard day's work or freezing, to "take a holy word into their mouths." Hardly one of these was up to the Gemarah part of the Talmud, and even the Mishnah only few could brave single-handed. They sat at their open books following their voluntary teacher, a large, heavy, middle-aged man—a mass of unkempt beard, flesh, and rags, ablaze with the intellectual fury of his enormous black eyes. He was reading aloud, with ferocious appetite, swaying and jerking his disheveled bulk, as he ever and anon tossed up his head to interpret the Mishna to his pupils, and every little while breaking off in the middle of a sentence, or even a word, to let his class shout the other half as a guaranty of proficiency. Some of his listeners plodded along the lines of their books, in humble silence, with their index fingers for fescues; the brighter ones boldly interrupted the ponderous man, joyously anticipating his explanations or pointing out some discrepancy; one old dissembler repeated unintelligible half-sentences with well-acted gusto; another little old fellow betrayed the fog in his mind by timid nods of assent, while still another was bravely kept from dozing off on his holy book by frequent neighborly nudges from the man next him. Standing behind the members of the class were some envying "boors," like our poor Asriel, to whom even the Mishnah was a luxury beyond their intellectual means.

One of the long tables in the adjoining room was covered with the open folios of the daily Gemarah class—some fifteen men of all ages and economical conditions from the doddering apple-vender, to whom the holy books are the only source of pleasure in this life as well as in the other, to the well-fed, overdressed young furniture-dealer, with whom the Talmud is a second nature, contracted in the darker days of his existence in Russia. There were several "keen brains" in the group, and a former "prodigy" or two, like Shaya. The class needed no guide, but one old man with a boyish face framed in snow-white hair, and wearing a sea of unstarched linen collar about his emaciated neck, was their chosen reader. He also left many sentences unuttered, but he did it merely because he thought them too well-known to need repetition. Whenever he had something to add to the text, he would address himself to the man by his side, snapping his fingers at him genially, and at times all but pinching him for ecstasy. The others participated now by a twirl of a finger, now by the swift repetition of a whole syllogism, now by an indescribable system of gestures, enacting, in dumb show, the whole logical process involved in a nice point. All at once the whole class would burst into a bedlam of voices and gesticulations. When the whirlwind of enthusiasm subsided, it might be followed by a bit of pleasantry—from the exuberance of good spirits at having got the better of a difficult point—and upon the whole the motley company looked like a happy family at the Sabbath table.

The other long tables in both rooms were occupied by *lomdim* (learned men), each intent upon the good deed of studying "for study's sake" by himself: some humming to their musty folios melodiously; others smiling and murmuring to them, like a fond mother to her babe; still others wailing or grumbling or expostulating with their books, or slapping them and yelling for delight, or roaring like a lion in a cage. A patriarch teaching his ten-year-old grandson and both shouting at the top of their voices, in an entanglement of pantomime; a swarthy little grammar-school boy going it on his own hook over a volume bigger than himself; a "fine householder" in reduced circumstances dignifiedly swinging his form and twirling his sidelock as if he were confiding a secret to his immense golden beard; one or two of the hollow-voiced *prooshim,* who had come to America in search of fortune, but who were now supported by the congregation for giving all their time to "the law and the service"; a knot of men engaged in a mixed discussion of "words of law" and "words of every-day life"—all these voices and murmurs mingled in one effervescence of the sublime and the ridiculous, with tragedy for a keynote—twenty centuries thrown pellmell in a chaos of sound and motion.

Asriel could have lived on the spectacle, and although unable to participate in it himself, he now, since the advent of the prodigy, looked upon it as a world in which he was not without a voice. He was seated in a remote corner of the Gemarah room, now watching the noisy scenes with open-mouthed reverence, now turning to admire Reb Tzalel by his side. The cadaverous face and burning eyes of the peddler were sneering at the drab-colored page before him, while his voice sounded melancholy, like a subdued bugle call.

Presently Reb Tzalel paused, and the two engaged in converse. As Asriel was boasting of Shaya's genius and kindliness of disposition, vainly courting his friend for a word of assent, the peddler, suddenly reddening in the face, interrupted him: "What's the use of playing

cat and rat, Mr. Stroon?" he burst out with his ghastly
smile. "I may as well tell you what lies like a heavy
stone on my heart. Your Shaya is going to the bad. He
is an *appikoros*."*

"An appikoros!" Asriel demanded, as if the word
had suddenly acquired a new meaning.

"Yes, an appikoros, and a Jeroboam the son of Ne-
bat—he sins, and leads others to sin," the Talmudist
declared tartly. "I hated to cause you the pain, Mr.
Stroon, but he has gone too far in Gentile books, and
when he is here and you are not about he talks to everybody he can get hold of concerning the way the
world swings around the sun, how rain and thunder,
day and night—everything—can be explained as a
matter of common sense, and that there is no God in
heaven, and all that sort of vile stuff that you hear from
every appikoros—may they all be hurled from one
end of the world to the other! Everything can be
explained—may the Angel of Death explain it to them,
may they——"

"Hold on, Reb Tzalel!" Asriel shouted: "You need
not curse him: you don't feed him, do you? And
what you say is a lie!—as big a lie as Og the King of
Bashan!" he concluded with calm ferocity, raising his
burly figure from the bench.

"A lie, is it? Very well, then—you shall know all.
Little Mendele saw your imported decoration smoking
a cigarette last Sabbath."

"Shaya smoke on the Sabbath!" Asriel echoed. The
practical, concrete nature of this sin came home to him
with a more forceful blow than all the peddler had said
about Shaya's ungodly theories. "Begone!" the surrounding chaos seemed to say to the "boor." "From
now on you have nothing to do here!"

"Shaya smoke a cigarette on the Sabbath!" he repeated. "Well, and I have this to say, that Mendele, and
yourself, and the whole lot of you are nothing but a set
of first-class liars and begrudging gossip-mongers. It
must give him a belly-ache to think that he could not

*Epicurean; atheist.

afford such a bridegroom for his girl and that I could. Well, I have got a prodigy for my daughter and he has licked the whole lot of you learned fellows to ground coffee. I have got him—see?—and let all my enemies and the boy's enemies burst for envy." He clicked his tongue and snapped his fingers, and for a moment stood glaring witheringly at his interlocutor.

"Well, I am not going to argue with a boor," said Reb Tzalel, in utter disgust.

His words were drowned in the noise, but the "boor" reached Asriel's ear and touched him on the raw. "Shut up, Reb Tzalel!" he said, paling.

"Why should I? This is not your house. It is God's dwelling. Here I am richer than you. I only wanted to say that it is not you I pity. You have been a boor, and that's what you are and will be. But the boy was about to become a great man in Israel, and you have brought him over here for bedeviled America to turn him into an appikoros. Woe! woe! woe!"

"Keep still, Reb Tzalel; take pity," Asriel implored, in a squeaking voice. "Don't spill any salt over my wounds. Forgive me—you know I am a boor. Do take pity and say no more; but all you have said—they have said—is a lie—the cholera choke me if it is not." And gasping for breath, he ran out of the synagogue.

When he found himself in the street he was conscious of some terrific blow having just been dealt him, but did not clearly realize its full meaning; and what had transpired a minute before, between him and Reb Tzalel, seemed to have occurred in the remote past. The clamor of the street peddlers, and the whole maze of squalor and noise through which he was now scurrying, he appeared to hear and to view at a great distance, as if it all were on the other side of a broad river, he hurrying on his lonely way along the deserted bank opposite.

"An appikoros! an appikoros!" he said to himself, vainly trying to grasp the meaning of the word which he knew but too well. "An appikoros, smoking on the Sabbath!" The spectacle smote him in cold blood. "Shaya smoke on the holy Sabbath! It's a lie!"

He started in the direction of Mendele's residence, bent upon thrashing the red-haired talebearer to death. Soon, however, he halted and turned homeward. The courage failed Asriel Stroon to face the man who had seen his daughter's fiancé smoke a cigarette on a Saturday. Then Shaya appeared to his mind as something polluted, sacrilegious, and although this something had nothing in common with his beloved prodigy, save the name, and the young man whitened in the distance, pure and lovely as ever, Asriel's rage surged in the direction of his home, and he mended pace to storm the house as soon as he could get there.

When he collected his wits he decided to wait till he found out everything for himself. For the first time, perhaps, he felt himself a coward. He quailed before the thought that what he had heard from the learned peddler might prove true, and he cringingly begged his own mind to put off the culminating agony of believing it.

Nevertheless, when he saw Shaya, at the supper table, his heart whispered to him, in dismay: "An appikoros!" and the unuttered word enveloped the prodigy in a forbidding, sinister atmosphere.

He now hated Shaya; he felt as though he feared him.

"Where have you been so late, papa?" Flora inquired.

"Deep in the earth. You care much where your papa is, do you?" he snarled.

"Papa!" she said deprecatingly; "are you mad?"

He made no response.

"Have you been to the Mariv service?" Shaya intervened. "I studied at the Souvalk Synagogue today."

Asriel remained grimly uncommunicative.

The young people, reinforced by Tamara, made several other attempts at conversation, but the dogged taciturnity of the head of the family cast a spell of misery over them all, and the meal passed in unsupportable silence.

"See if papa ain't getting on to what you are doing, Shayie," Flora said, when the two were alone.

"Pshaw! is it the first time you see him out of humor? He must have had some trouble with a tenant or janitor."

"He must have," she assented gloomily. "But what if he gets wind? I'm worrying the life out of myself about it."

"So am I. I love your father just the same as if he were my own papa. I wish the wedding were over, don't you?" he asked in his childish way.

X

On the following morning Asriel repaired to the Souvalk Synagogue to attend the service (his usual place of worship he had not the heart to visit), and, incidentally, to ascertain how Shaya had spent his time there the day before.

To his consternation he learned that his "daughter's bridegroom" had not been seen there for weeks.

Asriel held his counsel, and took to shadowing the young man.

He now had no doubt as to the accuracy of Reb Tzalel's story. But it gave him no pain. It was Shaya no longer; it was not his daughter's bridegroom; it was not the prodigy he had imported—it was an appikoros. But then Asriel's heart withered at the notion of being the victim of systematic deception. Shaya was an appikoros and a secret, sneaking enemy.

"That youngster trick Asriel Stroon!" He panted with hatred and thrilled with a detective-like passion to catch Shaya in the act of some grave violation of the Mosaic Law.

He went about the various synagogues where the young man was supposed to study the Talmud, with a keen foretaste of his vicious joy at finding that he had been playing truant. Yet each time his fervent expectations were realized he would, instead of triumph, experience an overpowering sense of defeat.

"You have been cheated out of your boots by a stripling, Asrielke—woe to your foolish head!" he tortured himself, reveling in an agony of fury. "Ah, a cholera into him! I'll show him how to fool Asriel Stroon!"

He discovered that Shaya's frequent companion was his former teacher of English, whom he often visited in his attic room on Clinton Street, and he impatiently awaited the next Saturday to raid the atheistic resort and to overtake Shaya smoking or writing on the holy day. But the climax came a day or two sooner.

After tracing Shaya to the Clinton Street house Asriel stood waiting around a corner, at a vantage point from which he could see the windows of the two garret rooms one of which was the supposed scene of the young man's ungodly pursuits. He had no definite purpose in view, for it was not Sabbath, and he would not spoil his game by apprehending his man in the mere act of reading Gentile books. Yet he was rooted to the place, and remained aimlessly waiting, with his eyes riveted to the windows which they could not penetrate. Tired at last, and overcome with a sense of having been engaged in a fool's errand, he returned home, and, reaching his bedroom, sank on the bed in a prostration of hurt pride and impotent rage.

On the following morning he returned to his post. The attic windows drew him like the evil one, as he put it to himself.

He had been keeping watch for some minutes when, to his fierce joy, Shaya and his accomplice sallied forth into the street. He dogged their steps to Grand Street, and thence, through the Bowery, to Lafayette Place, where they disappeared behind the massive doors of an imposing structure, apparently neither a dwelling place nor an office building.

"Dis a choych?" Asriel asked a passerby.

"A church? No, it's a library—the Astor Library," the stranger explained.

"Ah, a lot of Gentile books!" he exclaimed to himself, disappointed in one way and triumphant in another. The unaccustomed neighborhood and the novelty of his impressions increased the power of the "evil one" over him. He took up a position whence he could observe without being observed, and waited for the two young men to come out. What he would gain by tracing them back to the Jewish quarter he never asked himself. He waited because the "evil one" would not let him stir from the spot.

An hour passed. He was growing faint with hunger; yet he never moved. "He has not had his lunch, either," he thought. "Still, he can stand it. It's the witchcraft of the Gentile books—may he be burned to death!—keeping up his strength. They'll come out in a minute or two."

Many more minutes elapsed, and still Asriel waited. At last "Here, they are, the convert Jews! Look at them—how jolly! It's the Black Year shining out of their faces—may they shine on their death-beds! That beggar of a teacher I shall have arrested."

He followed them through Fourth Street back to the Bowery and down the rumbling thoroughfare, till—"a lamentation!"—they entered a Christian restaurant!

A terrific pang smote Asriel's heart. It was as if he saw his temple, the embodiment of many years of labor, the object of his fondest cares, just completed and ready to be dedicated, suddenly enveloped in flames. The prodigy, *his* prodigy, his Kaddish, his glory in this and the other world, plunged into the very thick of impurity!

He made to rush after them, but checked himself to wait till the *treife** food was served them. A few minutes later he made his entry, cool and collected as a regular customer.

Each of the two young men was bent on a veal cutlet. The collegian was dispatching his with the nonchalant appetite and ease of manner of an habitué, whereas poor Shaya looked like one affecting to relish his first plate of raw oysters. The smells proceeding from the kitchen made him dizzy, and the cutlet itself, partly because he was accustomed to meat of a better quality, but mainly through the consciousness of eating treife, inclined him to nausea.

Asriel took a vacant chair at the same table.

"Bless the sitter,† Shaya!" he said.

*Unclean; not prepared according to the laws of Moses.
†Form of greeting when the host is found at table.

The two young men were petrified.

"How is the pork—does it taste well?" Asriel pursued.

"It is not pork. It is veal cutlet," the teacher found tongue to retort.

"I am not speaking to you, am I?" Asriel hissed out. Murder was swelling in his heart. But at this point the waiter came up to his side.

"Vot'll ye have?"

"Notink!" Asriel replied, suddenly rising from his seat and rushing out, as if this were the most terrible sort of violence he could conceive.

XI

Asriel found his daughter playing.

"Stop that or I'll smash your Gentile piano to pieces!" he commanded her, feeling as though the instrument had all along been in the conspiracy and were now bidding him defiance.

"Why, what's the matter?" she questioned, getting up from her stool in stupefaction.

"Matter? Bluff a dead rooster, not me—my head is still on my shoulders. Here it is, you see?" he added, taking himself by the head. "It's all up, Flora."

"What do you mean?" she made out to inquire.

"I mean that if Shayke* ever enters this house I'll murder both of you. You thought your papa was a fool, didn't you? Well, you are a poor hand at figuring, Flora. I knew everything, but I wanted some particulars. I have got them all now here, in my pocket, and a minute ago I took the pleasure of bidding him 'bless the sitter' in a Gentile restaurant—may he be choked with his treife gorge!"

"You've got no business to curse him like that!" she flamed out, coloring violently.

"*I* have no business? And who is to stop me, pray?"

"*I* am. It ain't my fault. You know I did not care at first."

*Contemptuous diminutive of Shaya.

The implication that he had only himself to blame threw him into a new frenzy. But he restrained himself, and said with ghastly deliberation: "Flora, you are not going to marry him."

"I *am*. I can't live without him," she declared with quiet emphasis.

Asriel left her room.

"It's all gone, Tamara! My candle is blown out," he said, making his way from the dining room to the kitchen. "There is no Shaya any longer."

"A weeping, a darkness to me! Has an accident—mercy and peace!—befallen the child?"

"Yes, he is 'dead and buried, and gone from the market place.' Worse than that: a convert Jew is worse than a dead one. It's all gone, Tamara!" he repeated gravely. "I have just seen him eating treife in a Gentile restaurant. America has robbed me of my glory."

"Woe is me!" the housekeeper gasped, clutching at her wig. "Treife! Does he not get enough to eat here?" She then burst out, "Don't I serve him the best food there is in the world? Any king would be glad to get such dinners."

"Well, it seems treife tastes better," Asreil rejoined bitterly.

"A calamity upon my sinful head! We must have evil-eyed the child; we have devoured him with our admiring looks."

While Asriel was answering her volley of questions, Flora stealthily left the house.

When Stroon missed her he hurried off to Clinton Street. There he learned of the landlady that her lodger had left a short while before, in the company of his friend and a young lady whom the two young men had found waiting in her parlor. In his despair Asriel betook himself to the Astor Library, to some of Flora's friends, and even to the Bowery restaurant.

When he reached home, exhausted with fatigue and rage, he found his daughter in her room.

"Where have you been?"

"I am going to tell you, but don't blame Shaya. He

is awful fond of you. It's all my fault. He didn't want
to go, but I couldn't help it, papaly. We've been to the
city court and got married by a judge. Shaya didn't
want to."

"You married!"

"Yes, but don't be angry, papaly darlin'. We'll do
everything to please you. If you don't want him to be
a doctor, he won't."

"A doctor!" he resumed, still speaking like one in a
daze. "Is that what you have been up to? I see—you
have got the best of me, after all. You married, Flora?"
he repeated, unable to apply the meaning of the word
to his daughter. "In court—without Canopy and Dedication—like Gentiles? What have you done, Flora?"
He sank into a chair, gnashing his teeth and tearing at
his sidelocks.

"Papaly, papaly, don't!" she sobbed, hugging and
kissing him. "You know I ain't to blame for it all."

It dawned upon him that no serious wrong had been
committed, after all, and that it could all be mended by
a Jewish marriage ceremony; and so great was his relief at the thought that it took away all his anger, and
he even felt as if he were grateful to his daughter for
not being guilty of a graver transgression than she was.

"I know you are not to blame," he said, tragic in his
calmness. "America has done it all. But what is the use
talking! It's gone, and I am not going to take another
sin upon my soul. I won't let you be his wife without
Canopy and Dedication. Let the Jewish wedding come
off at once—this week—tomorrow. You have got the
best of me and I don't kick, do I? It seems God does
not want Asrielke the boor to have some joy in his old
age, nor a Kaddish for his soul, when the worms will
be feasting upon his silly bones——"

"Oh, don't say that, papa. It'll break my heart if you
do. You know Shaya is as good as a son to you."

"An appikoros my son? An appikoros my Kaddish?
No," he rejoined, shaking his head pensively.

As he said it he felt as if Flora, too, were a stranger
to him.

He descended to the basement in a state of mortal indifference.

"I have lost everything, Tamara," he said. "I have no daughter, either. I am all alone in the world—alone as a stone."

He had no sooner closed the kitchen door behind him, than Flora was out and away to Clinton Street to surprise her bridegroom with the glad news of her father's surrender.

The housekeeper was in the kitchen, sewing upon some silk vestments for the scrolls of her synagogue. Asriel stood by her side, leaning against the cupboard door, in front of the Palestine box. Speaking in a bleak, resigned undertone, he told her of Flora's escapade and of his determination to make the best of it by precipitating the Jewish ceremony. A gorgeous celebration was now, of course, out of the question. The proposed fête which was to have been the talk of the synagogues and which had been the center of his sweetest dreams had suddenly turned in his imagination to something like a funeral feast. Tamara bade him be of good cheer, and cited Rabbi Nochum And-This-Too, who would hail the severest blows of fate with the words: "And this, too, is for the best." But Asriel would not be comforted.

"Yes, Tamara, it is gone, all gone," he murmured forlornly. "It was all a dream—a last year's lemon pie. It has flown away and you can't catch it. Gone, and that's all. You know how I feel? As if some fellow had played a joke on me."

The pious woman was moved.

"But it is a sin to take things so close to heart," she said impetuously. "You must take care of your health. Bear up under your affliction like a righteous Jew, Reb Asriel. Trust to the Uppermost, and you will live to rejoice in your child and in her children, if God be pleased."

Asriel heaved a sigh and fell silent. He stood with his eyes upon the pilgrim box, listening to the whisper of her needle.

"You know what; let us go to the Land of Israel," he

presently said, as though continuing an interrupted sentence. "They have got the best of me. I cannot change the world. Let them live as they please and be responsible to the Uppermost for themselves. I don't care the kernel of a hollow nut. I shall give Flora half my property and the rest I'll sell. You are a righteous woman, Tamara. Why not marry and end our days serving God in the Holy Land together?"

Tamara plied her needle with redoubled zeal. He could see only her glossy black wig and the flaming dusk of her cheek.

"We'll have a comfortable living and plenty of money for deeds of charity," he pursued. "I know I am only a boor. Do I say I am not? But is a boor no human being at all? Can't I die a righteous Jew?" he pleaded piteously.

The glossy wig bent lower and the silk rustled busily.

"You know that I have on my tongue what I have on my lung. Tamara. I mean what I say, and we want no matchmakers. America is now treife to me. I can't show my head. The world is dark and empty to me. All is gone, gone, gone. I am a little baby, Tamara. Come, take pity. I shall see Flora married according to the law of Moses and Israel, and then let us put up a canopy and set out on our journey. I want to be born again. Well?"

There was no response.

"Well, Tamara?"

"Since it is the will of God," she returned resignedly, without raising her head from the vestments.

XII

Flora was all of a flutter with impatience to share her joy with Shaya, and yearning for his presence. She had not seen him since he had become her legal husband, and the two or three hours seemed a week.

When the German landlady of the little Clinton Street house told her that neither her lodger nor his friend were in the attic room the young woman's heart sank within her. Her message seemed to be bubbling over and her over-wrought mind too weak to bear it another minute. She mentally berated her absent bridegroom, and not knowing whither to bend her steps in quest of him she repaired to some girl friends to while away the time and to deliver herself of part of her burden to them.

"When he comes tell him he da's not leave for one second till I come back. Tell him I've got some grand news for him," she instructed the landlady, struggling hard against a wild temptation to unbosom herself to the stranger.

It was about eight o'clock when she returned. Shaya met her in the hallway.

"Well?" he inquired anxiously.

"Well?" she mocked him. "You are a daisy! Why didn't you wait? Couldn't you guess I'd come?"

"How should I? But tell me what your father says. Why should you torment me?"

"He says he don't want you," she replied. But her look told even a more encouraging tale than the one she had to deliver, and they flew into mutual embrace in an outburst of happiness which seemed to both of them unlike any they had ever experienced before.

"A life into your little eyes! A health into your little hands and feet!" he muttered, stroking her arm sheepishly. "You shall see how fine it will all come out. You don't know me yet. I tell you you don't begin to know me," he kept repeating with some braggadocio and without distinctly knowing what he meant.

They were to return home at once and to try to pacify Asriel as best they could. When Flora pressed him to take his hat and overcoat, however, he looked reluctant and then said: "Floraly, you know what; come upstairs for just one minute. We are reading the nicest book you ever saw, and there is a lot of such nice gentlemen there!—several genuine Americans—Christians. Do come, Floraly." He drew her up the two flights of stairs almost by force. "Don't be afraid: the landlady knows all about it," he whispered. "You'll see what nice people. I tell you they are so educated, and they love Jews so much! A Jew is the same as a Gentile to them—even better."

Flora felt a lump growing in her heart. The notion of Shaya being at this minute interested in anything outside of herself and their mutual happiness literally dazed her, and before she had time to recover from her shock she was in the over-crowded attic.

There were some ten or twelve men in the room, some seated—two on chairs, two on the host's trunk, and three on his bed—the others standing by the window or propping the sloping wall with their heads. They were clustered about a round table, littered with books, papers, and cigarette stumps. A tin can was hissing on the flat top of a little parlor stove, and some of the company were sipping Russian tea from tumblers, each with a slice of lemon floating in it. The group was made up of a middle-aged man with a handsome and intensely intellectual Scotch face, who was a laborer by day and a philosopher by night; a Swedish tailor with the face of a Catholic priest; a Zurich Ph.D. in blue eyeglasses; a young Hindoo who eked out a wretched existence by selling first-rate articles to second-rate weeklies, and several Russian Jews, all of them insatiable debaters and most of them with university or gymnasium diplomas. The group met every Thursday to read and discuss Harriet Martineau's *Auguste Comte,* under the guidance of the Scotchman, who was a leading spirit in positivist circles.

The philosopher surrendered his chair to the lady, in a flurry of chivalry, but a seat was made for him on the trunk, and he forthwith resumed his reading with well-bred impetuosity, the kerosene lamp in the center of the table casting a halo upon his frank, pleasant face.

His auditors were now listening with conscious attention, some of the younger men affecting an absorbed mien or interrupting the reader with unnecessary questions. Shaya's eyes were traveling between Flora and the Scotchman's audience. "Did you ever see such a beautiful and stylish young lady?" he seemed to be saying. "She is my bride—mine and nobody else's in the world," and, "Look at these great men, Flora—I am their chum." Presently, however, he became engrossed in the reading; and only half-conscious of Flora's presence, he sat leaning forward, his mouth wide open, his face rapt, and his fingers quietly reproducing the mental gymnastics of Comte's system in the air.

The young woman gazed about her in perplexity. The Scotchman and his reading inspired her with respect, but the rest of the company and the *tout ensemble* of the scene impressed her as the haunt of queer individuals, meeting for some sinister purpose. It was anything but the world of intellectual and physical elegance into which she had dreamed to be introduced by marriage to a doctor. Any society of "custom peddlers" was better dressed than these men, who appeared to her more like some of the grotesque and uncouth characters in Dickens's novels than an assemblage of educated people. For a moment even Shaya seemed a stranger and an enemy. Overcome by the stuffy, overheated atmosphere of the misshapen apartment, she had a sense of having been kidnaped into the den of some terrible creatures, and felt like crying for help. Next she was wondering what her Shaya could have in common with these shabby beings and what it all had to do with becoming a doctor and riding in a buggy.

"Shaya!" she whispered, tugging him by the coatsleeve.

"Just one moment, Floraly," he begged her. "Ah, it's so deep!"

A discussion engaged itself. The Russians fell to greedily. One of them, in particular, a young man with a dignified bass, was hateful to Flora. She could not have told you why, but his voice, coupled with the red embroidery of his Little-Russian shirt front, cut her to the quick.

The room was full of smoke and broken English.

Shaya was brimful of arguments and questions which he had not the courage to advance; and so he sat, now making a vehement gesture of despair at somebody else's absurdities, now nodding violent approval, and altogether fidgeting about in a St. Vitus's dance of impotent pugnacity.

"Shaya, it is getting late, and papa——"

"One second, do please, Floraly, may you live long," he implored her, with some irritation; and taking the book from the Scotchman's hand, he fell to turning over its leaves in a feverish search of what struck him as a misinterpreted passage.

Flora was going to protest and to threaten to leave without him, but she could neither speak nor stir from her seat. A nightmare of desolation and jealousy choked her—jealousy of the Scotchman's book, of the Little-Russian shirt, of the empty tea-glasses with the slices of lemon on their bottoms, of the whole excited crowd, and of Shaya's entire future, from which she seemed excluded.

A Providential Match

He is still known among his townspeople as Rouvke
Arbel. Rouvke they call him, because this name, in its
more respectful form of Rouven, was bestowed upon
him on the eighth day of his life, at the ceremony
which initiated him into Israel. As to the nickname of
Arbel, which is Yiddish for "sleeve," he is indebted for
it to the apparently never-to-be-forgotten fact that before he came to America, and when he still drove
horses and did all sorts of work for Peretz the distiller,
he was in the habit of assigning to the sleeves of his
sheepskin coat such duties as generally devolve upon a
pocket-handkerchief.

That was only about four years ago; and yet Rouvke
is now quite a different young man in quite a different
coat and with a handkerchief in its side pocket. The
face is precisely the same: the same everlasting frown,
the same pockmarks, hollow yet ruddy cheeks, snub
nose, and little gray eyes, at once timid and sly. But for
all that, such is the dissimilarity between the Rouvke
of four years ago and the Rouvke of today that recently, when his mother, who still peddles boiled pota-
toes in Kropovetz, Government of Kovno, had been
surprised by a photograph of her son, her first impulse
was to spit at the portrait and to repudiate it as the ungodly likeness of some unknown Gentile. But then this
photograph, which, by the way, Rouvke had taken by

mere chance and for the sole reason that it was no use
trying to get any cash from the Bowery photographer,
to whom he had sold, on the installment plan, "a pair
of pants made to order"—this photograph fully establishes its original's claim of not being a "greener" in
the New World. For this is what the portrait reveals.
Rouvke's hair is now entirely free from the pair of
sidelocks, or *peieths,* which dangled over his ears
when he first set foot on American soil; it is parted in
the middle and combed on either side in the shape of
a curled ostrich feather. He wears a collar; and this collar is so high and so much below the size of his neck
that it gives you the uncomfortable idea of its owner
having swallowed the handle of the whip with which
he used to rule over Peretz, the distiller's mare. The
flannel muffler, which seemed never to part company
with him while he lived in Kropovetz, has been supplanted by a gay necktie, and the sheepskin by a diagonal "cutaway."

Now, if you were conversant with the business of
"custom-peddling," you might perhaps conjecture,
upon inspecting Rouvke's photograph, that his cutaway, which seems to be at least one size too large for
him, had formerly encased the portly figure of a bartender. And so it had, although for no length of time;
for finding the bartender as backward in his payments
as the photographer had been, Rouvke soon contrived
to prevail upon his delinquent customer to exchange
the cutaway for a "mishfeet corkshcrew Printz Albert,"
which would "feet him like a glove," and carrying off
the diagonal in advance he let the bartender wait for
the glove-like garment until doomsday.

But "bishness is bishness," as Rouvke would put it.
Otherwise he is quite a fine fellow. His bills he pays
promptly. On the Eve of the Day of Atonement he sub-
scribes a dollar or two to the funds of the synagogue
"Sons of Kropovetz," and has been known to start a
newly arrived townsman in business by standing his
security in a perforated chair-seat store to the amount
of two dollars and a half. Nevertheless, since he visits
the Bowery Savings Bank on Saturdays with the same

punctuality with which he puts on his phylacteries and prays in his room every morning on weekdays, and since his townsfolk, who, unlike him, are blessed with families, cannot afford such excursions to the Bowery institution, these latter Kropovetz Americans begrudge him his bank account, as well as his credit in the peddler-supply stores, and out of sheer envy like to refer to him, not as Robert Friedman, as his business card reads, but as "Rouvke Arbel—what do you think of that slouch!"

Let us hope, however, that these invidious references never reach Rouvke's ears; for his susceptibilities in this direction are, it must be owned, rather keen. Indeed, if there be a weakness of which he is guilty, it is a rather intense love of approbation and a slight proneness to parade himself. I do not know what he would not give to have people say: "Robert is a smart fellow! Robert is no greenhorn! Robert is the best soul in the world!" It was this foible which, in translating his first name into English, caused him to prefer Robert to Reuben, on the ground that the former appellation seemed to have less of Kropovetz and more of a "tzibilized" sound to it.

The feminine element was until recently absent from Rouvke's life. True, while at home, in the domestic employ of Peretz the distiller, he would bestow an occasional pinch on Leike the servant-maid's cheek. But that was by no means a pinch of gallantry; it was never one of those pinches which a Kropovetz lad will accompany with a look of ostensible mock admiration in his half-shut eyes, and with the exclamation "Capital stuff, that! As sure as I am a Jew!" No! Leike the lame devil, Leike the scold, Rouvke hated from the deepest recesses of his driver's soul; and when he pinched her, as he often did in the kitchen, he did it, not from love, but simply that she might smart and "jump to heaven, the scarecrow." And Leike would so amply repay him with the ladle, that there would ensue a series of the most complex and the most ingenious oaths, attended by hair-tearing and by squeaking, till the mistress would come rushing in and terminate the war by boxing the ears of both belligerent parties.

To Hanele, his master's only daughter, Rouvke used to serve tea with more alacrity than to the rest of the family; and when Feive, the matchmaker, made his first appearance and the first suitor was introduced, Rouvke's appetite for sour cream and rye bread somehow disappeared for a few days, while Rouvke himself moved about as if out of gear, and on one occasion caught a slap in the face, because, upon being ordered to fetch a pail of water, he stood staring as if he did not understand Yiddish. But this seemed of no consequence, and Rouvke himself could not, for the life of him, explain this sudden disappearance both of his appetite and presence of mind. Indeed, how could he have dared to connect Hanele with it? What could there have been in common between the relish for sour cream of a mere driver, and the pet daughter of Reb* Peretz, the distiller, the son of Rabbi Berele, and the first citizen of Kropovetz?

The negotiations of which Hanele was the object were soon broken off, and Rouvke's truant appetite again fell into the line of drivers' appetites; with this difference, however, that, when Hanele asked for a glass of tea, he would now run to serve her with still more eagerness than before.

Suitor after suitor called and was dismissed, until a year rolled by, when Rouvke's name appeared in the military service-roll, and he packed off for America.

In America he passed his first four years in the school of peddling, among the most diligent and most successful of its students, and so had no mind for anything else in the world. Only during the first few months his heart would almost unremittingly be pining and yearning after Kropovetz—after his mother, his master's family, his master's apple tree, under which he had loved to steal a nap on summer days; the raised lawn in front of the house, where he would sit down of a Friday evening and show off his enormous top boots,

*Abbreviation of Rabbi, and used as equivalent of Mister.

just after he had given them a fresh coat of tar, "in honor of the Sabbath"; the well by the synagogue, where on Saturdays, during the intermission in the morning prayer, he used to indulge in a lark with his chums, while the elder members of the congregation were attending the reading of the scrolls. But of all the memories which at this early period of his life in New York troubled his busy mind and gnawed at his enterprising heart that of Hanele was the most excruciating and the most persistent. In due course, however, the waves of time drowned in his mind and in his heart Hanele as well as the apple tree, the lawn in front of the house, and the well by the synagogue. Only at rare intervals, when plying a new arrival from Kropovetz with questions as to the place where his cradle had been rocked, Rouvke would, after a cursory inquiry concerning the health of his mother and of the Peretz family in general, exact the most minute information about Hanele; and then he would for some time feel as if his heart was "stretching," as he himself would mentally define the effect of his stirred-up recollections.

For the rest, Rouvke followed the regular peddler course with undisturbed assiduity. From a handkerchief peddler he was promoted to "basket-peddling"—that is to say, his stock became plentiful enough and heterogeneous enough to call for a portable store in the shape of a basket. After a while he joined the class where the peddling is done on the "stairses" of tenement houses. The curriculum of this class includes the occasional experience of being sent head foremost down all the "stairses," of then picking one's self up and imperturbably knocking at some door on the ground floor, only to come face to face with the janitor and thus get into fresh trouble, and so on. Finally, Rouvke reached the senior grade of the institution, and graduated with the degree of custom peddler, and with the following business card for his diploma: "ROBERT FRIEDMAN, DEALER IN FURNITURE, CARPETS, JEWELRY, CLOTHING, LADIES' DRESS GOODS, ETC. WEEKLY PAYMENTS TAKEN."

As has been said, Rouvke was a stranger to the feminine world. He met a good many members of the gentle sex, but that was exclusively in a business way. The other peddlers he would often encounter on the street in company with nicely dressed "yoong laddas," with whom they loudly spoke in English. He also knew that these fellows attended dancing academies, balls, and picnics; but to him himself these entertainments were a *terra incognita.* And sometimes when Rouvke entered the house of a fellow countryman on business (Rouvke never visited his fellow countrymen except on business), and there happening to be an English-speaking young woman, the host said: "Miss Goldberg—Mr. Friedman; Mr. Friedman—Miss Goldberg," Mr. Friedman would blush crimson at the transaction, while the sentence, "I'm pleashed to meech you," which he well knew was then in order, stuck in his throat and would not budge. This, however, was no common occurrence, for Rouvke took care to avoid such predicaments. At all events, he never allowed these things to bother his head.

After a while, however, by the time the peddlers and his townsfolk estimated his capital in cash at five thousand dollars, and when he actually had over three thousand dollars in bank deposits and twenty-five summers behind his back, his heart somehow resumed its old stretching process. He was at a loss to account for it; but he became aware that each time he passed by a pretty young woman this stretching sensation forced him to outrun her, and, making a show of stopping to look at a window display, to allow his eyes to stray off under the brim of the fair one's hat.

He gradually became a new sort of Rouvke. Formerly, when he was subjected to the tortures of an introduction to a "yoong ladda," the ordeal would result in a mere blush, accompanied by one or two minutes' violent throbbing. Whereas now, every time a similar accident befell him, he would, after the calamity was over, hasten to find himself in front of a looking glass, and fall to inspecting his glaring necktie and more particularly the pockmarks on his nose. In times past he was hardly ever conscious of these traces of smallpox on his face; now they dwelt in his mind with such pertinacity that one night he dreamed of seeing a watermelon, which was somehow at the same time a dog with a huge nose all covered with pocks. And when he awoke in the morning he felt so sick at heart that he could not relish his breakfast, and was so dazed all that day that he had a carpet sent to an Irishwoman who had ordered some satin for a dress.

Rouvke enrolled in a public evening school for immigrants, and when he had achieved the wisdom of piecing together the letters in "cat," "rat," "mat," of the *First Reader*, he one afternoon bought a newspaper, and applied himself to looking for an advertisement of some physician who would undertake to remove the footprints of smallpox. He had an idea that the papers contained kindred advertisements. The undertaking proved a failure, however, for Rouvke could detect in the paper neither "cat" nor "rat," while the other words only swam before his eyes. And his heart was "stretching" and "stretching."

It would be unfair to Rouvke, however, to ascribe his attending evening school to the sole purpose of being able to make out a medical advertisement. His chief motive therefor was twofold. In the first place, he would often say to himself: "Robert, bear in mind that you are Rouvke no longer; the chances are that in a year or two you may open a peddler's supply-store of your own: now, you know that the owner of a store who cannot read and write is in danger of being robbed by his bookkeeper." In the second place, his "stretching" heart seemed to whisper: "Robert, remember those ladies have nothing but sneers for a gentleman who does not know how to read a newspaper."

Moreover, those of his fellow peddlers who had studied the Talmud in Russia, and having, therefore, some mental training, found no trouble in picking up some crumbs of broken English in its written form, would often rally him on the "iron head" he must possess to retain the ponderous load of the addresses and accounts of his numerous customers without committing them to writing. These pleasantries pierced

Rouvke to the heart; but the pain they gave him was not half so cruel as his moral pangs at the jokes which were showered at him on the subject of his shyness in the presence of ladies. Often he would be entrapped into the company of a "nearly American-born" daughter of Israel; but a still more frequent prank at his expense was for a facetious fellow to drag him out to the middle of the floor in a peddler-supply store, and to force him into a waltz, or to jestingly measure his legs, by way of ascertaining their potential adroitness in a dancing hall. "Eh, Robert!" they would torment him, "Buy a teecket for a ball, veel you? A ball fi'sht clesh, I tell you. Come, ven the laddas veel shee you, dey veel get shtuck—in de co'ners." Robert would struggle, scream, swear, and, after all, steal up to the front of the looking glass. And his heart would be "stretching" and "stretching."

Whenever he heard of a new marriage, he would apply for details as to the bride and the bridegroom—how much he earned a week, how they came to be engaged, what space of time interposed between the engagement and the wedding. One Saturday morning, while mounting the stairs which led to his miniature hall bedroom, he saw through an open door a young woman buttoning the shirt-collar for her husband; whereupon his heart swelled with a feeling of mixed envy and extreme friendliness for the young couple. "Who is he?" he remarked to himself, on reaching his room, which now seemed to him desolate and lonely. "Only a tailor, a penniless workman. When I am married I shall not live in a tenement house." And at this his fancy unfolded a picture: A parlor with bronze clock on the mantelpiece; a mirror between two lace window curtains; a dark-eyed little woman in a chocolate-colored wrapper sweeping a carpet of flaming red and yellow; and, behold! he, Robert, comes in from business, and the young woman addresses him in a piping little voice: "Hello, Rob! Will you have dinner?" just as he had the day before seen in the house of a newly married custom-peddler.

And it came to pass, in those days of "heart-stretching," that one Saturday morning Robert met at the "Sons of Kropovetz" Synagogue a new arrival from his native place in the person of Feive the *melamed*. As the Hebrew term implies, this tall and bony old gentleman, with the face of a martyr, had at home conducted one of the schools in which a Jewish boy passes the day, learning the Word of God. As is not unusual with melameds, Feive's profession yielded him an income which made it necessary for him to devote his spare hours to the business of *shadchen*, or *shidech* agent—that is, of matchmaker in the matrimonial sense of the word. In course of time the shadchen spirit had become so deeply imbedded in Reb Feive's soul that even on finding himself in New York, and before his draggling satin coat had had time to exhale its lingering traces of steerage odors, his long and snuff-stocked nose fell to smelling for shidechs.

"Ah, Reb Feive!" Rouvke accosted his townsman, "how do you do? Quite an unexpected guest, as sure as I am a Jew! When did you arrive?"

And after a perfunctory catechism upon the health of his mother and Kropovetz matters in general, he inquired about his old master.

"Peretz?" the old man echoed Rouvke's interrogation. "May the Uppermost have mercy on him! You have heard that he is now in reduced circumstances, have you not? The distillery is closed."

"You don't say so!"

"Yes, he is in a very bad way," Reb Feive resumed, curling one of his long yellowish-gray sidelocks. "You know what hard times the Jews are now having in Russia. Things are getting from bad to worse—may He whom I dare not mention without washing my hands deliver us and preserve!—a Jew can nowadays hardly engage in any business, much less in the liquor line. Poor Peretz, he looks so careworn!"

"Can it be true that the distillery has been closed? I am *very* sorry."

Rouvke was moved with profound pity for his old employer, who had been kind to him, and to whom he had been devoted. But this feeling of commiseration was instantly succeeded by a vague sense of triumph. "What have I lived to see!" Rouvke seemed to exclaim. "I am now richer than Reb Peretz, as sure as I am a Jew!" And at this he became aware of the bankbook in his breast pocket.

"Oh, I am *very, very* sorry for him!" he added, with renewed sincerity, after a slight pause. "Why, such an honest Jew! And how is Hanele?"

"As usual," the shadchen rejoined—"still unmarried. But it serves Peretz right. (May God not punish me for my hard words!) When I offered her the best matches in the world, he was hard to please. Nothing short of a king would have suited his ambition."

As the old shadchen spoke his right arm, hand, and fingers were busily engaged punctuating his words with a system of the most intricate and most diversified evolutions in the air.

"And how does she look?" Rouvke again broke in. "Is she still as pretty as she used to be?"

"That she is," the matchmaker returned grimly. "But all the worse for her. Would she were plainer looking, for then her father would not have been so fastidious about a young man for her, and she might be a mother of three children by this time."

"Oh, she will have no trouble in making a match; such a beauty!" Rouvke observed.

In the afternoon of the same day, Rouvke lay across his bed with his legs stretched on a chair, after his wont, and his head lost in recollections of Hanele. She had recently all but faded away from his memory, and when he did have occasion to recall her, her portrait before his mind's eye would be a mere faint-drawn outline. But now, singularly enough, he could somehow again vividly see her good-natured, deep, dark eyes, and her rosy lips perpetually exposing the dazzling whiteness of her teeth and illuminating her pallid face with inextinguishable good humor; he could hear the rustle of her fresh calico dress as she friskily ran up to answer her father's solemnly affectionate "Good Sabbath," on Reb Peretz's return from synagogue, the last Saturday before Rouvke's departure.

The image did not send a yearning thrill through Rouvke, as it would have done during his first few months in America; still, on the other hand, it now had for his wearied soul a quieting, benign charm, which it had never exercised before, and the more deeply to indulge in its soothing effect, he shut his eyes. "Suppose I marry her." The thought flashed through his mind, but was instantly dismissed as an absurdity too gross to be indulged even for a pastime. But the thought carried him back to his old days in Kropovetz, and he wished he could go there in flesh for a visit. What a glorious time it would be to let them see his stylish American dress, his businesslike manners and general air of prosperity and "echucation!" Ah, how they would be stupefied to see the once Rouvke Arbel thus elegantly attired, "like a regula' dood!" For who in all Kropovetz wears a cutaway, a brown derby, a necktie, and a collar like his? And would it not be lovely to donate a round sum to the synagogue? Oh, how he would be sought after and paraded!

"Poor Reb Peretz!" he said to himself, transferring his thoughts to the news of his old employer's adversity. "Poor Hanele!" Whereat the Kropovetz girl loomed up, her head lowered and tears trickling down her cheeks, as he had once seen her when she sat quietly lamenting her defeated expectation of a new dress. Rouvke conceived the vague idea of sending Reb Peretz fifty dollars, which would make the respectable sum of one hundred rubles. But the generous plan was presently lost in a labyrinth of figures, accounts of his customers, and reflections upon his prospective store, which the notion of fifty dollars called forth in his dollar-ridden brain.

He thus lay plunged in meditation until his reverie was broken by the door flying open.

"Good Sabbath! Good Sabbath!" Reb Feive greeted his young townsman with his martyr-like features relaxed into a significant smile, as he squeezed himself through the narrow space between the half-opened door and the foot of the bedstead. "Do not take ill my

not knocking at the door first. I am not yet used to
your customs here, greenhorn that I am."

"Ah, Reb Feive! Good Sabbath!" Rouvke returned,
starting up with an anxious air and foreboding an appeal for pecuniary assistance.

"Guess what brings me, Rouven."

"How can I tell?" the host rejoined, with a forced
simper. "And why should you not call just for a visit
in honor of the Sabbath? You are a welcome guest. Be
seated," he added, indicating his solitary chair and
himself keeping his seat on the bed, which rendered
the additional service of lounge.

"How dare these beggarly greenhorns beset me in
this manner?" he left unsaid. "Indeed, what business
have they to come to America at all?"

"Well, how are things going on in Kropovetz?" he
asked, audibly. "Business is very dull *here*—*very* dull,
indeed—may I not be punished for talking business on
Sabbath—"

"Well, *do* leave business alone! You had better hear
my errand, Rouven," the matchmaker said, working his
fingers. "Suppose I had a shidech for you, eh?"

"A shidech?" Rouvke ejaculated, much relieved
from his misgivings, only to become all of a flutter
with delicious surprise.

"Yes, a shidech; and what sort of a one! You never
dreamed of such a shidech, I can assure you. Never
mind blushing like that. Why, is it not high time for a
young man like you to get married?"

"I am not blushing at all," Rouvke protested, coloring still more deeply, and missing the sentence by
which he had been about to inform himself of the fair
one's name without betraying his feverish impatience.

"Well," Reb Feive resumed, with a smile, and twist-
ing his sidelock into a corkscrew, "it would be too
cruel to try your patience. Let us come straight to the
point, then. I mean—guess whom—well, I mean
Hanele, Peretz the distiller's Hanele! What do you
think of that?" the shadchen added in a whisper, as he
let go of his corkscrew, and started back in well-acted
ecstasy to watch the produced effect.

Rouvke flushed up to the roots of his hair, while his mouth opened in one of those embarrassed grins which seem to be especially adapted to the mouths of Kropovetz horse-drivers—one which makes the general expression of the face such that you are at a loss whether to take it for a smile or for the preliminary to a cry.

"You must be joking, Reb Feive. Why I a-a-a-I am not thinking of getting married as yet; a-a-you had better tell me some news," he faltered.

The fact is that the shadchen's attack had taken him so unawares that it gave him no time to analyze his own mind, and although the subject thrilled his soul with delightful curiosity, he dreaded the risk of committing himself. But Feive was not the man to let himself be put off so easily in matters of a professional nature; and so, warming up to the beloved topic, he launched out in a flood of garrulity, emphasizing his speech now by striking some figure in space, now by an energetic twirl of his yellowish gray appendages. He enlarged with real shadchenlike gusto on the prospective bride's virtues and accomplishments; on the love which, according to him, she had always professed for Rouvke; on the frivolity of American girls; on the honor it would confer upon his listener to marry into the family of Reb Peretz the distiller.

Rouvke followed Reb Feive with breathless attention, but never uttered a word or a gesture which might be interpreted into an encouragement. This, however, mattered but little to the old matrimonial commission agent, for, carried away with his own eloquence, he talked himself into the impression that Rouvke "was willing," if I may be permitted to borrow a phrase from a more famous horse-driver. At any rate, when Reb Feive suddenly bethought himself that he came near missing the afternoon service at the synagogue, and abruptly got up from his seat, Rouvke seemed anxious to detain him; and as he returned "What is your hurry, Reb Feive?" to his departing visitor's "Good-pie!—is that the way you say here on leaving?" he felt for the old man a kind of filial tenderness.

Choson is a term applied to a Jewish young man, embracing the period from the time he is placed on the matrimonial market down to the termination of the nuptial festivities. There is all the difference in the world between a choson and a common unmarried mortal of the male sex, who is left to the bare designation of *bocher,* the very sound of the hymeneal title possessing an indefinable charm, an element of solemnity, which seems to invest its bearer with a glittering halo.

Reb Feive thus suddenly, as if by a magic wand, converted Rouvke from a simple bocher into a choson. And so keenly alive was Rouvke to his unexpected transformation, that for some time after the wizard's departure his face was wreathed in bashful smiles, as if his new self, by its dazzling presence, embarrassed him. He felt the change in himself in a general way, however, and quite apart from the idea of Hanele. As to Peretz's daughter, the notion of her assenting to marry him again seemed preposterous. Besides, admitting for argument's sake, as the phrase goes, that she would accept him, Rouvke reflected that he would then not be fool enough to enter into wedlock with a portionless girl; that if he waited a year or two longer (although it seemed much too long to wait), that is, until he was a prospering storekeeper, he could get for a wife the daughter of some Division Street merchant with two or three thousand dollars into the bargain.

So he relinquished the thought of Hanele as a thing out of the question and proceeded to picture himself the choson of some American girl. But as he was making that effort, the image of the Kropovetz maiden kept intruding upon his imagination, interfering with the mental process, and his heart seemed all the while to be longing after the dismissed subject and filled with the desire that he might have both matches to choose from. Finally, he yielded and resumed the discussion of Reb Feive's project. The idea of a Division Street business man for a father-in-law, beside the assumption of becoming the son-in-law of Reb Peretz, appeared prosaic and vulgar. Those New York merchants had risen from

the mire, like himself, while his old master looked at
the world from the lofty height of distinguished birth,
added to Talmudical learning and exceeding social importance. And here the ties of traditional reverence and
adoration which bound Rouvke to his former employer
made themselves keenly felt in his heart. Ah, for the
privilege of calling Reb Peretz father-in-law! To think
of the stir the news would make among his townsfolk,
both in Kropovetz and here in New York! Besides, the
American-born or "nearly American-born" girls inspire
him with fear. These young ladies are brought up at picnics and balls, while to him the very thought of inviting
a lady for a dance is embarrassing. What are they good
for, anyway? They look more Christian than Jewish,
and are only great hands at squandering their husbands'
money on candy, dresses, and theatres. A woman like
that would domineer over him, treat him haughtily, and
generally make life a burden to him. Hanele, dear
Hanele, on the other hand, is a true daughter of Israel.
She would make a good housekeeper; would occasionally also mind the store; would accompany him to synagogue every Saturday; and that is just what a man like
him wants in a wife. An English-speaking Mrs. Friedman he would have to call "darling," a word barren of
any charm or meaning for his heart, whereas Hanele he
would address in the melodious terms of *"Kreinele
meine! Gold meine!"** Ah, the very music of these
sounds would make him cry with happiness!

The thought of a walk to synagogue with Hanele,
dressed in a plush cloak and an enormous hat, by his
side, and of whispering these words of endearment in
her ear was enchanting enough; but then, enchantment-
like, the spectacle soon faded away before the hard,
retrospective fact of Rouvke, the horse-driver, in top
boots, serving tea to Hanele, the only daughter of Reb
Peretz the distiller. "Oh, it cannot be! Feive *is a
greener* to take such a match into his head!" he mentally exclaimed in black despair. And forthwith he once
more sought consolation in the prospect of a marriage

*"My little crown! My gold!"

portion which a New York wife would bring him, and fell to adding the probable amount to his own future capital. Hanele will reject him? Why, so much the better! That makes it impossible for him to commit the folly of sacrificing at least two thousand dollars. And his spirits rose at the narrow escape he was having from a ruinous temptation. Still, lurking in a deeper corner of his heart, there lingered something which wounded his pride and made him feel as if he would much rather have *that* means of escape cut off from him and the temptation left for himself to grapple with.

Feive, the melamed, had another talk with Rouvke; but although he did not hesitate to speak authoritatively of Reb Peretz's and Hanele's assent, he utterly failed to elicit from his interlocutor any positive hint. Nothing daunted, however, the shadchen dispatched a lengthy epistle to Reb Peretz. He went off in raptures over Rouvke's wealth, social rank in America, and religious habits, and gave him credit for newly acquired education. "It is not the Rouvke of yore," read at least one line on each of the ten pages of the letter. The installment peddling business was elevated to the dignity of a combination of large concerns in furniture, jewelry, and clothing. The owner of this thriving establishment was depicted as panting with love for Hanele, and this again was pointed out as proof that the match had been foreordained by Providence.

Reb Peretz's answer had not reached its destination when in New York there occurred two events which came to the daring matchmaker's assistance.

The daughter of a Seventh Ward landlord had been betrothed to a successful custom peddler, her father promising one thousand dollars in cash, in addition to a complete household outfit, as her marriage portion. As the fixed wedding day drew near, the choson was one day shocked to receive from his would-be father-in-law the intimation that his girl and the household outfit were good enough on their own merits, and that the thousand dollars would have to be dispensed with. The young man immediately cut short his visits to the landlord's daughter; but a fortnight had hardly elapsed before he found himself behind prison bars on an action brought in the name of his broken-hearted sweetheart. How the matter was compromised does not concern our story; but the news, which for several days was the main topic of gossip in the peddler stores, reached Rouvke; and the effect it had on him the reader may well imagine: it riddled to pieces the only unfavorable argument in his discussion of Feive's offer.

A still more powerful element in reaching a conclusion was with Rouvke the following incident.

One day he went to see the shadchen, who had his lodging in the house of a fellow townsman. While he stood behind the door adjusting his necktie, as he now invariably did before entering a house, he overheard a loud dialogue between the housewife and her boarder. Catching his own name, Rouvke paused with bated breath to listen.

"Pray, don't be talking nonsense, Reb Feive," came to the ears of our eavesdropper. "Peretz the distiller give his Hanele in marriage to Rouvke Arbel!—That pock-pitted bugbear and Hanele! Such a beauty, such a pampered child! Why, anybody would be glad to marry her, penniless as she may be. She marry that horrid thing, sloptub, cholera that he is!"

Rouvke was cut to the quick; and shivering before the prospect of hearing some further uncomplimentary allusions to himself, he was on the point of beating retreat; but the very thought of those epithets continuing to be uttered at his expense, even though beyond his hearing, was too painful to bear; and so he put a stop to them by a knock at the door.

"But are you really sure, Reb Feive, that Reb Peretz will have me?" he queried, after a little, all of a flutter, in a private conversation with the shadchen, in the bedroom.

"Leave it to me," the marriage-broker replied. "I have managed greater things in my lifetime. It is as good as settled."

"See if I do not marry Hanele after all, if only to spite you, grudging witch that you are!" Rouvke, in his heart, addressed to his townswoman, on emerging from the pitchy darkness of the little bedroom.

"Good-bye, Mrs. Kohen!" his tongue then said, as his eyes looked daggers at her.

Reb Peretz concluded the reading of Reb Feive's letter by good naturedly calling him "foolish melamed." Little by little, however, the very fact that the shadchen could now dare conceive such a match at all began to mortify him. It took him back to the time when Rouvke used to sit behind his mare, and when he, Reb Peretz, was the most prosperous Jew for miles around, and it wrung his heart with pity both for himself and for Hanele. He became aware that it was over a year since a young man had come to offer himself, and instead of becoming irritated with his daughter, as had latterly been frequently the case with him, he was overpowered by an acute twinge of hurt pride, as well as by compunction for the splendid matrimonial opportunities which he had brushed aside from her. It occurred to Reb Peretz that Hanele was now in her twenty-fifth year, whereupon his fancy reproachfully pointed at his cherished child in the form of a grayhaired old maid. A shudder ran through his veins at the vision, and he began to seek refuge in commercial air castles, but the aerial structures were presently blown away, only to leave him face to face with the wretched ramshackle edifice of his actual affairs. His attention reverted to the American letter, but the collocation of Rouvke Arbel with Hanele sickened Reb Peretz. His self-respect suddenly rushed back upon him, and he felt like "tearing out the beard and sidelocks" of the impudent shadchen.

Nevertheless, he took up the letter once more. This time the matchmaker's eulogies of Rouvke's flourishing business made a deeper impression on him, and brought the indistinct reflection that in course of time he might have to emigrate to America himself with his whole family.

"Pooh, nonsense!" he ultimately concluded, after a third or fourth reading of Reb Feive's missive. "America makes a new man of every young fellow. There had not been a more miserable wretch than Tevke, the watchman; and yet when he recently came back from America for a visit, he looked like a prince. Let her go and be a mother of children, as behooves a daughter of Israel. We must trust to God. The match does look like a Providential affair."

Reb Peretz was a whole day in mustering courage for an explanation with Hanele. But when he had at last broached the subject to her, by means of rendering Feive's Hebrew letter into Yiddish, his undertaking proved easier of achievement than he had anticipated.

Hanele was really a "true daughter of Israel," and this implies that her education was limited to the reading of a Yiddish version of the Five Books of Moses, and that her knowledge of the world did not extend beyond "Kropovetz and its goats," as the phrase runs in her native town. She was a taciturn, good-natured, and tractable girl, and her greatest pleasure was to be knitting fancy tablecloths and brooding over daydreams. Moreover, the repeated appearance and disappearance of chosons, by recurrently unsettling her hitherto calm and easy heart, had left it in a state of perpetual unrest. She had not fallen in love with any of the young men who had sought her hand and her marriage portion, for, according to a rigid old rule of propriety to which her father clung, she never had been allowed the chance of interchanging a word with any of them, even while the suit was pending. Still, when a month passed without a shadchen putting in an appearance, she would often, when the latch gave a click, raise her eyes to the door in the eager hope that it would admit a member of that profession. In her reveries she now frequently dwelt on her girl friends who had married out of Kropovetz, and then her soul would be yearning and longing, she knew not after what. With all the tender affection which tied her to her family, with all her attachment to her native surroundings, her father's house became dreary and lonely to her; she grew tired of her home and homesick after the rest of the world.

To be sure, the first intimation as to her marrying Rouvke Arbel shocked her, and on realizing the full meaning of the offer she dropped her head on her father's shoulder and burst into tears. But as Reb Peretz stroked her hair, while he presented the matter in an aspect which was even an improvement on Feive's plea, he gradually hypnotized her into a lighter mood, and she recalled Rouvke's photograph, which his mother had on several occasions flaunted before her. The match now assumed a somewhat romantic phase. She let her jaded imagination waft her away to an unknown far-off land, where she saw herself glittering with gold and pearls and nestling up to a masculine figure in sumptuous attire. It was a bewitching, thrilling scene only slightly marred by the dim outline of Rouvke in topboots and sheepskin rising in the background. Ah, it was such a pity to have that taint on the otherwise fascinating picture! And, in order to remove the sickly blotch, Hanele essayed to rig Rouvke out in a "cutaway," stand-up collar, and necktie after the model of the photograph. But then her effort produced a total stranger with features she could not make out, while Rouvke Arbel, topboots, sheepskin and all, seemed to have dodged the elegant attire and to remain aloof both from the stranger and the photograph. Well, it is not Rouvke, then, who is proposed to her, she settled, with the three images crowding each other in her mind. It is an entirely new man. Besides, who can tell what may transpire? Let her first get to America and then—who knows, but she may in truth marry another man, a nice young fellow who had never been her father's servant? And Hanele felt that such would be the case. At all events, did not Baske David, the flour merchant's daughter, marry a former blacksmith in America, and is she not happy? Ah, the letters she writes to her!

"Say yes or no. Speak out, my little dove," Reb Peretz insisted, in conclusion of a second conversation on the same subject. "It is not my destiny which is to be decided. It is for you to say," he added, feeling that

Hanele had no business to render any but an affirmative decision.

"Yes," she at last whispered, drooping her head and bursting into a cry.

The shadchen gave himself no rest, and letters sailed over the Atlantic by the dozen. In his first reply Reb Peretz took care to appear oscillating. His second contained a hint as to the attachment which Hanele had always felt for Rouvke, whom they had treated like one of the family. There were also letters with remote allusions to money which Hanele would want for some dresses and to pay her way. And thus, with every message he penned, the conviction gained on Reb Peretz that his daughter would be happy in America, and that the match was really of Providential origin.

These letters operated on Rouvke's heart as an ointment does on a wound, to cite his own illustration; and in spite of the money hints, which constituted the fly in this ointment, he felt happy. He thought of Hanele; he dreamed of her; and, above all, he thought and dreamed of the sensation which her departure from home would create at Kropovetz, and of his glory on her arrival in New York. "Good luck to you, Robert!" the peddlers repeatedly congratulated him. "Have you ever dreamed of becoming the son-in-law of Peretz the distiller? There should be no end to the treats which you ought to stand now." And Robert stood treat and was wreathed in chosonlike smiles.

It was a busy day at Castle Garden. Several transatlantic steamers had arrived, and the railed enclosure within the vast shed was alive with a motley crowd of freshly landed steerage passengers. Outside, there was a cluster of empty merchandise trucks waiting for their human loads, while at a haughty distance from these stood a pair of highly polished carriages—quite a rare sight in front of the immigrant landing station. It was Rouvke who had engaged these superior vehicles. He had come in them with Reb Feive, and with two or three others of his fellow countrymen and brothers in business, to meet Hanele. He was dressed in his Saturday clothes and in a brand-new brown derby hat, and even wore a huge red rose which one of the party, a gallant custom peddler, had stuck into the lapel of his "cutaway" before starting.

The atmosphere of the barn-like garden was laden with nauseating odors of steerage and of carbolic acid, and reeking with human wretchedness. Leaning against the railing or sitting on their baggage, there were bevies of unkempt men and women in shabby dress of every cut and color, holding on to ragged, bulging parcels, baskets, or sacks, and staring at space with a look of forlorn, stupefied, and cowed resignation. The cry of children in their mothers' arms, blending in jarring discord with the gruff yells of the uniformed officers, jostling their way through the crowd, and with the general hum and buzz inside and outside the inclosure, made the scene as painful to the ear as it was to the eye and nostrils, and completed the impression of misery and desolation.

Rouvke and his companions, among a swarm of other residents of the East Side, who, like themselves, had come to meet newly landed friends, stood gazing through the railing. Rouvke was nervously biting his fingernails, and now and then brushing his new derby with his coat-sleeve or adjusting his necktie. Reb Feive was winding his sidelock about his finger, while the young peddlers were vying with each other in pleasantries appropriate to the situation. Our choson was lost in a tumult of emotions. He made repeated attempts at collecting his wits and devising a befitting form of welcome; he tried to figure to himself Hanele's present appearance and to forecast her conduct on first catching sight of him; he also essayed to analyze the whole situation and to think out a plan for the immediate future. But all his efforts fell flat. His thoughts were fragmentary, and no sooner had he laid hold of an idea or an image than it would flee from his mind again and his attention would, for spite, as it were, occupy itself with the merest trifle, such as the size of the whiskers of one of the officers or the sea-biscuit at which an immigrant urchin was nibbling.

At last Rouvke's heart gave a leap. His eyes had fallen on Hanele. She was still more beautiful and charming than before. Instead of the spare and childish-looking girl whom he had left at Kropovetz, there stood before him a stately, well-formed young woman of twenty-five.

"Ha—Ha—Hanele!" he gasped out, all but melting away with emotion, and suddenly feeling, not like Robert Friedman, but like Rouvke Arbel.

Hanele turned her head toward him, but she did not see him. So at least it seemed, for instead of pushing her way to the part of the railing where he stood, she started back and obliterated herself in the crowd.

Presently her name was called, together with other names, and she emerged from a stream of fellow immigrants. More dead than alive, Rouvke ran forward to meet her; but he had advanced two steps when his legs refused to proceed, and his face became blank with amazement. For, behold, snugly supporting Hanele's arm, there was a young man in spectacles and in a seedy gray uniform overcoat of a Russian collegian, with its brass buttons superseded by new ones of black celluloid.

The pair marched up to Rouvke, she with her eyes fixed at the floor, as she clung to her companion, and the collegian with his head raised in timid defiance.

"How do you do, Rouven?" she began. "This is *Gospodin** Levinsky—my choson. Do not take it ill, Rouven. I am not to blame, as true as I am a child of Israel. You see, it is my Providential match, and I could not help it," she rattled off in a trembling voice and like an embarrassed schoolboy reciting a lesson which he has gotten well by heart.

"I'll pay you every copeck, you can rest assured," the collegian interposed, turning as white as a sheet. "I have a rich brother in Buffalo."

---

*Russian for Mister.

Hanele had met the young man in the steerage of the Dutch vessel which brought them across the ocean; and they passed a fortnight there, walking or sitting together on deck, and sharing the weird overawing whispers of the waves, the stern thumping of the engine, and the soothing smiles of the moon—that skillfulest of shadchens in general, and on ship's deck in particular. The long and short of it is that the matchmaking luminary had cut Reb Feive out of his job.

Hanele's explanation at first stunned Rouvke, and he stood for some time eyeing her with a grin of stupid distraction. But presently, upon recovering his senses, he turned as red as fire, and making a face like that of a child when suddenly robbed of its toy, he wailed out in a husky voice:

"I want my hundred and fifty dollars back!" And then in English: "I call a politzman. I vant my hoondered an' fifty dollar!"

"*Ai, ai*—murderess! murderess!" Reb Feive burst out at Hanele. "I am going to get your father to come over here, *ai, ai*!" he lamented, all but bursting into tears with rage. And presently, in caressing tones: "Listen to me, Hanele! I know you are a good and God-fearing Jewish girl. Fie! drop that abominable beggar. Leave that Gentile-like shaven mug, I tell you. Rouven is your Providential match. Look at him, the prince that he is! You will live like a queen with him, you will roll in gold and jewels, Hanele!"

But Hanele only clung to the collegian's arm the faster, and the two were about to leave the Garden, when Rouvke grasped his successful rival by the lapels of his overcoat, crying as he did so: "Politzman! Politzman!"

The young couple looked a picture of helplessness. But at this juncture a burly shaven-faced "runner" of an immigrant hotel, who had been watching the scene, sprang to their rescue. Brushing Rouvke aside with a thrust of his mighty arm, accompanied by a rasping "Git out, or I'll punch your pockmarked nose, ye monkey!" he marched Hanele and his choson away, leaving

Rouvke staring as if he were at a loss to realize the situation, while Reb Feive, violently wringing his hands, gasped, "Ai! ai! ai!" and the young peddlers bandied whispered jokes.

A Sweatshop Romance

Leizer Lipman was one of those contract tailors who are classed by their hands under the head of "cockroaches," which—translating the term into lay English—means that he ran a very small shop, giving employment to a single team of one sewing-machine operator, one baster, one finisher, and one presser.

The shop was one of a suite of three rooms on the third floor of a rickety old tenement house on Essex Street, and did the additional duty of the family's kitchen and dining room. It faced a dingy little courtyard, and was connected by a windowless bedroom with the parlor, which commanded the very heart of the Jewish markets. Bundles of cloth, cut to be made into coats, littered the floor, lay in chaotic piles by one of the walls, cumbered Mrs. Lipman's kitchen table and one or two chairs, and formed, in a corner, an improvised bed upon which a dirty two-year-old boy, Leizer's heir apparent, was enjoying his siesta.

Dangling against the door or scattered among the bundles, there were cooking utensils, dirty linen, Lipman's velvet skullcap, hats, shoes, shears, cotton-spools, and whatnot. A red-hot kitchen stove and a blazing grate full of glowing flatirons combined to keep up the overpowering temperature of the room, and helped to justify its nickname of sweatshop in the literal sense of the epithet.

Work was rather scarce, but the designer of the Broadway clothing firm, of whose army of contractors Lipman was a member, was a second cousin to the latter's wife, and he saw to it that his relative's husband was kept busy. And so operations in Leizer's shop were in full swing. Heyman, the operator, with his bared brawny arms, pushed away at an unfinished coat, over which his head, presenting to view a wealth of curly brown hair, hung like an eagle bent on his prey. He swayed in unison to the rhythmic whirr of his machine, whose music, supported by the energetic thumps of Meyer's press iron, formed an orchestral accompaniment to the sonorous and plaintive strains of a vocal duet performed by Beile, the finisher girl, and David, the baster.

Leizer was gone to the Broadway firm's offices, while Zlate, his wife, was out on a prolonged haggling expedition among the tradeswomen of Hester Street. This circumstance gave the hands a respite from the restrictions usually placed on their liberties by the presence of the "boss" and the "Missis," and they freely beguiled the tedium and fatigue of their work, now by singing, now by a bantering match at the expense of their employer and his wife, or of each other.

"Well, I suppose you might as well quit," said Meyer, a chubby, red-haired, freckled fellow of forty, emphasizing his remark by an angry stroke of his iron. "You have been over that song now fifty times without taking breath. You make me tired."

"Don't you like it? Stuff up your ears, then," Beile retorted, without lifting her head from the coat in her lap.

"Why, I do like it, first-rate and a half," Meyer returned, "but when you keep your mouth shut I like it better still, see?"

The silvery tinkle of Beile's voice, as she was singing, thrilled Heyman with delicious melancholy, gave him fresh relish for his work, and infused additional activity into his limbs; and as her singing was interrupted by the presser's gibe, he involuntarily stopped his machine with that annoying feeling which is experienced by dancers when brought to an unexpected standstill by an abrupt pause of the music.

"And you?"—he addressed himself to Meyer, facing about on his chair with an irritated countenance. "It's all right enough when you speak, but it is much better when you hold your tongue. Don't mind him, Beile. Sing away!" he then said to the girl, his dazzlingly fair face relaxing and his little eyes shutting into a sweet smile of self-confident gallantry.

"You had better stick to your work, Heyman. Why, you might have made half a cent the while," Meyer fired back, with an ironical look, which had reference to the operator's reputation of being a niggardly fellow, who overworked himself, denied himself every pleasure, and grew fat by feasting his eyes on his savings-bank book.

A sharp altercation ensued, which drifted to the subject of Heyman's servile conduct toward his employer.

"It was you, wasn't it," Meyer said, "who started that collection for a birthday present for the boss? Of course, we couldn't help chipping in. Why is David independent?"

"Did I compel you?" Heyman rejoined. "And am I to blame that it was to me that the boss threw out the hint about that present? It is so slack everywhere, and you ought to thank God for the steady job you have here," he concluded, pouncing down upon the coat on his machine.

David, who had also cut short his singing, kept silently playing his needle upon pieces of stuff which lay stretched on his master's dining table. Presently he paused to adjust his disheveled jet-black hair, with his fingers for a comb, and to wipe the perspiration from his swarthy, beardless and typically Israelitic face with his shirtsleeve.

While this was in progress, his languid hazel eyes were fixed on the finisher girl. She instinctively became conscious of his gaze, and raised her head from the needle. Her fresh buxom face, flushed with the heat of the room and with exertion, shone full upon the

young baster. Their eyes met. David colored, and, to
conceal his embarrassment, he asked: "Well, is he going to raise your wages?"

Beile nodded affirmatively, and again plunged her
head into her work.

"He is? So you will now get five dollars a week. I
am afraid you will be putting on airs now, won't you?"

"Do you begrudge me? Then I am willing to swap
wages with you. I'll let you have my five dollars, and
I'll take your twelve dollars every week."

Lipman's was a task shop, and, according to the sig-
nification which the term has in the political economy
of the sweating world, his operator, baster, and finisher, while nominally engaged at so much a week,
were in reality paid by the piece, the economical week
being determined by a stipulated quantity of made-up
coats rather than by a fixed number of the earth's rev-
olutions around its axis; for the sweatshop day will not
coincide with the solar day unless a given amount of
work be accomplished in its course. As to the presser,
he is invariably a pieceworker, pure and simple.

For a more lucid account of the task system in the
tailoring branch, I beg to refer the reader to David, although his exposition happens to be presented rather in
the form of a satire on the subject. Indeed, David,
while rather inclined to taciturnity, was an inveterate
jester, and what few remarks he indulged in during his
work would often cause boisterous merriment among
his shopmates, although he delivered them with a nonchalant manner and with the same look of good-
humored irony, mingled in strange harmony with a
general expression of gruffness, which his face usually
wore.

"My twelve dollars every week?" David echoed.
"Oh, I see; you mean a week of twelve days!" And his
needle resumed its duck-like sport in the cloth.

"How do you make it out?" Meyer demanded, in order to elicit a joke from the witty young man by his
side.

"Of course, *you* don't know how to make that out.
But ask Heyman or Beile. The three of us do."

"Tell him, then, and he will know too," Beile urged, laughing in advance at the expected fun.

A request coming from the finisher was—yet unknown to herself—resistless with David, and in the present instance it loosened his tongue.

"Well, I get twelve dollars a week, and Heyman fourteen. Now a working week has six days, but—hem—that 'but' gets stuck in my throat—but a day is neither a Sunday nor a Monday nor anything unless we make twelve coats. The calendars are a lot of liars."

"What do you mean?"

"They say a day has twenty-four hours. That's a bluff. A day has twelve coats."

Beile's rapturous chuckle whetted his appetite for persiflage, and he went on: "They read the Tuesday Psalm in the synagogue this morning, but I should have read the Monday one."

"Why?"

"You see, Meyer's wife will soon come up with his dinner, and here I have still two coats to make of the twelve that I got yesterday. So it's still Monday with me. My Tuesday won't begin before about two o'clock this afternoon."

"How much will you make this week?" Meyer questioned.

"I don't expect to finish more than four days' work by the end of the week, and will only get eight dollars on Friday—that is, provided the Missis has not spent our wages by that time. So when it's Friday I'll call it Wednesday, see?"

"When I am married," he added, after a pause, "and the old woman asks me for Sabbath expenses, I'll tell her it is only Wednesday—it isn't yet Friday—and I have no money to give her."

David relapsed into silence, but mutely continued his burlesque, hopping from subject to subject.

David thought himself a very queer fellow. He often wondered at the pranks which his own imagination was in the habit of playing, and at the grotesque combinations it frequently evolved. As he now stood, leaning forward over his work, he was striving to make out how it was that Meyer reminded him of the figure "7."

"What nonsense!" he inwardly exclaimed, branding himself for a crank. "And what does Heyman look like?" his mind queried, as though for spite. He contemplated the operator askance, and ran over all the digits of the Arabic system, and even the whole Hebrew alphabet, in quest of a counterpart to the young man, but failed to find anything suitable. "His face would much better become a girl," he at last decided, and mentally proceeded to envelop Heyman's head in Beile's shawl. But the proceeding somehow stung him, and he went on to meditate upon the operator's chunky nose. "No, that nose is too ugly for a girl. It wants a little planing. It's an unfinished job, as it were. But for that nose Heyman would really be the nice fellow they say he is. His snow-white skin—his elegant heavy mustache—yes, if he did not have that nose he would be all right," he maliciously joked in his heart. "And I, too, would be all right if Heyman were noseless," he added, transferring his thoughts to Beile, and wondering why she looked so sweet. "Why, *her* nose is not much of a beauty, either. Entirely too straight, and too—too foolish. Her eyes look old and as if constantly on the point of bursting into tears. Ah, but then her lips—that kindly smile of theirs, coming out of one corner of her mouth!" And a strong impulse seized him to throw himself on those lips and to kiss them, which he did mentally, and which shot an electric current through his whole frame. And at this Beile's old-looking eyes both charmed and pierced him to the heart, and her nose, far from looking foolish, seemed to contemplate him contemptuously, triumphantly, and knowingly, as if it had read his thoughts.

While this was going on in David's brain and heart, Beile was taken up with Heyman and with their mutual relations. His attentions to her were an open secret. He did not go out of his way to conceal them. On the contrary, he regularly escorted her home after work, and took her out to balls and picnics—a thing involving great sacrifices to a fellow who trembled over every cent he spent, and who was sure to make up for these losses to his pocketbook by foregoing his meals. While alone with her in the hallway of her mother's residence, his voice would become so tender, so tremulous, and on several occasions he even addressed her by the endearing form of Beilinke. And yet all this had been going on now for over three months, and he had not as much as alluded to marriage, nor even bought her the most trifling present.

Her mother made life a burden to her, and urged the point-blank declaration of the alternative between a formal engagement and an arrest for breach of promise. Beile would have died rather than make herself the heroine of such a sensation; and, besides, the idea of Heyman handcuffed to a police detective was too terrible to entertain even for a moment.

She loved him. She liked his blooming face, his gentleman-like mustache, the quaint jerk of his head, as he walked; she was fond of his company; she was sure she was in love with him: her confidant, her fellow country girl and playmate, who had recently married Meyer, the presser, had told her so.

But somehow she felt disappointed. She had imagined love to be a much sweeter thing. She had thought that a girl in love admired *everything* in the object of her affections, and was blind to all his faults. She had heard that love was something like a perpetual blissful fluttering of the heart.

"I feel as if something was melting here," a girl friend who was about to be married once confided to her, pointing to her heart. "You see, it aches and yet it is so sweet at the same time." And here she never feels anything melting, nor can she help disliking some things about Heyman. His smile sometimes appears to her fulsome. Ah, if he did not shut his eyes as he does when smiling! That he is so slow to spend money is rather one of the things she likes in him. If he ever marries her she will be sure to get every cent of his wages. But then when they are together at a ball he never goes up to the bar to treat her to a glass of soda, as the other fellows do to their girls, and all he offers her is an apple or a pear, which he generally stops to buy on the street on their way to the dancing hall. Is she in love at all? Maybe she is mistaken? But no! he is after all so dear to her. She must have herself to blame. It is not in vain that her mother calls her a whimpering, nagging thing, who gives no peace to herself nor to anybody around her. But why does he not come out with his declaration? Is it because he is too stingy to wish to support a wife? Has he been making a fool of her? What does he take her for, then?

In fairness to Heyman, it must be stated that on the point of his intentions, at least, her judgment of him was without foundation, and her misgivings gratuitous. Pecuniary considerations had nothing to do with his slowness in proposing to her. And if she could have watched him and penetrated his mind at the moments when he examined his bankbook—which he did quite often—she would have ascertained that little images of herself kept hovering before his eyes between the figures of its credit columns, and that the sum total conjured up to him a picture of prospective felicity with her for a central figure.

Poor thing; she did not know that when he lingeringly fondled her hand, on taking his leave in the hallway, the proposal lay on the tip of his tongue, and that lacking the strength to relieve himself of its burden he every time left her consoling himself that the moment was inopportune, and that "tomorrow he would surely settle it." She did not know that only two days ago the idea had occurred to him to have recourse to the aid of a messenger in the form of a lady's watch, and that while she now sat worrying lest she was being made a fool of, the golden emissary lay in Heyman's vest pocket, throbbing in company with his heart with impatient expectation of the evening hour, which had been fixed for the delivery of its message.

"I shall let mother speak to him," Beile resolved, in her musings over her needle. She went on to picture the scene, but at this point her meditations were suddenly broken by something clutching and pulling at her hair. It was her employer's boy. He had just got up from his after-dinner nap, and, for want of any other occupation, he passed his dirty little hand into her raven locks.

"He is practicing to be a boss," observed David, whose attention was attracted to the spectacle by the finisher's shriek.

Beile's voice brought Heyman to his feet, and disentangling the little fellow's fingers from the girl's hair, he fell to "plastering his nasty cheeks for him," as he put it. At this juncture the door opened to admit the little culprit's father. Heyman skulked away to his seat, and, burying his head in his work, he proceeded to drown, in the whir-r, whir-r of his machine, the screams of the boy, who would have struck a much higher key had his mamma happened on the spot.

Lipman took off his coat, substituted his greasy velvet skullcap for his derby, and lighting a cigar with an air of good-natured businesslike importance, he advanced to Meyer's corner and fell to examining a coat.

"And what does *he* look like?" David asked himself, scrutinizing his task-master. "Like a broom with its stick downward," he concluded to his own satisfaction. "And his snuffbox?"—meaning Lipman's huge nose— "A perfect fiddle!—And his mouth? Deaf-mutes usually have such mouths. And his beard? He has entirely too much of it, and it's too pretty for his face. It must have got there by mistake."

Presently the door again flew open, and Mrs. Lipman, heavily loaded with parcels and panting for breath, came waddling in with an elderly couple in tow.

"Greenhorns," Meyer remarked. "Must be fellow townspeople of hers—lately arrived."

"She looks like a teakettle, and she is puffing like one, too," David thought, after an indifferent gaze at the newcomers, looking askance at his stout, dowdyish little "Missis." "No," he then corrected himself, "she rather resembles a broom with its stick out. That's it! And wouldn't it be a treat to tie a stick to her head and to sweep the floor with the horrid thing! And her mouth? Why, it makes me think she does nothing but sneeze."

"Here is Leizer! Leizer, look at the guests I have brought you!" Zlate exclaimed, as she threw down her bundles. "Be seated, Reb Avrom; be seated, Basse. This is our factory," she went on, with a smile of mixed welcome and triumph, after the demonstrative greetings were over. "It is rather too small, isn't it? but we are going to move into larger and better quarters."

Meyer was not mistaken. Zlate's visitors had recently arrived from her birthplace, a poor town in Western Russia, where they had occupied a much higher social position than their present hostess, and Mrs. Lipman, coming upon them on Hester Street, lost no time in inviting them to her house, in order to overwhelm them with her American achievements.

"Come, I want to show you my parlor," Mrs. Lipman said, beckoning to her country people, and before they were given an opportunity to avail themselves of the chair which she had offered them, they were towed into the front room.

When the procession returned, Leizer, in obedience to an order from his wife, took Reb Avrom in charge and proceeded to initiate him into the secrets of the "American style of tailoring."

"Oh, my!" Zlate suddenly ejaculated, with a smile. "I came near forgetting to treat. Beilke!" she then addressed herself to the finisher girl in a tone of imperious nonchalance, "here is a nickel. Fetch two bottles of soda from the grocery."

"Don't go, Beile!" David whispered across his table, perceiving the girl's reluctance.

It was not unusual for Beile to go on an errand for the wife of her employer, though she always did it unwillingly, and merely for fear of losing her place; but then Zlate generally exacted these services as a favor. In the present instance, however, Beile felt mortally offended by her commanding tone, and the idea of being paraded before the strangers as a domestic cut her to the quick, as a stream of color rushing into her face indicated. Nevertheless the prospect of having to look

for a job again persuaded her to avoid trouble with
Zlate, and she was about to reach out her hand for
the coin, when David's exhortation piqued her sense
of self-esteem, and she went on with her sewing.
Heyman, who, being interrupted in his work by the
visitor's inspection, was a witness of the scene, at this
point turned his face from it, and cringing by his machine, he made a pretense of busying himself with the
shuttle. His heart shrank with the awkwardness of his
situation, and he nervously grated his teeth and shut
his eyes, awaiting still more painful developments. His
veins tingled with pity for his sweetheart and with
deadly hatred for David. What could he do? he apologized to himself. Isn't it foolish to risk losing a steady
job at this slack season on account of such a trifle as
fetching up a bottle of soda? What business has David
to interfere?

"You are not deaf, are you? I say go and bring some
soda, quick!" Mrs. Lipman screamed, fearing lest she
was going too far.

"Don't budge, Beile!" the baster prompted, with fire
in his eyes.

Beile did not.

"I say go!" Zlate thundered, reddening like a beet, to
use a phrase in vogue with herself.

"Never mind, Zlate," Basse interposed, to relieve the
embarrassing situation. "We just had tea."

"Never mind. It is not worth the trouble," Avrom
chimed in.

But this only served to lash Zlate into a greater fury,
and unmindful of consequences, she strode up to the
cause of her predicament, and tearing the coat out of
her hands, she squeaked out: "Either fetch the soda, or
leave my shop at once!"

Heyman was about to say, to do something, he knew
not exactly what, but his tongue seemed seized with
palsy, the blood turned chill in his veins, and he could
neither speak nor stir.

Leizer, who was of a quiet, peaceful disposition, and
very much under the thumb of his wife, stood nervously smiling and toying with his beard.

David grew ashen pale, and trembling with rage he said aloud and in deliberate accents: "Don't mind her, Beile, and never worry. Come along. I'll find you a better job. This racket won't work, Missis. Your friends see through it, anyhow, don't you?" he addressed himself to the newcomers. "She wanted to brag to you. That's what she troubled you for. She showed off her parlor carpet to you, didn't she? But did she tell you that it had been bought on the installment plan, and that the custom peddler threatened to take it away unless she paid more regularly?"

"Leizer! are you—are you drunk?" Mrs. Lipman gasped, her face distorted with rage and desperation.

"Get out of here!" Leizer said, in a tone which would have been better suited to a cordial invitation.

The command was unnecessary, however, for by this time David was buttoning up his overcoat, and had his hat on. Involuntarily following his example, Beile also dressed to go. And as she stood in her new beaver cloak and freshly trimmed large old hat by the side of her discomfited commander, Basse reflected that it was the finisher girl who looked like a lady, with Zlate for her servant, rather than the reverse.

"See that you have our wages ready for Friday, and all the arrears, too!" was David's parting shot as the two left the room with a defiant slam of the door.

"That's like America!" Zlate remarked, with an attempt at a scornful smile. "The meanest beggar girl will put on airs."

"Why *should* one be ordered about like that? She is no servant, is she?" Heyman murmured, addressing the corner of the room, and fell to at his machine to smother his misery.

When his day's work was over, Heyman's heart failed him to face Beile, and although he was panting to see her, he did not call at her house. On the following morning he awoke with a headache, and this he used as a pretext to himself for going to bed right after supper.

On the next evening he did betake himself to the Division Street tenement house, where his sweetheart lived with her mother on the top floor, but on coming in front of the building his courage melted away. Added to his cowardly part in the memorable scene of two days before, there now was his apparent indifference to the finisher, as manifested by his two evenings' absence at such a critical time. He armed himself with a fib to explain his conduct. But all in vain; he could not nerve himself up to the terrible meeting. And so day after day passed, each day increasing the barrier to the coveted visit.

At last, one evening, about a fortnight after the date of Mrs. Lipman's fiasco, Heyman, forgetting to lose courage, as it were, briskly mounted the four flights of stairs of the Division Street tenement. As he was about to rap for admission he was greeted by a sharp noise within of something, like a china plate or a bowl, being dashed to pieces against the very door which he was going to open. The noise was followed by merry voices: "Good luck! Good luck!" and there was no mistaking its meaning. There was evidently an engagement party inside. The Rabbi had just read the writ of betrothment, and it was the mutual pledges of the contracting parties which were emphasized by the "breaking of the plate."

Presently Heyman heard exclamations which dissipated his every doubt as to the identity of the chief actors in the ceremony which had just been completed within.

"Good luck to you, David! Good luck to you, Beile! May you live to a happy old age together!" "Feige, why don't you take some cake? Don't be so bashful!" "Here is luck!" came through the door, piercing a muffled hum inside.

Heyman was dumbfounded, and with his head swimming, he made a hasty retreat.

Ever since the tragi-comical incident at Lipman's shop, Heyman was not present to Beile's thoughts except in the pitiful, cowering attitude in which he had sat through that awful scene by his machine. She was sure she hated him now. And yet her heart was, during the first few days, constantly throbbing with the expectation of his visit; and as she settled in her mind that even if he came she would have nothing to do with him, her deeper consciousness seemed to say, with a smile of conviction: "Oh no, you know you would not refuse him. You wouldn't risk to remain an old maid, would you?" The idea of his jilting her harrowed her day and night. Did he avail himself of her leaving Lipman's shop to back out of the proposal which was naturally expected of him, but which he never perhaps contemplated? Did he make game of her?

When a week had elapsed without Heyman's putting in an appearance, she determined to let her mother see a lawyer about breach-of-promise proceedings. But an image, whose outlines had kept defining themselves in her heart for several days past, overruled this decision. It was the image of a pluckier fellow than Heyman—of one with whom there was more protection in store for a wife, who inspired her with more respect and confidence, and, what is more, who seemed on the point of proposing to her.

It was the image of David. The young baster pursued his courtship with a quiet persistency and a suppressed fervor which was not long in winning the girl's heart. He found work for her and for himself in the same shop; saw her home every evening; regularly came after supper to take her out for walk, in the course of which he would treat her to candy and invite her to a coffee saloon—a thing which Heyman had never done;—kept her chuckling over his jokes; and at the end of ten days, while sitting by her side in Central Park, one night, he said, in reply to her remark that it was so dark that she knew not where she was: "I'll tell you where you are—guess."

"Where?"

"Here, in my heart, and keeping me awake nights, too. Say, Beile, what have I ever done to you to have my rest disturbed by you in that manner?"

Her heart was beating like a sledge hammer. She tried to laugh, as she returned: "I don't know—You can never stop making fun, can you?"

"Fun? Do you want me to cry? I will, gladly, if I

only know that you will agree to have an engagement party," he rejoined deeply blushing under cover of the darkness.

"When?" she questioned, the word crossing her lips before she knew it.

"On my part, tomorrow."

Circumstances

Tatyana Markovna Lurie had just received the July number of *Russian Thought,* and was in a flurry. She felt like devouring all the odd dozen of articles in the voluminous book at once; and the patience failing her to cut the leaves, she fell to prying between them on the rocking chair which she had drawn up close to one of the two windows of the best room.

Altogether, the residence of the Luries consisted of three small uncarpeted and scantily furnished apartments, and occupied a fourth of the top floor of a veteran tenement house on Madison Street.

Ultimately, Tatyana Markovna settled on an extensive review of a new translation of Guy de Maupassant's stories. But here again she was burning to glance over the beginning, the middle, and the end of the article simultaneously. And so she sat, feverishly skipping and hopping over the lines, until a thought expressed by the critic, and which struck her as identical with one she had set forth in a recent discussion with her husband, finally fixed her attention and overspread her youthful little face with radiance. She was forerelishing her triumph when, upon Boris's return from work, she would show him the passage; for in their debate he had made light of her contention, and met her irresolute demurrer with the patronizing and slightly ironical tone which he usually took while discussing book questions with her.

But at the thought of Boris she suddenly remembered her soup, and growing pale she put the magazine aside, and darted into the semi-obscurity of the kitchen.

Tatyana, or Tanya, as her husband would fondly call her, was the daughter of a merchant and Hebrew writer in Kieff, who usually lost upon his literary ventures what he would save from his business. It was not long after she had graduated from one of the female gymnasiums of her native city that she met Boris Lurie, then a law student at the University of St. Vladimir.

He was far from being what Russian college girls would call "a dear little soul"; for he was tall and lank, awkwardly nearsighted, and rather plain of feature, and the scar over his left eyebrow, too, added anything but beauty to his looks. But for all that, the married young women of his circle voted him decidedly interesting.

Tanya was attracted by his authoritative tone and rough sort of impetuosity upon discussing social or literary topics; by his reputation for being one of the best-read men at the university, as well as a leading spirit in student "circles," and by the perfect Russian way in which his coal-black hair fell over his commanding forehead. As to him, he was charmed by that in her which had charmed many a student before him: the delicate freshness of her pink complexion, which, by the time we first find her in the Madison Street tenement, had only partially faded; the enthusiastic smile beaming from her every feature as she spoke; and the way her little nose, the least bit retroussé, would look upward, and her beautiful hazel eyes would assume a look of childlike curiosity, while she was listening to her interlocutor.

They were married immediately after his graduation, with the intention of settling in Kremenchug, where he had every prospect of a large practice. But when he presented himself for admission to the bar, as a "private attorney," he encountered obstacle after obstacle. He tried another district, but with no better success. By that time it had become clear that the government was bent upon keeping the Jews out of the forensic profession, although it had not officially placed it upon the list of vocations proscribed to their race.

After a year of peregrination and petitioning he came, a bundle of nerves, to Jitomir to make a last attempt in the province of Volyn.

A high judiciary officer who received him rather politely made, in the course of their interview, the semi-jocular remark that the way to the bar lay through the baptismal font.

"Villain!" Lurie thundered, his fists clenched and his eyes flashing.

Luckily the functionary was a cool-headed old man who knew how to avoid unsavory publicity. And so, when Lurie defiantly started to stalk out of the room, he was not stopped.

A month or two later, Boris and Tanya arrived in New York.

II

It was near seven o'clock when Boris came from the pearl-button factory where he earned, at piecework, from six to seven dollars a week. As Tanya heard his footsteps through the door she sprang to her feet and, with a joyous gleam in her eye, she ran out to meet him at the head of the stairs. In her delight she at once forgot the Maupassant article.

After an affectionate greeting she said, with burlesque supplication: "Don't get angry, Borya, but I am afraid I have flunked on my soup again."

His fatigued smile expanded.

"The worst of it," she pursued, "is the fact that this time my negligence resulted from something which is against you. Yes, I have got something that will show you that Mr. Boris has not monopolized all the wisdom in the world; that other people know something, too. Yes, sir!" she beamingly concluded, in English.

"You must have received the July number, have you?" he burst out, flushing with anticipated delight.

"Not your booseeness" (business), she replied in English, playfully pronouncing the words as in Russian. "You know you can't get it before supper is over; so what is the use asking?" she added, in the tongue of her native country. With which she briskly busied herself about the table and the stove, glowing with happiness, every inch of her a woman in the long-awaited presence of the man she loves.

Boris's shabby working clothes, his few days' growth of beard and general appearance of physical exhaustion vainly combined, as it were, to extinguish the light of culture and intellectuality from his looks; they only succeeded in adding the tinge of martyrdom to them. As to Tatyana, she had got so far habituated to the change that she was only occasionally aware of it. And when she was, it would move her to pity and quicken her love for him. At such moments his poor workaday clothes would appear to her as something akin to the prison garb of the exiled student in Siberia.

"Let me just take a glance at the table of contents," he begged, brokenly, washing himself at the sink.

"After supper."

"Then do you tell me what there is to read. Anything interesting?"

"After supper."

"Or is it that you begrudge me the few minutes' talk we have together?" she resumed more earnestly, after a slight pause. "The whole day I am all alone, and when he comes he plunges into some book or other or falls asleep like a murdered man. All there remains is the half hour at supper; so that, too, he would willingly deprive me of."

It was Tanya's standing grievance, and she would deliver herself of it on the slightest provocation, often quite irrelevantly.

After supper she read to him the passage which she regarded as an endorsement of her view upon Maupassant. When she had finished and turned to him a face full of triumphant inquiry, she was rather disappointed by the lukewarm readiness of his surrender.

"Oh, I see. It is rather an interesting point," he remarked lazily.

He was reclining on the stiff carpet-covered lounge in the front room, while she was seated in the rocker, in front of him. It flashed across her mind that such unusual tractability in him might augur some concession to be exacted from her. She flew into a mild little passion in advance, but made no inquiries, and only said, with good-natured sarcasm: "Of course, once it is printed in *Russian Thought*, it is 'rather an interesting point,' but when it was only Tanya who made it, why then it was mere rubbish."

"You know I never said it was rubbish, Tanya," he returned deprecatingly.

After a slight pause, he resumed listlessly: "Besides, I am sick of these 'interesting points.' They have been the ruin of us, Tanychka; they eat us up alive, these 'interesting points'—the deuce grab them. If I cared less about 'interesting points' "—he articulated the two words with venomous relish—"and a little more about your future and mine, I might not now have to stick in a button factory."

She listened to him with an amused air, and when he paused, she said flippantly: "We have heard it before."

"So much the worse for both of us. If you at least took a more sober view of things! Seriously, Tanya, you ought to make life a burden to me until I begin to do something to get out of this devilish—of this villainous, unpardonable position."

"You should have married Cecilia Trotzky, then," she said, laughing.

Cecilia Trotzky was the virago among the educated Russo-Jewish immigrants, who form a numerous colony within a colony in the Ghetto of New York. She was described as a woman who had placed her husband in a medical college, then made a point of sending him supperless to bed every time he failed to study his lessons, and later, when he was practicing, fixed the fees with his patients.

"Well, what is the use of joking?" he said gloomily, suppressing a smile. "Every illiterate nonentity," he went on, letting the words filter through his teeth with languid bitterness, "every shop clerk, who at home hardly knew there was such a thing as a university in the world, goes to college here; and I am serving the community by supplying it with pearl buttons for six dollars a week. Would this were regular, at least! But it is not. I forgot to tell you, but we may again have a slack season, Tanya. Oh! I will not let things go on like this. If I don't begin to do something at once, I shall send a bullet through my forehead. You may laugh, but this time it is not idle talk. From this day on I shall be a different man. I have a plan; I have considered everything carefully. If we wish to get rid of our beggarly position, of this terrible feeling of insecurity and need," he proceeded, as he raised himself to a sitting posture, his voice gathering energy and his features becoming contorted with an expression of disgust; "if we really mean to free ourselves from this constant trembling lest I lose my job, from these excursions to the pawn shops—laugh away! laugh away!—but, as I say, if we seriously wish to make it possible for me to enter some college here, we must send all literature and magazines and all gush about Russia to the deuce, and do as others do. I have a splendid plan. Everything depends upon you, Tanya."

At this the childlike look of curiosity came into her face. But he seemed in no hurry to come to the point.

"People who hang about pawn shops have no right to 'interesting points' and Guy de Maupassant and that sort of luxury. Poverty *is* a crime! Well, but from now on, everything will be different. Listen, Tanychka; the greatest trouble is the rent, is it not? It eats up the larger part of my wages—that is, provided I work full time; and you know how we tremble and are on the verge of insanity each time the first of the month is drawing near. If we wish to achieve something, we must be satisfied to pinch ourselves and to put up with some inconvenience. Above all, we must not forget that I am a common workingman. Well, every workingman's family around here keeps a boarder or two; let us also take one. There is no way out of it, Tanya."

He uttered the concluding words with studied nonchalance, but without daring to look her in the face.

"Bor-ya!" she exclaimed, with a bewildered air.

Her manner angered him.

"There, now! I expected as much!" he said irascibly. And continuing in softer accents, he forced her to listen to the details of his project. The boarder's pay would nearly come up to their rent. If they lived more economically than now they could save up enough for his first year's tuition at a New York college, or, as a steppingstone, for a newspaper stand. Free from worry about their rent, he would be in a fitter mood to study English after work. In course of time he would know the language enough to teach it to the uneducated workingmen of the Jewish quarter; and so he would be liberated from his factory yoke, as many an immigrant of his class had been. Dalsky, a friend of theirs, and a former classmate of Boris's, who was studying medicine, earned his living by giving such lessons in English, and, by the way, he was now looking for a lodging. Why should they not offer him their parlor? They could do with the kitchen and the bedroom. Besides, Dalsky would be one of the family, and would have only partial use of the parlor.

As the plan assumed a personified form in her mind—the face of a definite boarder—her realization of its horrors was so keen that she shut her ears and begged Boris to take pity on her and desist. Whereupon he flew into a rage and charged her with nursing aristocratic instincts which in their present position they could not afford. She retorted, tearfully, that she was ready to put up with any amount of additional work and discomfort, but that she did not care to have a "constant cataract on the eye."

"God knows you give me little enough of your company, as it is. I must have tired you capitally, if you seek somebody to talk to and to save you from being alone with me."

"You know it is the rankest nonsense you are saying!" he flamed out. "And what is the use crying like that? As if I took a delight in the whole affair! Cry to our circumstances, not to me. Circumstances, circumstances, Tanya!" he repeated, with pleading vehemence.

Little by little he relented, however, and eventually he promised never to mention the matter again, although inwardly both of them felt that he would. He sat by her side on the lounge, fondling her little hands and murmuring love, when suddenly bending upon him an imploring face, she said, in a tremulous, tearful voice: "Borinka, dear! I shall also go to some factory. We will get along without boarders," with which she fell upon his shoulder in a fit of heart-rending sobbing.

He clasped her to him, whispering: "You know, my angel, that I would commit suicide before letting you go to work. Don't worry, my joy, we *will* get along without boarders."

"I want no strangers to hang around the house all the time; I want to be with you alone, I want nobody, nobody, nobody else in the world!" she said, pressing him tightly to her heart.

III

On the following evening, as Boris was musingly trudging on his way home, after work, it suddenly came over him that his manner with the foreman of the shop was assuming a rather obsequious nature. Work was scarce, and the distribution of it was, to a considerable extent, a matter of favoritism. He recalled how the Czech foreman, half tipsy with beer, had been making some stupid efforts at being witty, and how he, Boris Lurie, standing by, in greedy expectation of work, had smiled a broad, ingratiating smile of approbation. At the moment he had been so far merged in the surroundings and in his anxiety about work that he had not been aware of doing anything unnatural. But now, as it all came back to him, with inexorable vividness, and he beheld his own wretched, artificial smile, he was overcome with disgust. "Vil-lain!" he broke out at himself, gnashing his teeth; and at the next moment he was at the point of bursting into tears for self-pity.

To think of him, who had not hesitated to call the president of a Russian court "rogue" to his face, simpering like a miserable time-server at every stupidity and nastiness of a drunken brute! Is that what circumstances had made of him?

He reached home out of temper, and before supper was well over he reopened the discussion of his scheme. It again led to a slight quarrel, which was again made up by his surrender, as in the previous instance.

A few days later he was "laid off" for a fortnight.

To eke out their rent they had to forego meat. For several consecutive days they lived on bread and butter and coffee. Boris grew extremely nervous and irritable.

One morning, coming back from the pawn shops, Boris, pale and solemn, quietly laid on the kitchen table the package which he had under his arm.

"They wouldn't take it," he said almost in a whisper. "It is not worth anything, they say."

Tanya only raised at him a meek glance, and went on with her work. Boris fell to pacing the front room. They could not speak.

Presently she stepped up to his side and said, with rueful tenderness: "Well, what is the good of grieving, Borya?"

Their hands clasped tightly, and their eyes fixed themselves forlornly on the floor.

"I have promised Dalsky an answer," he said, after a little.

"Let him move in," she returned lugubriously, with a slight shrug of her shoulder, as if submitting to fate.

IV

It was about nine in the morning, and Dalsky, slowly pacing the front room, *Quiz-Compend* in hand, was reviewing his lesson. He had a certain dignity and nobleness of feature which consorted well with the mysterious pallor of his oval face, and to which, by the way, his moral complexion gave him perfect right. Then, too, his middle-sized form was exceedingly well proportioned. But for the rest, his looks, like everything else about him, presented nothing to produce an impression.

Presently he deliberately closed the book, carefully placed it on his whatnot, and, his eye falling upon the little flowerpot on the window, he noiselessly stepped into the kitchen, where Tanya was ironing some trifles on the dining table.

"What are you looking for, Monsieur Dalsky?" she inquired amiably, turning her flushed face to the boarder, who was then gazing about the kitchen.

"Nothing—do not trouble yourself, Tatyana Markovna—I have got it," he answered politely, resting the soft look of his good gray eyes at her, and showing the enameled cup which he was carrying to the water tap.

"It is high time to give my flowerpot its breakfast; it must have grown hungry," he remarked unobtrusively, retracing his steps to the front room, with the cup half filled with water.

"It gets good board with you, your little flowerpot," Tanya returned, in her plaintive soprano, speaking through the open window, which sometimes served to separate and sometimes to connect the kitchen and the front room. "By the way, it is time for its master to have its breakfast, too. Shall I set the table, Monsieur Dalsky?"

"All rightissimo!" answered the student jestingly, with the remotest suggestion of a chivalrous smile and a bow of his head.

As he ate, she made a playful attempt at reading the portly textbook, which he had brought with him. Whenever she happened to mispronounce an English word, he would set her right, in a matter-of-fact way; whereupon she accepted his correction with a slight blush and a smile, somewhat bashful and somewhat humorous.

Hardly a fortnight had elapsed since Dalsky had installed himself and his scanty effects at the Luries', yet he seemed to have grown into the family, and the three felt as if they had dwelt together all their lives. His presence in the house produced a change that was at once striking and imperceptible. When free from college and from teaching, an hour or two in the morning and a few hours during the afternoon, he would stay at home studying or reading, humming, between whiles, some opera tune, or rolling up a cigarette and smoking it as he paced up and down the floor—all of which he did softly, unobtrusively, with a sort of pleasing fluency. Often he would bring from the street some useful or decorative trifle—a matchbox, a towel-ring, a bit of bric-a-brac for the mantelpiece, a flowerpot. At supper he, Boris and Tanya would have a friendly chat over the contents of the newspapers, or the gossip of the colony, or some Russian book, although Boris was apt to monopolize the time for his animadversions upon the occurrences in the pearl-button shop, which both Tanya and Dalsky were beginning to think rather too minute and uninteresting. "Poor fellow; the pearl-button environment *has* eaten him up," the medical student would say to himself, with heartfelt commiseration. As to his own college, he would scarcely ever refer to it. After supper he usually left for his private lessons, after which he would perhaps drop in at the Russian Students' Club; and altogether his presence did not in the least encroach upon the privacy of the Luries' life, while, on the other hand, it seemed to have breathed an easier and pleasanter atmosphere into their home.

"Well, was there any ground for making so much ado?" Boris once said triumphantly. "We are as much alone as ever, and you are not lonely all day, into the bargain."

Dalsky had come to America with the definite purpose of studying and then practicing medicine. He had landed penniless, yet in a little over two years, and before his friends in the colony had noticed it, he was in a position to pay his first year's tuition and to meet all the other bills of his humble, but well-ordered and, to him, gratifying living.

He was a normally constituted and well-regulated young man of twenty-five, a year or two Lurie's junior.

There was nothing bright nor deep about him, but he was seldom guilty of a gross want of tact. He would be the last man to neglect his task on account of a ball or an interesting book, yet he was never classed among the "grinds." He was endowed with a light touch for things as well as for men, and with that faculty for ranking high in his class, which, as we all know, does not always precede distinction in the school of life. This sort of people give the world very little, ask of it still less, but get more than they give.

As he neither intruded too far into other people's souls, nor allowed others too deep into his own confidence, he was at peace with himself and everybody else in the colony.

v

Three months more had passed. The button factory was busy. Boris's hard, uncongenial toil was deepening its impress upon him. When he came from work he would be so completely fagged out that an English grammar was out of the question.

He grew more morose every day.

Tanya was becoming irritable with him.

One afternoon after six she was pensively rocking and humming a Russian folksong, one of her little white hands resting on an open Russian book in her lap. Dalsky was out, for it was one of those days when he would stay at college until six and come home at about the same time as Boris.

Presently she was awakened from her reverie by the sound of footsteps. The door opened before she had time to make out whose they were, and as her eye fell upon Boris, a shadow of disappointment flitted across her brow.

Still, at the sight of his overworked face, her heart was wrung with pity, and she greeted him with a commiserating, nervous, exaggerated sort of cordiality.

After a little he took to expounding a plan, bearing upon their affairs, which he had conceived while at work. She started to listen with real interest, but her attention soon wandered away, and as he went on she gazed at him blankly and nodded irrelevant assent.

"What is the use of talking, since you are not listening anyway?" he said, mildly.

She was about to say softly, "Excuse me, Borya, say it again, I'll listen," but she said resentfully, "Suit yourself!"

His countenance fell.

"Any letters from home?" he demanded, after a while, to break an awkward stillness.

"No," she replied, with an impatient jerk of her shoulder.

He gave a perplexed shrug, and took up his grammar.

When Dalsky came he found them plainly out of sorts with each other. Tanya returned his "Good health to you," only partly relaxing the frown on her face. Boris raised his black head from his book; his brusque "Good health, Dalsky!" had scarcely left his lips when his short-sighted eyes again nearly touched the open grammar.

"You must excuse me; I am really sorry to have kept you waiting," the boarder apologized, methodically taking off his overcoat and gently brushing its velvet collar before hanging it up, "but I was unavoidably detained at the lecture, and then I met Stern, and you know how hard it is to shake oneself free from him."

"It is not late at all," Tanya observed, unnecessarily retaining a vestige of the cloud upon her countenance. "What does he want, Stern? Some new scheme again?"

"You hit it there, Tatyana Markovna; and, by the way, you two are to play first violin in it."

"I?" asked Tanya, her countenance suddenly blazing up with confused animation. "What is it?" Boris laid down his book and pricked up his ears.

"He has unearthed some remarkable dialogue in Little Russian—you know everything Stern comes across is remarkable. Well, and he wants the two of you to recite it or act it—that's your business—at the New Year's gathering."

"What an idiotic plan!" was Boris's verdict, which his countenance belied unceremoniously.

"Who else is going to participate?" inquired Tanya.

Fixing his mild gray eyes on his youthful landlady, Dalsky proceeded to describe the prospective entertainment in detail. Presently he grew absent-minded and lost the thread of a sentence. He noticed that, as his listener's eyes met his, her gaze became unsteady, wandering, as though she were out of countenance.

She confusedly transferred her glance to his fresh, clean-shaven face and then to his neatly tied scarf and immaculate shirt front.

Boris wore a blue flannel shirt, and, as usual in the middle of the week, his face was overgrown with what he jocosely called underbrush. As he had warmed up to Dalsky's subject and rose to his feet to ply him with questions, the contrast which the broad, leaf-shaped gas flame illuminated was striking. It was one between a worn, wretched workingman and a trim, fresh-looking college student.

Supper passed in animated conversation, as usual. When it was over and the boarder was gone to his pupils, Boris, reclining on the lounge, took up his *Dombey and Son* and Alexandroff's Dictionary. In a quarter of an hour he was fast asleep and snoring. It attracted the attention of Tanya, who sat near by, reading her Russian novel. She let the book rest on her lap and fell to contemplating her husband. His sprawling posture and his snores at once revolted her and filled her with pity. She looked at the scar over his eyebrow, and it pained her; and yet, somehow, she could not divert her eyes from it. At the same time she felt a vague reminiscence stirring in her mind. What was it? She seemed to have seen or heard or read something somewhere which had a certain bearing upon the painful feeling which she was now nursing, in spite of herself, as she was eyeing the scar over Boris's eyebrow. What could it be?

A strenuous mental effort brought to her mind the passage in Tolstoy's novel where Anna Karenina, after having fallen under Vronsky's charm, is met by her husband upon her return to St. Petersburg, whereupon the first thing that strikes her about him is the uncouth hugeness of his ears.

It was not the first time her thoughts had run in this direction. She had repeatedly caught herself dwelling upon such apparently silly subjects as the graceful trick which Dalsky had in knocking off the ashes of his cigarette, or the way he would look about the cupboard for the cup with which he watered his plant, or, again, the soft ring of his voice as he said, "Tatyana Markovna!"—the thoroughly Russian form of address, not much in vogue in the colony. Once, upon touching his flower on the window sill, she became conscious of a thrill, deliciously disquieting and as if whispering something to her. And yet, as the case of Anna Karenina now came to her mind, as an illustration of her own position, it smote her consciousness as a startling discovery.

"And so I am a married woman in love with another man!" was her first thought; and with her soul divided between a benumbing terror and the sweet titillation produced by a sense of tasting forbidden fruit, she involuntarily repeated the mental exclamation: "Yes, I am a married woman in love with another man!"

And with a painful, savage sort of relish she went on staring at her husband's scar and listening to his fatigued breathing. There was a moment when a wave of sympathy suddenly surged to her heart and nearly moved her to tears; but at the next moment it came back to her that it was at Boris's insistence, and in spite of her sobs, that the boarder had been taken into the house; whereupon her heart swelled with a furious sense of revenge. The image of Dalsky floated past her mental vision and agitated her soul with a novel feeling. When a moment or two after she threw a glance at the looking glass she seemed a stranger to herself.

"Is this Tanya? Is this the respectable, decorous young woman that she has been?" she seemed to soliloquize. "What nonsense; why not? What have I done? Dalsky himself does not even suspect anything." It seemed as if she were listening to the depth of her own soul for a favorable answer to her question, and as if the favorable answer did not come.

She became fearful of herself, and, with another sudden flow of affection for her husband, she stepped up to his side to wake him; but as she came into close contact with him, the wave of tenderness ebbed away and she left the room.

"It *is* nonsense," she decided; "still, I must invent some pretext for insisting upon his removal. Then I'll forget him, anyway."

Whether she would have had the courage to carry out her resolve or not, is not known, for the task soon became superfluous.

A few days later, as Dalsky was drawing on his overcoat to leave for his lessons, he said, rather awkwardly, addressing himself to both, while looking at Boris: "By the way, I have to tell you something. I am afraid that devilish college will make it impossible for me to live downtown."

Both Boris and Tanya grew pale.

"You see," Dalsky pursued, "the lectures and the work in the dissecting room are so scattered throughout the day that I don't see my way out unless I get a room in the neighborhood of the college." And to talk himself out of the embarrassing position, he went on to explain college affairs with unnecessary detail.

As a matter of fact, however, his whole explanation, although not based on an untruth, was not the real cause of his determination to leave the Luries. He had known Boris in his better days, and now sympathized with him and Tanya keenly. The frequent outbreaks of temper between husband and wife, and the cloud which now almost constantly hung over the house, heavily bore down upon him as a friend, and made his life there extremely uncomfortable. At last he had perceived the roving, nonplussed look in her eyes as their glances met. Once become observant in this direction, he noticed a thousand and one other little things which seemed to confirm his suspicion. "Can it be that she is interested in me?" he said to himself. For a moment the thought caressed his vanity and conjured up the image of Tanya in a novel aspect, which lured him and spoke of the possibility of reciprocating her feeling—of an adventure.

It was on the very next day that he announced his intention to move.

VI

The house became so dreary to Tanya that her loneliness during the day frightened her, though the presence of Boris irritated her more than ever. She felt as if some member of the household had died. Wherever she turned she beheld some trace of the student; worse than anything else was the window plant, which Dalsky had left behind him. She avoided looking at it, lest it should thrill her with a crushing sense of her desolation, of her bereavement, as it were. Yet, when she was about to remove it, she had not the heart to do it. She strayed about like a shadow, and often felt as though it were enough to touch her to make her melt away in tears.

One evening, after an unbearable silence, succeeding a sharp altercation, Boris asked, pleadingly: "What has become of you, Tanya? I simply fail to recognize you."

"If you understand, then it is foolish to ask," she retorted, with a smile of mild sarcasm, eyeing the floor.

"I understand nothing." But as the words left his lips, something suddenly dawned upon him which made his blood run cold. An array of situations which had produced an impression upon him, but which had been lost upon his consciousness, now uprose in his mind. He grew ashen pale.

"Well, so much the worse," said she.

"Tell me, and I will know," he rejoined, with studied irony, while in his heart he was praying Heaven that his misgivings might prove baseless.

"Oh! I think you do understand; you are not so blind." Her voice now sounded alien in his ears, and she herself seemed to him suddenly changed—as if she had in one moment become transmuted into an older, wiser, sterner, and more beautiful, fiercely beautiful, woman.

"I swear to you that I do not know anything."

"Very well, then; I shall write it," she said, with a sudden determination, rising to produce paper, pen, and ink.

"All right," he said, in abject cowardice, with a meaningless smile.

She wrote: "I am your best friend in the world. I have been thinking, and thinking, and have arrived at the conclusion that the best thing for us to do is to part for a time. I do not blame anybody but myself, but I cannot help it. I have no moral right to live with you as long as my mind is constantly occupied with somebody else. I have struggled hard to keep out the thoughts of him, but it is of no avail."

The phlegmatic ticking of the cheap alarm clock was singing a solemn accompaniment to the impressive stillness of the surroundings. Boris, gazing at the corner of the room with a faint, stolid smile, was almost trembling. Tanya's face was burning with excitement. She went on: "I repeat, I have only myself to blame, and I am doing my best to struggle out of this state of mind. But while it lasts, my false, my dishonest position in this house aggravates things. I wish to be alone, for a while, at least. Then, under new conditions, I hope I shall soon get over it. For the sake of everything that is good, do not attempt to persuade me to stay. It is all thought out and decided. Nor do you need offer to support me. I have no right to it, and will not accept it under any circumstances. I can work and earn my own living. I am prepared to bear the cross. Besides, shall I be the only Russian college woman to work in an American factory? Above all, do not let anybody know anything—the person to whom I have referred not excluded, *of course*. I am sure he does not suspect anything. Do not let him surmise the cause of it all, if you do not wish to see my corpse. We can invent some explanation."

VII

It was the early part of bleak wintry evening. The interior of Silberman's shop, crowded with men and women and their sewing machines, every bit of space truckled up with disorderly piles of finished shirts or bundles of stuff, was dappled with cheerless gaslight. The spacious, barn-like loft rang and trembled with a chaos of mournful and merry song, vying with the insolent rattle of the machines. There were synagogue airs in the chorus and airs of the Jewish stage; popular American airs, airs from the dancing schools, and time-honored airs imported from Russia, Poland, Galicia, Roumania, Hungary.

Only Tanya was not singing. Bent upon her machine, in a remote corner, she was practicing a straight stitch upon some cuttings. She was making marked progress, and, flushed with her success, had almost grown oblivious of the heavy lump at her heart, and the pricking pain which seemed to fill her every limb. Presently the girl next her, who had been rapturously singing "I have a girl in Baltimore" in a sort of cross-tune between the song's own melody and the highly melancholy strains of a Hebrew prayer, suddenly switched off into one of the most Russian of Russian folksongs:

> By the little brook,
> By the little bridge,
> Grass was growing

This she sang with such an un-Russian flavor, and pronounced the words with such a strong Yiddish accent, and so illiterately, that Tanya gnashed her teeth as if touched to the quick, and closed her eyes and ears. The surroundings again grew terrible to her. Commencement Day at the Kieff Gymnasium loomed before her imagination, and she beheld herself one of a group of blooming young maidens, all in fresh brown dresses with black aprons, singing that very song, but in sturdy, ringing, charming Russian. A cruel anguish choked her. Everybody and everything about her was

so strange, so hideously hostile, so exile-like! She once
more saw the little home where she had recently
reigned. "How do I happen here?" she asked herself.
She thought of Boris, and was tempted to run back to
him, to fly into his arms and beg him to establish a
home again. But presently came the image of Dalsky,
neat, polite, dignified, and noiseless; and she once
more fell to her machine, and with a furious cruelty for
herself, she went on working the treadle. Whereupon
her mind gradually occupied itself with the New Year's
entertainment, with the way the crowd would be com-
menting upon her separation, and above all, with her
failure to appear on the platform to recite in Little Russian and to evoke a storm of applause in the presence
of Dalsky.

At that time Boris was on his way from work, in the
direction of Madison Street. It was the second day after he had cleared the rooms by selling the furniture
and cooking utensils to the neighbors, who rushed at
them like flies at a drop of molasses. But he still had
his books and some other effects to remove. When he
entered the rooms, there was light enough from the
street to show the unwanted darkness in them. A silvery streak fell upon the black aperture which had the
day before been filled with the pipe of a little parlor
stove. This and the weird gloom of the rest of the
apartment overwhelmed him with distress and terror.
He hastened to light the gas. The dead emptiness of the
three rooms which so recently had been full of life, the
floors littered with traces of Tanya and their life
together—every corner and recess had a look of doleful, mysterious reproach.

For the first time he seemed to realize what had befallen him; and for the first time in many years he
burst into tears. Hot tears they were, and they fell in
vehement drops, as, leaning his wearied form against
the doorpost and burying his face in his arm, he whispered brokenly, "Tanychka! Tanychka!"

A Ghetto Wedding

Had you chanced to be in Grand Street on that starry February night, it would scarcely have occurred to you that the Ghetto was groaning under the culmination of a long season of enforced idleness and distress. The air was exhilaratingly crisp, and the glare of the cafés and millinery shops flooded it with contentment and kindly good will. The sidewalks were alive with shoppers and promenaders, and lined with peddlers.

Yet the dazzling, deafening chaos had many a tale of woe to tell. The greater part of the surging crowd was out on an errand of self-torture. Straying forlornly by inexorable window displays, men and women would pause here and there to indulge in a hypothetical selection, to feast a hungry eye upon the object of an imaginary purchase, only forthwith to pay for the momentary joy with all the pangs of awakening to an empty purse.

Many of the peddlers, too, bore piteous testimony to the calamity which was then preying upon the quarter. Some of them performed their task of yelling and gesticulating with the desperation of imminent ruin; others implored the passers-by for custom with the abject effect of begging alms; while in still others this feverish urgency was disguised by an air of martyrdom or of shamefaced unwontedness, as if peddling were beneath the dignity of their habitual occupations, and they had been driven to it by sheer famine—by the hopeless dearth of employment at their own trades.

One of these was a thick-set fellow of twenty-five or twenty-six, with honest, clever blue eyes. It might be due to the genial, inviting quality of his face that the Passover dishes whose praises he was sounding had greater attraction for some of the women with an "effectual demand" than those of his competitors. Still, his comparative success had not as yet reconciled him to his new calling. He was constantly gazing about for a possible passer-by of his acquaintance, and when one came in sight he would seek refuge from identification in closer communion with the crockery on his pushcart.

"Buy nice dishes for the holidays! Cheap and strong! Buy dishes for Passover!" When business was brisk, he sang with a bashful relish; when the interval between a customer and her successor was growing too long, his singsong would acquire a mournful ring that was suggestive of the psalm-chanting at an orthodox Jewish funeral.

He was a cap-blocker, and in the busy season his earnings ranged from ten to fifteen dollars a week. But he had not worked full time for over two years, and during the last three months he had not been able to procure a single day's employment.

Goldy, his sweetheart, too, who was employed in making knee breeches, had hardly work enough to pay her humble board and rent. Nathan, after much hesitation, was ultimately compelled to take to peddling; and the longed-for day of their wedding was put off from month to month.

They had become engaged nearly two years before; the wedding ceremony having been originally fixed for a date some three months later. Their joint savings then amounted to one hundred and twenty dollars—a sum quite adequate, in Nathan's judgment, for a modest, quiet celebration and the humble beginnings of a household establishment. Goldy, however, summarily and indignantly overruled him.

"One does not marry every day," she argued, "and

when I have at last lived to stand under the bridal canopy with my predestined one, I will not do so like a beggar maid. Give me a respectable wedding, or none at all, Nathan, do you hear?"

It is to be noted that a "respectable wedding" was not merely a casual expression with Goldy. Like its antithesis, a "slipshod wedding," it played in her vocabulary the part of something like a well-established scientific term, with a meaning as clearly defined as that of "centrifugal force" or "geometrical progression." Now, a slipshod wedding was anything short of a gown of white satin and slippers to match; two carriages to bring the bride and the bridegroom to the ceremony, and one to take them to their bridal apartments; a wedding bard and a band of at least five musicians; a spacious ballroom crowded with dancers, and a feast of a hundred and fifty covers. As to furniture, she refused to consider any which did not include a pierglass and a Brussels carpet.

Nathan contended that the items upon which she insisted would cost a sum far beyond their joint accumulations. This she met by the declaration that he had all along been bent upon making her the target of universal ridicule, and that she would rather descend into an untimely grave than be married in a slipshod manner. Here she burst out crying; and whether her tears referred to the untimely grave or to the slipshod wedding, they certainly seemed to strengthen the cogency of her argument; for Nathan at once proceeded to signify his surrender by a kiss, and when ignominiously repulsed he protested his determination to earn the necessary money to bring things to the standard which she held up so uncompromisingly.

Hard times set in. Nathan and Goldy pinched and scrimped; but all their heroic economies were powerless to keep their capital from dribbling down to less than one hundred dollars. The wedding was postponed again and again. Finally the curse of utter idleness fell upon Nathan's careworn head. Their savings dwindled apace. In dismay they beheld the foundation of their happiness melt gradually away. Both were tired of boarding. Both longed for the bliss and economy of married life. They grew more impatient and restless every day, and Goldy made concession after concession. First the wedding supper was sacrificed; then the pier-mirror and the bard were stricken from the program; and these were eventually succeeded by the hired hall and the Brussels carpet.

After Nathan went into peddling, a few days before we first find him hawking chinaware on Grand Street, matters began to look brighter, and the spirits of our betrothed couple rose. Their capital, which had sunk to forty dollars, was increasing again, and Goldy advised waiting long enough for it to reach the sum necessary for a slipshod wedding and establishment.

It was nearly ten o'clock. Nathan was absently drawling his "Buy nice dishes for the holidays!" His mind was engrossed with the question of making peddling his permanent occupation.

Presently he was startled by a merry soprano mocking him: "Buy nice di-i-shes! Mind that you don't fall asleep murmuring like this. A big lot you can make!"

Nathan turned a smile of affectionate surprise upon a compact little figure, small to drollness, but sweet in the amusing grace of its diminutive outlines—an epitome of exquisite femininity. Her tiny face was as comically lovely as her form; her applelike cheeks were firm as marble, and her inadequate nose protruded between them like the result of a hasty tweak; a pair of large, round black eyes and a thick-lipped little mouth inundating it all with passion and restless, good-natured shrewdness.

"Goldy! What brings *you* here?" Nathan demanded, with a fond look which instantly gave way to an air of discomfort. "You know I hate you to see me peddling."

"Are you really angry? Bite the feather bed, then. Where is the disgrace? As if you were the only peddler in America! I wish you were. Wouldn't you make heaps of money then! But you had better hear what *does* bring me here. Nathan, darling-dearest little heart, dearest little crown that you are, guess what a plan I have hit upon!" she exploded all at once. "Well, if you hear me out, and you don't say that Goldy has the head of a cabinet minister, then—well, then you will be a big hog, and nothing else."

And without giving him time to put in as much as an interjection, she rattled on, puffing for breath and smacking her lips for ecstasy. Was it not stupid of them to be racking their brains about the wedding while there was such a plain way of having both a "respectable" celebration and fine furniture—Brussels carpet, pier-glass, and all—with the money they now had on hand?

"Come, out with it, then," he said morosely.

But his disguised curiosity only whetted her appetite for tormenting him, and she declared her determination not to disclose her great scheme before they had reached her lodgings.

"You have been yelling long enough today, anyhow," she said, with abrupt sympathy. "Do you suppose it does not go to my very heart to think of the way you stand out in the cold screaming yourself hoarse?"

Half an hour later, when they were alone in Mrs. Volpiansky's parlor, which was also Goldy's bedroom, she set about emptying his pockets of the gross results of the day's business, and counting the money. This she did with a preoccupied, matter-of-fact air, Nathan submitting to the operation with fond and amused willingness; and the sum being satisfactory, she went on to unfold her plan.

"You see," she began, almost in a whisper, and with the mien of a care-worn, experience-laden old matron, "in a week or two we shall have about seventy-five dollars, shan't we? Well, what is seventy-five dollars? Nothing! We could just have the plainest furniture, and no wedding worth speaking of. Now, if we have no wedding, we shall get no presents, shall we?"

Nathan shook his head thoughtfully.

"Well, why shouldn't we be up to snuff and do this way? Let us spend all our money on a grand, respectable wedding, and send out a big lot of invitations, and

then—well, won't uncle Leiser send us a carpet or a
parlor set? And aunt Beile, and cousin Shapiro, and
Charley, and Meyerke, and Wolfke, and Bennie, and
Sore-Gitke—won't each present something or other, as
is the custom among respectable people? May God
give us a lump of good luck as big as the wedding
present each of them is sure to send us! Why, did not
Beilke get a fine carpet from uncle when she got married? And am I not a nearer relative than she?"

She paused to search his face for a sign of approval,
and, fondly smoothing a tuft of his dark hair into place,
she went on to enumerate the friends to be invited and
the gifts to be expected from them.

"So you see," she pursued, "we will have both a respectable wedding that we shan't have to be ashamed
of in after years and the nicest things we could get if
we spent two hundred dollars. What do you say?"

"What *shall* I say?" he returned dubiously.

The project appeared reasonable enough, but the in-
vestment struck him as rather hazardous. He pleaded
for caution, for delay; but as he had no tangible argument to produce, while she stood her ground with the
firmness of conviction, her victory was an easy one.

"It will all come right, depend upon it," she said
coaxingly. "You just leave everything to me. Don't be
uneasy, Nathan," she added. "You and I are orphans,
and you know the Uppermost does not forsake a bride
and bridegroom who have nobody to take care of them.
If my father were alive, it would be different," she concluded, with a disconsolate gesture.

There was a pathetic pause. Tears glistened in
Goldy's eyes.

"May your father rest in a bright paradise," Nathan
said feelingly. "But what is the use of crying? Can you
bring him back to life? I will be a father to you."

"If God be pleased," she assented. "Would that
mamma, at least—may she be healthy a hundred and
twenty years—would that she, at least, were here to attend our wedding! Poor mother! it will break her heart
to think that she has not been foreordained by the Uppermost to lead me under the canopy."

There was another desolate pause, but it was presently broken by Goldy, who exclaimed with unexpected buoyancy, "By the way, Nathan, guess what I did! I am afraid you will call me braggart and make fun of me, but I don't care," she pursued, with a playful pout, as she produced a strip of carpet from her pocketbook. "I went into a furniture store, and they gave me a sample three times as big as this. I explained in my letter to mother that this is the kind of stuff that will cover my floor when I am married. Then I enclosed the sample in the letter, and sent it all to Russia."

Nathan clapped his hands and burst out laughing. "But how do you know that is just the kind of carpet you will get for your wedding present?" he demanded, amazed as much as amused.

"How do I know? As if it mattered what sort of carpet! I can just see mamma going the rounds of the neighbors, and showing off the 'costly tablecloth' her daughter will trample upon. Won't she be happy!"

Over a hundred invitations, printed in as luxurious a black and gold as ever came out of an Essex Street hand press, were sent out for an early date in April. Goldy and Nathan paid a month's rent in advance for three rooms on the second floor of a Cherry Street tenement house. Goldy regarded the rent as unusually low, and the apartments as the finest on the East Side.

"Oh, haven't I got lovely rooms!" she would ejaculate, beaming with the consciousness of the pronoun. Or, "You ought to see *my* rooms! How much do you pay for yours?" Or again, "I have made up my mind to have my parlor in the rear room. It is as light as the front one, anyhow, and I want that for a kitchen, you know. What do you say?" For hours together she would go on talking nothing but rooms, rent, and furniture; every married couple who had recently moved into new quarters, or were about to do so, seemed bound to her by the ties of a common cause; in her imagination, humanity was divided into those who were interested in the question of rooms, rent and furniture and those who were not—the former, of whom she was one, constituting the superior category; and whenever her eye fell upon a bill announcing rooms to let, she would experience something akin to the feeling with which an artist, in passing, views some accessory of his art.

It is customary to send the bulkier wedding presents to a young couple's apartments a few days before they become man and wife, the closer relatives and friends of the betrothed usually settling among themselves what piece of furniture each is to contribute. Accordingly, Goldy gave up her work a week in advance of the day set for the great event, in order that she might be on hand to receive the things when they arrived.

She went to the empty little rooms, with her lunch, early in the morning, and kept anxious watch till after nightfall, when Nathan came to take her home.

A day passed, another, and a third, but no express-man called out her name. She sat waiting and listening for the rough voice, but in vain.

"Oh, it is too early, anyhow. I am a fool to be expecting anything so soon at all," she tried to console herself. And she waited another hour, and still another; but no wedding gift made its appearance.

"Well, there is plenty of time, after all; wedding presents do come a day or two before the ceremony," she argued; and again she waited, and again strained her ears, and again her heart rose in her throat.

The vacuity of the rooms, freshly cleaned, scrubbed, and smelling of whitewash, began to frighten her. Her overwrought mind was filled with sounds which her over-strained ears did not hear. Yet there she sat on the window sill, listening and listening for an express-man's voice.

"Hush, hush-sh, hush-sh-sh!" whispered the walls; the corners muttered awful threats; her heart was ever and anon contracted with fear; she often thought herself on the brink of insanity; yet she stayed on, waiting, waiting, waiting.

At the slightest noise in the hall she would spring to her feet, her heart beating wildly, only presently to sink in her bosom at finding it to be some neighbor or a peddler; and so frequent were these violent throbbings that Goldy grew to imagine herself a prey to heart disease. Nevertheless the fifth day came, and she was again at her post, waiting, waiting, waiting for her wedding gifts. And what is more, when Nathan came from business, and his countenance fell as he surveyed the undisturbed emptiness of the rooms, she set a merry face against his rueful inquiries, and took to bantering him as a woman quick to lose heart, and to painting their prospects in roseate hues, until she argued herself, if not him, into a more cheerful view of the situation.

On the sixth day an expressman did pull up in front of the Cherry Street tenement house, but he had only a cheap huge rocking chair for Goldy and Nathan; and as it proved to be the gift of a family who had been set down for nothing less than a carpet or a parlor set, the joy and hope which its advent had called forth turned to dire disappointment and despair. For nearly an hour Goldy sat mournfully rocking and striving to picture how delightful it would have been if all her anticipations had come true.

Presently there arrived a flimsy plush-covered little corner table. It could not have cost more than a dollar. Yet it was the gift of a near friend, who had been relied upon for a pier-glass or a bedroom set. A little later a cheap alarm clock and an icebox were brought in. That was all.

Occasionally Goldy went to the door to take in the entire effect; but the more she tried to view the parlor as half finished, the more cruelly did the few lonely and mismated things emphasize the remaining emptiness of the apartments: whereupon she would sink into her rocker and sit motionless, with a drooping head, and then desperately fall to swaying to and fro, as though bent upon swinging herself out of her woebegone, wretched self.

Still, when Nathan came, there was a triumphant twinkle in her eye, as she said, pointing to the gifts, "Well, mister, who was right? It is not very bad for a start, is it? You know most people do send their wedding presents after the ceremony—why, of course!" she added, in a sort of confidential way. "Well, we have invited a big crowd, and all people of no mean sort, thank God; and who ever heard of a lady or a gentleman attending a respectable wedding and having a grand wedding supper, and then cheating the bride and the bridegroom out of their presents?"

The evening was well advanced; yet there were only a score of people in a hall that was used to hundreds.

Everybody felt ill at ease, and ever and anon looked about for the possible arrival of more guests. At ten o'clock the dancing preliminary to the ceremony had not yet ceased, although the few waltzers looked as if they were scared by the ringing echoes of their own footsteps amid the austere solemnity of the surrounding void and the depressing sheen of the dim expanse of floor.

The two fiddles, the cornet, and the clarinet were shrieking as though for pain, and the malicious superabundance of gaslight was fiendishly sneering at their tortures. Weddings and entertainments being scarce in the Ghetto, its musicians caught the contagion of misery: hence the greedy, desperate gusto with which the band plied their instruments.

At last it became evident that the assemblage was not destined to be larger than it was, and that it was no use delaying the ceremony. It was, in fact, an open secret among those present that by far the greater number of the invited friends were kept away by lack of employment: some having their presentable clothes in the pawn shop; others avoiding the expense of a wedding present, or simply being too cruelly borne down by their cares to have a mind for the excitement of a wedding; indeed, some even thought it wrong of Nathan to have the celebration during such a period of hard times, when everybody was out of work.

It was a little after ten when the bard—a tall, gaunt man, with a grizzly beard and a melancholy face—donned his skullcap, and, advancing toward the dancers, called out in a synagogue intonation, "Come, ladies, let us veil the bride!"

An odd dozen of daughters of Israel followed him and the musicians into a little side room where Goldy was seated between her two brideswomen (the wives of two men who were to attend upon the groom). According to the orthodox custom she had fasted the whole day, and as a result of this and of her gnawing grief, added to the awe-inspiring scene she had been awaiting, she was pale as death; the effect being heightened by the wreath and white gown she wore. As the procession came filing in, she sat blinking her round dark eyes in dismay, as if the bard were an executioner come to lead her to the scaffold.

The song or address to the bride usually partakes of the qualities of prayer and harangue, and includes a melancholy meditation upon life and death; lamenting the deceased members of the young woman's family, bemoaning her own woes, and exhorting her to discharge her sacred duties as a wife, mother, and servant of God. Composed in verse and declaimed in a solemn, plaintive recitative, often broken by the band's mournful refrain, it is sure to fulfill its mission of eliciting tears even when hearts are brimful of glee. Imagine, then, the funereal effect which it produced at Goldy's wedding ceremony.

The bard, half starved himself, sang the anguish of his own heart; the violins wept, the clarinet moaned, the cornet and the double-bass groaned, each reciting the sad tale of its poverty-stricken master. He began:

> Silence, good women, give heed to *my* verses!
> Tonight, bride, thou dost stand before the
>   Uppermost.
> Pray to him to bless thy union,
> To let thee and thy mate live a hundred and
>   twenty peaceful years,
> To give you your daily bread,
> To keep hunger from your door.

Several women, including Goldy, burst into tears,
the others sadly lowering their gaze. The band sounded
a wailing chord, and the whole audience broke into
loud, heartrending weeping.

The bard went on sternly:

> Wail, bride, wail!
> This is a time of tears.
> Think of thy past days:
> Alas! they are gone to return nevermore.

Heedless of the convulsive sobbing with which the
room resounded, he continued to declaim, and at last,
his eye flashing fire and his voice tremulous with emotion, he sang out in a dismal, uncanny high key:

> And thy good mother beyond the seas,
> And thy father in his grave
> Near where thy cradle was rocked,
> Weep, bride, weep!
> Though his soul is better off
> Than we are here underneath
> In dearth and cares and ceaseless pangs,
> Weep, sweet bride, weep!

Then, in the general outburst that followed the extemporaneous verse, there was a cry—"The bride is
fainting! Water! quick!"

"Murderer that you are!" flamed out an elderly matron, with an air of admiration for the bard's talent as
much as of wrath for the far-fetched results it achieved.

Goldy was brought to, and the rest of the ceremony
passed without accident. She submitted to everything
as in a dream. When the bridegroom, escorted by two
attendants, each carrying a candelabrum holding
lighted candles came to place the veil over her face,
she stared about as though she failed to realize the situation or to recognize Nathan. When, keeping time to
the plaintive strains of a time-honored tune, she was
led, blindfolded, into the large hall and stationed beside the bridegroom under the red canopy, and then

marched around him seven times, she obeyed instructions and moved about with the passivity of a hypnotic. After the Seven Blessings had been recited, when the cantor, gently lifting the end of her veil, presented the wineglass to her lips, she tasted its contents with the air of an invalid taking medicine. Then she felt the ring slip down her finger, and heard Nathan say, "Be thou dedicated to me by this ring, according to the laws of Moses and Israel."

Whereupon she said to herself, "Now I am a married woman!" But somehow, at this moment the words were meaningless sounds to her. She knew she was married, but could not realize what it implied. As Nathan crushed the wineglass underfoot, and the band struck up a cheerful melody, and the gathering shouted, "Good luck! Good luck!" and clapped their hands, while the older women broke into a wild hop, Goldy felt the relief of having gone through a great ordeal. But still she was not distinctly aware of any change in her position.

Not until fifteen minutes later, when she found herself in the basement, at the head of one of three long tables, did the realization of her new self strike her consciousness full in the face, as it were.

The dining room was nearly as large as the dancing hall on the floor above. It was as brightly illuminated, and the three tables, which ran almost its entire length, were set for a hundred and fifty guests. Yet there were barely twenty to occupy them. The effect was still more depressing than in the dancing room. The vacant benches and the untouched covers still more agonizingly exaggerated the emptiness of the room, in which the sorry handful of a company lost themselves.

Goldy looked at the rows of plates, spoons, forks, knives, and they weighed her down with the cold dazzle of their solemn, pompous array.

"I am not the Goldy I used to be," she said to herself. "I am a married woman, like mamma, or auntie, or Mrs. Volpiansky. And we have spent every cent we had on this grand wedding, and now we are left without money for furniture, and there are no guests to send us any, and the supper will be thrown out, and everything is lost, and I am to blame for it all!"

The glittering plates seemed to hold whispered converse and to exchange winks and grins at her expense. She transferred her glance to the company, and it appeared as if they were vainly forcing themselves to partake of the food—as though they, too, were looked out of countenance by that ruthless sparkle of the unused plates.

Nervous silence hung over the room, and the reluctant jingle of the score of knives and forks made it more awkward, more enervating, every second. Even the bard had not the heart to break the stillness by the merry rhymes he had composed for the occasion.

Goldy was overpowered. She thought she was on the verge of another fainting spell, and, shutting her eyes and setting her teeth, she tried to imagine herself dead. Nathan, who was by her side, noticed it. He took her hand under the table, and, pressing it gently, whispered, "Don't take it to heart. There is a God in heaven."

She could not make out his words, but she felt their meaning. As she was about to utter some phrase of endearment, her heart swelled in her throat, and a piteous, dovelike, tearful look was all the response she could make.

By-and-by, however, when the foaming lager was served, tongues were loosened, and the bard, although distressed by the meager collection in store for him, but stirred by an ardent desire to relieve the insupportable wretchedness of the evening, outdid himself in offhand acrostics and witticisms. Needless to say that his efforts were thankfully rewarded with unstinted laughter; and as the room rang with merriment, the gleaming rows of undisturbed plates also seemed to join in the general hubbub of mirth, and to be laughing a hearty, kindly laugh.

Presently, amid a fresh outbreak of deafening hilarity, Goldy bent close to Nathan's ear and exclaimed with sobbing vehemence, "My husband! My husband! My husband!"

"My wife!" he returned in her ear.

"Do you know what you are to me now?" she resumed. "A husband! And I am your wife! Do you know what it means—*do* you, *do* you, Nathan?" she insisted, with frantic emphasis.

"I do, my little sparrow; only don't worry over the wedding presents."

It was after midnight, and even the Ghetto was immersed in repose. Goldy and Nathan were silently wending their way to the three empty little rooms where they were destined to have their first joint home. They wore the wedding attire which they had rented for the evening: he a swallowtail coat and high hat, and she a white satin gown and slippers, her head uncovered—the wreath and veil done up in a newspaper, in Nathan's hand.

They had gone to the wedding in carriages, which had attracted large crowds both at the point of departure, and in front of the hall; and of course they had expected to make their way to their new home in a similar "respectable" manner. Toward the close of the last dance, after supper, they found, however, that some small change was all they possessed in the world.

The last strains of music were dying away. The guests, in their hats and bonnets, were taking leave. Everybody seemed in a hurry to get away to his own world, and to abandon the young couple to their fate.

Nathan would have borrowed a dollar or two of some friend. "Let us go home as behooves a bride and bridegroom," he said. "There is a God in heaven: he will not forsake us."

But Goldy would not hear of betraying the full measure of their poverty to their friends. "No! no!" she retorted testily. "I am not going to let you pay a dollar and a half for a few blocks' drive, like a Fifth Avenue nobleman. We can walk," she pursued, with the grim determination of one bent upon self-chastisement. "A poor woman who dares spend every cent on a wedding must be ready to walk after the wedding."

When they found themselves alone in the deserted

street, they were so overcome by a sense of loneliness, of a kind of portentous, haunting emptiness, that they could not speak. So on they trudged in dismal silence; she leaning upon his arm, and he tenderly pressing her to his side.

Their way lay through the gloomiest and roughest part of the Seventh Ward. The neighborhood frightened her, and she clung closer to her escort. At one corner they passed some men in front of a liquor saloon.

"Look at dem! Look at dem! A sheeny fellar an' his bride, I'll betch ye!" shouted a husky voice. "Jes' comin' from de weddin'."

"She ain't no bigger 'n a peanut, is she?" The simile was greeted with a horse-laugh.

"Look a here, young fellar, what's de madder wid carryin' dat lady of yourn in your vest pocket?"

When Nathan and Goldy were a block away, something like a potato or a carrot struck her in the back. At the same time the gang of loafers on the corner broke into boisterous merriment. Nathan tried to face about, but she restrained him.

"Don't! They might kill you!" she whispered, and relapsed into silence.

He made another attempt to disengage himself, as if for a desperate attack upon her assailants, but she nestled close to his side and held him fast, her every fiber tingling with the consciousness of the shelter she had in him.

"Don't mind them, Nathan," she said.

And as they proceeded on their dreary way through a somber, impoverished street, with here and there a rustling tree—a melancholy witness of its better days—they felt a stream of happiness uniting them, as it coursed through the veins of both, and they were filled with a blissful sense of oneness the like of which they had never tasted before. So happy were they that the gang behind them, and the bare rooms toward which they were directing their steps, and the miserable failure of the wedding, all suddenly appeared too insignificant to engage their attention—paltry matters alien to their new life, remote from the enchanted world in which they now dwelt.

The very notion of a relentless void abruptly turned to a beatific sense of their own seclusion, of there being only themselves in the universe, to live and delight in each other.

"Don't mind them, Nathan darling," she repeated mechanically, conscious of nothing but the tremor of happiness in her voice.

"I should give it to them!" he responded, gathering her still closer to him. "I should show them how to touch my Goldy, my pearl, my birdie!"

They dived into the denser gloom of a sidestreet.

A gentle breeze ran past and ahead of them, proclaiming the bride and the bridegroom. An old tree whispered overhead its tender felicitations.

II

Yekl

*A Tale of the
New York Ghetto*

1896

1

JAKE AND YEKL

The operatives of the cloak shop in which Jake was employed had been idle all the morning. It was after twelve o'clock and the "boss" had not yet returned from Broadway, whither he had betaken himself two or three hours before in quest of work. The little sweltering assemblage—for it was an oppressive day in midsummer—beguiled their suspense variously. A rabbinical-looking man of thirty, who sat with the back of his chair tilted against his sewing machine, was intent upon an English newspaper. Every little while he would remove it from his eyes—showing a dyspeptic face fringed with a thin growth of dark beard—to consult the cumbrous dictionary on his knees. Two young lads, one seated on the frame of the next machine and the other standing, were boasting to one another of their respective intimacies with the leading actors of the Jewish stage. The board of a third machine, in a corner of the same wall, supported an open copy of a socialist magazine in Yiddish, over which a cadaverous young man absorbedly swayed to and fro droning in the Talmudical intonation. A middle-aged operative, with huge red side whiskers, who was perched on the presser's table in the corner opposite, was mending his own coat. While the thick-set presser and all the three women of the shop, occupying the three machines ranged against an adjoining wall, formed an attentive audience to an impromptu lecture upon the comparative merits of Boston and New York by Jake.

He had been speaking for some time. He stood in the middle of the overcrowded stuffy room with his long but well-shaped legs wide apart, his bulky round head aslant, and one of his bared mighty arms akimbo. He spoke in Boston Yiddish, that is to say, in Yiddish more copiously spiced with mutilated English than is the language of the metropolitan Ghetto in which our story lies. He had a deep and rather harsh voice, and his r's could do credit to the thickest Irish brogue.

"When I was in Boston," he went on, with a contemptuous mien intended for the American metropolis, "I knew a *feller,** so he was a *preticly* friend of John Shullivan's. He is a Christian, that feller is, and yet the two of us lived like brothers. May I be unable to move from this spot if we did not. How, then, would you have it? Like here, in New York, where the Jews are a *lot* of *greenhorns* and can not speak a word of English? Over there every Jew speaks English like a stream."

"*Say,* Dzake," the presser broke in, "John Sullivan is *tzampion* no longer, is he?"

"Oh, no! Not always is it holiday!" Jake responded, with what he considered a Yankee jerk of his head. "Why, don't you know? Jimmie Corbett *leaked* him, and Jimmie *leaked* Cholly Meetchel, too. *You can betch you' bootsh!* Johnnie could not leak Chollie, *becaush* he is a big *bluffer,* Chollie is," he pursued, his clean-shaven florid face beaming with enthusiasm for his subject, and with pride in the diminutive proper nouns he flaunted. "But Jimmie *pundished* him. *Oh, didn't he knock him out off shight!* He came near making a meat ball of him"—with a chuckle. "He *tzettled* him in three *roynds.* I knew a feller who had seen the fight."

"What is a *rawnd,* Dzake?" the presser inquired.

Jake's answer to the question carried him into a minute exposition of "right-handers," "left-handers,"

---

*English words incorporated in the Yiddish of the characters of this narrative are given in italics.

"sending to sleep," "first blood," and other commodities of the fistic business. He must have treated the subject rather too scientifically, however, for his female listeners obviously paid more attention to what he did in the course of the boxing match, which he had now and then, by way of illustration, with the thick air of the room, than to the verbal part of his lecture. Nay, even the performances of his brawny arms and magnificent form did not charm them as much as he thought they did. For a display of manly force, when connected—even though in a purely imaginary way—with acts of violence, has little attraction for a "daughter of the Ghetto." Much more interest did those arms and form command on their own merits. Nor was his chubby high-colored face neglected. True, there was a suggestion of the bulldog in its make up; but this effect was lost upon the feminine portion of Jake's audience, for his features, illuminated by a pair of eager eyes of a hazel hue, and shaded by a thick crop of dark hair, were, after all, rather pleasing than otherwise. Strongly Semitic naturally, they became still more so each time they were brightened up by his good-natured boyish smile. Indeed, Jake's very nose, which was fleshy and pear-shaped and decidedly not Jewish (although not decidedly anything else), seemed to join the Mosaic faith, and even his shaven upper lip looked penitent, as soon as that smile of his made its appearance.

"Nice fun that!" observed the side-whiskered man, who had stopped sewing to follow Jake's exhibition. "Fighting—like drunken moujiks in Russia!"

"Tarrarra-boom-de-ay!" was Jake's merry retort; and for an exclamation mark he puffed up his cheeks into a balloon, and exploded it by a *"pawnch"* of his formidable fist.

"Look, I beg you, look at his dog's tricks!" the other said in disgust.

"Horse's head that you are!" Jake rejoined good-naturedly. "Do you mean to tell me that a moujik understands how to *fight*? A disease he does! He only knows how to strike like a bear [Jake adapted his voice and gesticulation to the idea of clumsiness], *an' dot' sh ull*! What does he *care* where his paw will land, so he strikes. *But* here one must observe *rulesh* [rules]."

At this point Meester Bernstein—for so the rabbinical-looking man was usually addressed by his shopmates—looked up from his dictionary.

"Can't you see?" he interposed, with an air of assumed gravity as he turned to Jake's opponent, "America is an educated country, so they won't even break bones without grammar. They tear each other's sides according to 'right and left,'* you know." This was a thrust at Jake's right-handers and left-handers, which had interfered with Bernstein's reading. "Nevertheless," the latter proceeded, when the outburst of laughter which greeted his witticism had subsided, "I do think that a burly Russian peasant would, without a bit of grammar, crunch the bones of Corbett himself; and he would not *charge* him a cent for it, either."

"*Is dot sho?*" Jake retorted, somewhat nonplussed. "*I betch you* he would not. The peasant would lie bleeding like a hog before he had time to turn around."

"*But* they might kill each other in that way, *ain't it,* Jake?" asked a comely, milk-faced blonde whose name was Fanny. She was celebrated for her lengthy tirades, mostly in a plaintive, nagging strain, and delivered in her quiet, piping voice, and had accordingly been dubbed "The Preacher."

"Oh, that will happen but very seldom," Jake returned rather glumly.

The theatrical pair broke off their boasting match to join in the debate, which soon included all except the socialist; the former two, together with the two girls and the presser, espousing the American cause, while Malke the widow and "De Viskes" sided with Bernstein.

"Let it be as you say," said the leader of the minority, withdrawing from the contest to resume his news-

---

*A term relating to the Hebrew equivalent of the letter *s,* whose pronounciation depends upon the right or left position of a mark over it.

paper. "My grandma's last care it is who can fight best."

"Nice pleasure, *anyhull*," remarked the widow. "*Never min'*, we shall see how it will lie in his head when he has a wife and children to *support*."

Jake colored. "What does a *chicken* know about these things?" he said irascibly.

Bernstein again could not help intervening. "And you, Jake, can not do without 'these things,' can you? Indeed, I do not see how you manage to live without them."

"Don't you like it? I do," Jake declared tartly. "Once I live in America," he pursued, on the defensive, "I want to know that I live in America. *Dot'sh a' kin' a man I am!* One must not be a *greenhorn*. Here a Jew is as good as a Gentile. How, then, would you have it? The way it is in Russia, where a Jew is afraid to stand within four ells of a Christian?"

"Are there no other Christians than *fighters* in America?" Bernstein objected with an amused smile. "Why don't you look for the educated ones?"

"Do you mean to say the *fighters* are not *ejecate*? Better than you, *anyhoy*," Jake said with a Yankee wink, followed by his Semitic smile. "Here you read the papers, and yet *I'll betch you* you don't know that Corbett *findished college*."

"I never read about fighters," Bernstein replied with a bored gesture, and turned to his paper.

"Then say that you don't know, and *dot'sh ull*!"

Bernstein made no reply. In his heart Jake respected him, and was now anxious to vindicate his tastes in the judgment of his scholarly shopmate and in his own.

"*Alla right,* let it be as you say; the *fighters* are not *ejecate*. No, not a bit?" he said ironically, continuing to address himself to Bernstein. "But what will you say to *baseball*? All *college boys* and *tony peoplesh* play it," he concluded triumphantly. Bernstein remained silent, his eyes riveted to his newspaper. "Ah, you don't answer, *shee*?" said Jake, feeling put out.

The awkward pause which followed was relieved by one of the playgoers who wanted to know whether it was true that to pitch a ball required more skill than to catch one.

"*Sure!* You must know how to *peetch,*" Jake rejoined with the cloud lingering on his brow, as he lukewarmly delivered an imaginary ball.

"And I, for my part, don't see what wisdom there is to it," said the presser with a shrug. "I think I could throw, too."

"He can do everything!" laughingly remarked a girl named Pessé.

"How hard can you hit?" Jake demanded sarcastically, somewhat warming up to the subject.

"As hard as you at any time."

"*I betch you a dullar to you' ten shent* you can not," Jake answered, and at the same moment he fished out a handful of coin from his trousers pocket and challengingly presented it close to his interlocutor's nose.

"There he goes!—betting!" the presser exclaimed, drawing slightly back. "For my part, your *pitzers* and *catzers* may all lie in the earth. A nice entertainment, indeed! Just like little children—playing ball! And yet people say America is a *smart* country. I don't see it."

" '*F caush* you don't, *becaush* you are a bedraggled *greenhorn,* afraid to budge out of Heshter Street." As Jake thus vented his bad humor on his adversary, he cast a glance at Bernstein, as if anxious to attract his attention and to re-engage him in the discussion.

"Look at the Yankee!" the presser shot back.

"More of a one than you, *anyhoy.*"

"He thinks that *shaving* one's mustache makes a Yankee!"

Jake turned white with rage.

" '*Pon my vord,* I'll ride into his mug and give such a *shaving* and planing to his pig's snout that he will have to pick up his teeth."

"That's all you are good for."

"Better don't answer him, Jake," said Fanny, intimately.

"Oh, I came near forgetting that he has somebody to take his part!" snapped the presser.

The girl's milky face became a fiery red, and she retorted in vituperative Yiddish from that vocabulary which is the undivided possession of her sex. The presser jerked out an innuendo still more far-reaching than his first. Jake, with bloodshot eyes, leaped at the offender, and catching him by the front of his waist-coat, was aiming one of those bearlike blows which but a short while ago he had decried in the moujik, when Bernstein sprang to his side and tore him away, Pessé placing herself between the two enemies.

"Don't get excited," Bernstein coaxed him.

"Better don't soil your hands," Fanny added.

After a slight pause Bernstein could not forbear a re-mark which he had stubbornly repressed while Jake was challenging him to a debate on the education of baseball players: "Look here, Jake; since fighters and baseball men are all educated, then why don't you try to become so? Instead of *spending* your money on fights, dancing, and things like that, would it not be better if you paid it to a teacher?"

Jake flew into a fresh passion. "*Never min'* what I do with my money," he said; "I don't steal it from you, do I? Rejoice that you keep tormenting your books. Much does he know! Learning, learning, and learn-ing, and still he can not speak English. I don't learn and yet I speak quicker than you!"

A deep blush of wounded vanity mounted to Bernstein's sallow cheek. "*Ull right, ull right!*" he cut the conversation short, and took up the newspaper.

Another nervous silence fell upon the group. Jake felt wretched. He uttered an English oath, which in his heart he directed against himself as much as against his sedate companion, and fell to frowning upon the leg of a machine.

"Vill you go by Joe tonight?" asked Fanny in En-glish, speaking in an undertone. Joe was a dancing master. She was sure Jake intended to call at his "acad-emy" that evening, and she put the question only in or-der to help him out of his sour mood.

"No," said Jake, morosely.

"Vy, today is Vensday."

"And without you I don't know it!" he snarled in Yiddish.

The finisher girl blushed deeply and refrained from any response.

"He does look like a *regely* Yankee, doesn't he?" Pessé whispered to her after a little.

"Go and ask him!"

"Go and hang yourself together with him! Such a nasty preacher! Did you ever hear—one dares not say a word to the noblewoman!"

At this juncture the boss, a dwarfish little Jew, with a vivid pair of eyes and a shaggy black beard, darted into the chamber.

"It is *no used!*" he said with a gesture of despair. "There is not a stitch of work, if only for a cure. Look, look how they have lowered their noses!" he then added with a triumphant grin. "*Vel*, I shall not be teasing you. 'Pity living things!' The expressman is *darn stess*. I would not go till I saw him *start*, and then I caught a car. No other *boss* could get a single jacket even if he fell upon his knees. *Vell*, do you appreciate it at least? Not much, ay?"

The presser rushed out of the room and presently came back laden with bundles of cut cloth which he threw down on the table. A wild scramble ensued. The presser looked on indifferently. The three finisher women, who had awaited the advent of the bundles as eagerly as the men, now calmly put on their hats. They knew that their part of the work wouldn't come before three o'clock, and so, overjoyed by the certainty of employment for at least another day or two, they departed till that hour.

"Look at the rush they are making! Just like the locusts of Egypt!" the boss cried half sternly and half with self-complacent humor, as he shielded the treasure with both his arms from all except "De Viskes" and Jake—the two being what is called in sweatshop parlance, *"chance-mentshen,"* i.e., favorites. "Don't be snatching and catching like that," the boss went on. "You may burn your fingers. Go to your machines, I say! The soup will be served in separate plates. Never fear, it won't get cold."

The hands at last desisted gingerly, Jake and the whiskered operator carrying off two of the largest bundles. The others went to their machines empty-handed and remained seated, their hungry glances riveted to the booty, until they, too, were provided.

The little boss distributed the bundles with dignified deliberation. In point of fact, he was no less impatient to have the work started than any of his employees. But in him the feeling was overriden by a kind of malicious pleasure which he took in their eagerness and in the demonstration of his power over the men, some of whom he knew to have enjoyed a more comfortable past than himself. The machines of Jake and "De Viskes" led off in a duet, which presently became a trio, and in another few minutes the floor was fairly dancing to the ear-piercing discords of the whole frantic sextet.

In the excitement of the scene called forth by the appearance of the bundles, Jake's gloomy mood had melted away. Nevertheless, while his machine was delivering its first shrill staccatos, his heart recited a vow: "As soon as I get my pay I shall call on the installment man and give him a deposit for a ticket." The prospective ticket was to be for a passage across the Atlantic from Hamburg to New York. And as the notion of it passed through Jake's mind it evoked there the image of a dark-eyed young woman with a babe in her lap. However, as the sewing machine throbbed and writhed under Jake's lusty kicks, it seemed to be swiftly carrying him away from the apparition which had the effect of receding, as a wayside object does from the passenger of a flying train, until it lost itself in a misty distance, other visions emerging in its place.

It was some three years before the opening of this story that Jake had last beheld that very image in the flesh. But then at that period of his life he had not even suspected the existence of a name like Jake, being known to himself and to all Povodye—a town in northwestern Russia—as Yekl or Yekelé.

It was not as a deserter from military service that he had shaken off the dust of the town where he had passed the first twenty-two years of his life. As the only son of aged parents he had been exempt from the duty of bearing arms. Jake may have forgotten it, but his mother still frequently refers to the day when he came rushing home, panting for breath, with the "red certificate" assuring his immunity in his hand. She nearly fainted for happiness. And when, stroking his dishevelled sidelocks with her bony hand and feasting her eye on his chubby face, she whispered, "My recovered child! God be blessed for his mercy!" there was a joyous tear in his eye as well as in hers. Well does she remember how she gently spat on his forehead three times to avert the effect of a possible evil eye on her "flourishing tree of a boy," and how his father standing by made merry over what he called her crazy woman-ish tricks, and said she had better fetch some brandy in honor of the glad event.

But if Yekl was averse to wearing a soldier's uniform on his own person he was none the less fond of seeing it on others. His ruling passion, even after he had become a husband and a father, was to watch the soldiers drilling on the square in front of the white-washed barracks near which stood his father's smithy. From a cheder* boy he showed a knack at placing himself on terms of familiarity with the Jewish members of the local regiment, whose uniforms struck terror into the hearts of his schoolmates. He would often play truant to attend a military parade; no lad in town knew so many Russian words or was as well versed in army terminology as Yekelé "Beril the blacksmith's;" and after he had left cheder, while working his father's bellows, Yekl would vary synagogue airs with martial song.

Three years had passed since Yekl had for the last time set his eyes on the whitewashed barracks and on his father's rickety smithy, which, for reasons indi-

---

*A school where Jewish children are instructed in the Old Testament or the Talmud.

rectly connected with the Government's redoubled discrimination against the sons of Israel, had become inadequate to support two families; three years since that beautiful summer morning when he had mounted the spacious *kibitka* which was to carry him to the frontierbound train; since, hurried by the driver, he had leaned out of the wagon to kiss his half-year-old son good-bye amid the heart-rending lamentations of his wife, the tremulous "Go in good health!" of his father, and the startled screams of the neighbors who rushed to the relief of his fainting mother. The broken Russian learned among the Povodye soldiers he had exchanged for English of a corresponding quality, and the bellows for a sewing machine—a change of weapons in the battle of life which had been brought about both by Yekl's tender religious feelings and robust legs. He had been shocked by the very notion of seeking employment at his old trade in a city where it is in the hands of Christians, and consequently involves a violation of the Mosaic Sabbath. On the other hand, his legs had been thought by his early American advisers eminently fitted for the treadle. Unlike New York, the Jewish sweatshops of Boston keep in line, as a rule, with the Christian factories in observing Sunday as the only day of rest. There is, however, even in Boston a lingering minority of bosses—more particularly in the "pants"-making branch—who abide by the Sabbath of their fathers. Accordingly, it was under one of these that Yekl had first been initiated into the sweatshop world.

Subsequently Jake, following numerous examples, had given up "pants" for the more remunerative cloaks, and having rapidly attained skill in his new trade he had moved to New York, the center of the cloak-making industry.

Soon after his arrival in Boston his religious scruples had followed in the wake of his former first name; and if he was still free from work on Saturdays he found many another way of "desecrating the Sabbath."

Three years had intervened since he had first set foot on American soil, and the thought of ever having been a Yekl would bring to Jake's lips a smile of patronizing commiseration for his former self. As to his Russian family name, which was Podkovnik, Jake's friends had such rare use for it that by mere negligence it had been left intact.

2

THE NEW YORK GHETTO

It was after seven in the evening when Jake finished his last jacket. Some of the operators had laid down their work before, while others cast an envious glance on him as he was dressing to leave, and fell to their machines with reluctantly redoubled energy. Fanny was a week worker and her time had been up at seven; but on this occasion her toilet had taken an uncommonly long time, and she was not ready until Jake got up from his chair. Then she left the room rather suddenly and with a demonstrative "Good-night all!"

When Jake reached the street he found her on the sidewalk, making a pretense of brushing one of her sleeves with the cuff of the other.

"So kvick?" she asked, raising her head in feigned surprise.

"You cull dot kvick?" he returned grimly. "Goodbye!"

"Say, ain't you goin' to dance tonight, really?" she queried shamefacedly.

"I tol' you I vouldn't."

"What does *she* want of me?" he complained to himself proceeding on his way. He grew conscious of his low spirits, and, tracing them with some effort to their source, he became gloomier still. "No more fun for me!" he decided. "I shall get them over here and begin a new life."

After supper, which he had taken, as usual, as his lodgings, he went out for a walk. He was firmly determined to keep himself from visiting Joe Peltner's dancing academy, and accordingly he took a direction opposite to Suffolk Street, where that establishment was situated. Having passed a few blocks, however, his feet, contrary to his will, turned into a side street and thence into one leading to Suffolk. "I shall only drop in to tell Joe that I can not sell any of his ball tickets, and return them," he attempted to deceive his own conscience. Hailing this pretext with delight he quickened his pace as much as the overcrowded sidewalks would allow.

He had to pick and nudge his way through dense swarms of bedraggled half-naked humanity; past garbage barrels rearing their overflowing contents in sickening piles, and lining the streets in malicious suggestion of rows of trees; underneath tiers and tiers of fire escapes, barricaded and festooned with mattresses, pillows, and featherbeds not yet gathered in for the night. The pent-in sultry atmosphere was laden with nausea and pierced with a discordant and, as it were, plaintive buzz. Supper had been despatched in a hurry, and the teeming populations of the cyclopic tenement houses were out in full force "for fresh air," as even these people will say in mental quotation marks.

Suffolk Street is in the very thick of the battle for breath. For it lies in the heart of that part of the East Side which has within the last two or three decades become the Ghetto of the American metropolis, and, indeed, the metropolis of the Ghettos of the world. It is one of the most densely populated spots on the face of the earth—a seething human sea fed by streams, streamlets, and rills of immigration flowing from all the Yiddish-speaking centers of Europe. Hardly a block but shelters Jews from every nook and corner of Russia, Poland, Galicia, Hungary, Roumania; Lithuanian Jews, Volhynian Jews, south Russian Jews, Bessarabian Jews; Jews crowded out of the "pale of Jewish settlement"; Russified Jews expelled from Moscow, St. Petersburg, Kieff, or Saratoff; Jewish runaways from justice; Jewish refugee from crying political and economical injustice; people torn from a hard-gained foothold in life and from deep-rooted attachments by the caprice of intolerance or the wiles of demagoguery—innocent scapegoats of a guilty Government for its outraged populace to misspend its blind fury upon; stu-

dents shut out of the Russian universities, and come to
these shores in quest of learning; artisans, merchants,
teachers, rabbis, artists, beggars—all come in search of
fortune. Nor is there a tenement house but harbors in
its bosom specimens of all the whimsical metamorpho-
ses wrought upon the children of Israel of the great
modern exodus by the vicissitudes of life in this their
Promised Land of today. You find there Jews born to
plenty, whom the new conditions have delivered up to
the clutches of penury; Jews reared in the straits of
need, who have here risen to prosperity; good people
morally degraded in the struggle for success amid an
unwonted environment; moral outcasts lifted from the
mire, purified, and imbued with self-respect; educated
men and women with their intellectual polish tarnished
in the inclement weather of adversity; ignorant sons of
toil grown enlightened—in fine, people with all sorts
of antecedents, tastes, habits, inclinations, and speaking all sorts of subdialects of the same jargon, thrown
pellmell into one social caldron—a human hodgepodge
with its component parts changed but not yet fused
into one homogeneous whole.

And so the "stoops," sidewalks, and pavements of
Suffolk Street were thronged with panting, chattering,
or frisking multitudes. In one spot the scene received a
kind of weird picturesqueness from children dancing
on the pavement to the strident music hurled out into
the tumultuous din from a row of the open and brightly
illuminated windows of what appeared to be a new tenement house. Some of the young women on the sidewalk opposite raised a longing eye to these windows,
for floating by through the dazzling light within were
young women like themselves with masculine arms
round their waists.

As the spectacle caught Jake's eye his heart gave a
leap. He violently pushed his way through the waltzing
swarm, and dived into the half-dark corridor of the
house whence the music issued. Presently he found
himself on the threshold and in the overpowering air of
a spacious oblong chamber, alive with a damp-haired,
dishevelled, reeking crowd—an uproarious human vor-

tex, whirling to the squeaky notes of a violin and the thumping of a piano. The room was, judging by its untidy, once-whitewashed walls and the uncouth wooden pillars supporting its bare ceiling, more accustomed to the whir of sewing machines than to the noises which filled it at the present moment. It took up the whole of the first floor of a five-story house built for large sweatshops, and until recently it had served its original purpose as faithfully as the four upper floors, which were still the daily scenes of feverish industry. At the further end of the room there was now a marble soda fountain in the charge of an unkempt boy. A stocky young man with a black entanglement of coarse curly hair was bustling about among the dancers. Now and then he would pause with his eyes bent upon some two pairs of feet, and fall to clapping time and drawling out in a preoccupied sing-song: "Von, two, tree! Leeft you' feet! Don' so kvick—sloy, sloy! Von, two, tree, von, two, tree!" This was Professor Peltner himself, whose curly hair, by the way, had more to do with the success of his institution than his stumpy legs, which, according to the unanimous dictum of his male pupils, moved about "like a *regely* pair of bears."

The throng showed but a very scant sprinkling of plump cheeks and shapely figures in a multitude of haggard faces and flaccid forms. Nearly all were in their workaday clothes, very few of the men sporting a wilted white shirt front. And while the general effect of the kaleidoscope was one of boisterous hilarity, many of the individual couples somehow had the air of being engaged in hard toil rather than as if they were dancing for amusement. The faces of some of these bore a wondering martyrlike expression, as who should say, "What have we done to be knocked about in this manner?" For the rest, there were all sorts of attitudes and miens in the whirling crowd. One young fellow, for example, seemed to be threatening vengeance to the ceiling, while his partner was all but exultantly exclaiming: "Lord of the universe! What a world this be!" Another maiden looked as if she kept murmuring, "You don't say!" whereas her cavalier mutely ejaculated, "Glad to try my best, your noble birth!"—after the fashion of a Russian soldier.

The prevailing stature of the assemblage was rather below medium. This does not include the dozen or two of undergrown lasses of fourteen or thirteen who had come surreptitiously, and—to allay the suspicion of their mothers—in their white aprons. They accordingly had only these articles to check at the hat box, and hence the nickname of "apron-check ladies," by which this truant contingent was known at Joe's academy. So that as Jake now stood in the doorway with an or- phaned collar button glistening out of the band of his collarless shirt front and an affected expression of *en- nui* overshadowing his face, his strapping figure tow- ered over the circling throng before him. He was immediately noticed and became the target for hellos, smiles, winks, and all manner of pleasantry: "Vot you stand like dot? You vont to loin dantz?" or "You a detectiff?" or "You vont a job?" or, again, "Is it hot anawff for you?" To all of which Jake returned an in- variable "Yep!" each time resuming his bored mien.

As he thus gazed at the dancers, a feeling of envy came over him. "Look at them!" he said to himself be- grudgingly. "How merry they are! Such *shnoozes,* they can hardly set a foot well, and yet they are free, while I am a married man. But wait till you get married, too," he perspectively avenged himself on Joe's pupils; "We shall see how you will then dance and jump!"

Presently a wave of Joe's hand brought the music and the trampling to a pause. The girls at once took their seats on the "ladies' bench," while the bulk of the men retired to the side reserved for "gents only." Several ap- parent post-graduates nonchalantly overstepped the boundary line, and, nothing daunted by the professor's repeated "Zents to de right an' ladess to the left!" unre- strainedly kept their girls chuckling. At all events, Joe soon desisted, his attention being diverted by the soda department of his business. "Sawda!" he sang out. "Ull kin's! Sam, you ought ashamed you'selv; vy don'tz you treat you' lada?"

In the meantime Jake was the center of a growing

bevy of both sexes. He refused to unbend and to enter into their facetious mood, and his morose air became the topic of their persiflage.

By-and-by Joe came scuttling up to his side. "Goot-evenig, Dzake!" he greeted him; "I didn't seen you at ull! Say, Dzake, I'll take care dis site an' you take care dot site—ull right?"

"Alla right!" Jake responded gruffly. "Gentsh, getch you partnesh, hawrry up!" he commanded in another instant.

The sentence was echoed by the dancing master, who then blew on his whistle a prolonged shrill warble, and once again the floor was set straining under some two hundred pounding, gliding, or scraping feet.

"Don' bee 'fraid. Gu right aheat an' getch you partner!" Jake went on yelling right and left. "Don' be 'shamed, Mish Cohen. Dansh mit dot gentlemarn!" he said, as he unceremoniously encircled Miss Cohen's waist with "dot gentlemarn's" arm. "Cholly! vot's de madder mitch *you*? You do hop like a Cossack, as true as I am a Jew," he added, indulging in a momentary lapse into Yiddish. English was the official language of the academy, where it was broken and mispronounced in as many different ways as there were Yiddish dialects represented in that institution. "Dot'sh de vay, look!" With which Jake seized from Charley a lanky fourteen-year-old Miss Jacobs, and proceeded to set an example of correct waltzing, much to the unconcealed delight of the girl, who let her head rest on his breast with an air of reverential gratitude and bliss, and to the embarrassment of her cavalier, who looked at the evolutions of Jake's feet without seeing.

Presently Jake was beckoned away to a corner by Joe, whereupon Miss Jacobs, looking daggers at the little professor, sulked off to a distant seat.

"Dzake, do me a faver; hask Mamie to gib dot feller a couple a dantzes," Joe said imploringly, pointing to an ungainly young man who was timidly viewing the pandemonium-like spectacle from the further end of the "gent's bench." "I hasked 'er myself, but se don'

vonted. He's a beesness man, you 'destan', an' he kan
a lot o' fellers an' I vonted make him satetzfiet."

"Dot monkey?" said Jake. "Vot you talkin' aboyt!
She vouldn't lishn to me neider, honesht."

"Say dot you don' vonted and dot's ull."

"Alla right; I'm goin' to ashk her, but I know it
vouldn't be of naw used."

"Never min', you hask 'er foist. You knaw se
vouldn't refuse *you*!" Joe urged, with a knowing grin.

"Hoy much vill you bet she will refushe shaw?"
Jake rejoined with insincere vehemence, as he whipped
out a handful of change.

"Vot kin' foon a man you are! Ulleways like to bet!"
said Joe, deprecatingly. "'F cuss it depend mit vot kin'
a mout' you vill hask, you 'destan'?"

"By gum, Jaw! Vot you take me for? Ven I shay I
ashk, I ashk. You knaw I don' like no monkey beesh-
nesh. Ven I promish anytink I do it shquare, dot'sh a
kin' a man *I* am!" And once more protesting his firm
conviction that Mamie would disregard his request, he
started to prove that she would not.

He had to traverse nearly the entire length of the
hall, and, notwithstanding that he was compelled to
steer clear of the dancers, he contrived to effect the
passage at the swellest of his gaits, which means that
he jauntily bobbed and lurched, after the manner of a
blacksmith tugging at the bellows, and held up his
enormous bullet head as if he were bidding defiance
to the whole world. Finally he paused in front of a
girl with a super-abundance of pitch-black side bangs
and with a pert, ill-natured, pretty face of the most
strikingly Semitic cast in the whole gathering. She
looked twenty-three or more, was inclined to plump-
ness, and her shrewd deep dark eyes gleamed out of a
warm gipsy complexion. Jake found her seated in a fatigued attitude on a chair near the piano.

"Good-evening, Mamie!" he said, bowing with
mock gallantry.

"Rats!"

"Shay, Mamie, give dot feller a tvisht, vill you?"

"Dot slob again? Joe must tink if you ask me I'll get

scared, ain't it? Go and tell him he is too fresh," she said with a contemptuous grimace. Like the majority of the girls of the academy, Mamie's English was a much nearer approach to a justification of its name than the gibberish spoken by the men.

Jake felt routed; but he put a bold face on it and broke out with studied resentment:

"Vot you kickin' aboyt, anyhoy? Jaw don't mean notin' at ull. If you don't vonted never min', an' dot'sh ull. It don't cut a figger, shee?" And he feignedly turned to go.

"Look how kvick he gets excited!" she said, surrenderingly.

"I ain't get ekshitet at ull; but vot'sh de used a makin' monkey beesnesh?" he retorted with triumphant acerbity.

"You are a monkey you'self," she returned with a playful pout.

The compliment was acknowledged by one of Jake's blandest grins.

"An' you are a monkey from monkeyland," he said. "Vill you dansh mit dot feller?"

"Rats! Vot vill you give me?"

"Vot should I give you?" he asked impatiently.

"Vill you treat?"

"Treat? Ger-rr oyt!" he replied with a sweeping kick at space.

"Den I von't dance."

"All right. I'll treat you mit a coupel a waltch."

"Is dot so? You must really tink I am swooning to dance vit you," she said, dividing the remark between both jargons.

"Look at her, look! she is a *regely* getzke*: one must take off one's cap to speak to her. Don't you always say you like to *dansh* with me *becush* I am a good *dansher*?"

"You must tink you are a peach of a dancer, ain't it? Bennie can dance a —— sight better dan you," she recurred to her English.

*A crucifix.

"Alla right!" he said tartly. "So you don' vonted?"

"O sugar! He is gettin' mad again. Vell, who is de getzke, me or you? All right, I'll dance vid de slob. But it's only becuss you ask me, mind you!" she added fawningly.

"Dot'sh all right!" he rejoined, with an affectation of gravity, concealing his triumph. "But you makin' too much fush. I like to shpeak plain, shee? Dot'sh a kin'a man *I* am."

The next two waltzes Mamie danced with the ungainly novice, taking exaggerated pains with him. Then came a lancers, Joe calling out the successive movements huckster fashion. His command was followed by less than half of the class, however, for the greater part preferred to avail themselves of the same music for waltzing. Jake was bent upon giving Mamie what he called a "sholid good time"; and, as she shared his view that a square or fancy dance was as flimsy an affair as a stick of candy, they joined or, rather, led the seceding majority. They spun along with all-forgetful gusto; every little while he lifted her on his powerful arm and gave her a "mill," he yelping and she squeaking for sheer ecstasy, as he did so; and throughout the performance his face and his whole figure seemed to be exclaiming, "Dot'sh a kin' a man *I* am!"

Several waifs stood in a cluster admiring or begrudging the antics of the star couple. Among these was lanky Miss Jacobs and Fanny the Preacher, who had shortly before made her appearance in the hall, and now stood pale and forlorn by the "apron-check" girl's side.

"Look at the way she is stickin' to him!" the little girl observed with envious venom, her gaze riveted to Mamie, whose shapely head was at this moment reclining on Jake's shoulders, with her eyes half shut, as if melting in a transport of bliss.

Fanny felt cut to the quick.

"You are jealous, ain't you?" she jerked out.

"Who, me? Vy should I be jealous?" Miss Jacobs protested, coloring. "On my part let them both go to ——. *You* must be jealous. Here, here! See how your eyes are creeping out looking! Here, here!" she teased her offender in Yiddish, poking her little finger at her as she spoke.

"Will you shut your scurvy mouth, little piece of ugliness, you? Such a piggish apron check!" poor Fanny burst out under breath, tears starting to her eyes.

"Such a nasty little runt!" another girl chimed in.

"Such a little cricket already knows what 'jealous' is!" a third of the bystanders put in. "You had better go home or your mamma will give you a spanking." Whereat the little cricket made a retort, which had better be left unrecorded.

"To think of a bit of a flea like that having so much *cheek*! Here is America for you!"

"America for a country and *'dod'll do'* [that'll do] for a language!" observed one of the young men of the group, indulging one of the stereotype jokes of the Ghetto.

The passage at arms drew Jake's attention to the little knot of spectators, and his eye fell on Fanny. Whereupon he summarily relinquished his partner on the floor, and advanced toward his shopmate, who, seeing him approach, hastened to retreat to the girls' bench, where she remained seated with a dropping head.

"Hello, Fanny!" he shouted briskly, coming up in front of her.

"Hello!" she returned rigidly, her eyes fixed on the dirty floor.

"Come, give ush a tvisht, vill you?"

"But you ain't goin' by Joe tonight!" she answered, with a withering curl of her lip, her glance still on the ground. "Go to your lady, she'll be mad atch you."

"I didn't vonted to gu here, honesht, Fanny. I o'ly come to tell Jaw shometin', an' dot'sh ull," he said guiltily.

"Why should you apologize?" she addressed the tip of her shoe in her mother tongue. "As if he was obliged to apologize to me! *For my part* you can *dance* with her day and night. *Vot do I care?* As if I *cared*! I have only come to see what a *bluffer* you are. Do you think I am a *fool*? As *smart* as your Mamie, *anyvay*. As if I had not known he wanted to make me stay at home! What are you afraid of? Am I in your way then? As if I was in his way! What business have I to be in your way? Who is in your way?"

While she was thus speaking in her voluble, querulous, harassing manner, Jake stood with his hands in his trousers' pockets, in an attitude of mock attention. Then, suddenly losing patience, he said:

"*Dot'sh alla right!* Your will finish your sermon afterward. And in the meantime *lesh have a valtz* from the land of *valtzes!*" With which he forcibly dragged her off her seat, catching her round the waist.

"But I don't need it, I don't wish it! Go to your Mamie!" she protested, struggling. "I tell you I don't need it, I don't—" The rest of the sentence was choked off by her violent breathing; for by this time she was spinning with Jake like a top. After another moment's pretense at struggling to free herself she succumbed, and presently clung to her partner, the picture of triumph and beatitude.

Meanwhile Mamie had walked up to Joe's side, and without much difficulty caused him to abandon the lancers party to themselves, and to resume with her the waltz which Jake had so abruptly broken off.

In the course of the following intermission she diplomatically seated herself beside her rival, and paraded her tranquility of mind by accosting her with a question on shop matters. Fanny was not blind to the maneuver, but her exultation was all the greater for it, and she participated in the ensuing conversation with exuberant geniality.

By-and-by they were joined by Jake.

"Vell, vill you treat, Jake?" said Mamie.

"Vot you vant, a kish?" he replied, putting his offer in action as well as in language.

Mamie slapped his arm.

"May the Angel of Death kiss you!" said her lips in Yiddish. "Try again!" her glowing face overruled them in a dialect of its own.

Fanny laughed.

"Once I am *treating,* both *ladas* must be *treated* alike, *ain'it*?" remarked the gallant, and again he proved himself as good as his word, although Fanny struggled with greater energy and ostensibly with more real indignation.

"But vy don't you treat, you stingy loafer you?"

"Vot elsh you vant? A peench?" He was again on the point of suiting the action to the word, but Mamie contrived to repay the pinch before she had received it, and added a generous piece of profanity into the bargain. Whereupon there ensued a scuffle of a character which defies description in more senses than one.

Nevertheless Jake marched his two "ladas" up to the marble fountain, and regaled them with two cents' worth of soda each.

An hour or so later, when Jake got out into the street, his breast pocket was loaded with a fresh batch of "Professor Peltner's Grand Annual Ball" tickets, and his two arms—with Mamie and Fanny respectively.

"As soon as I get my wages I'll call on the installment agent and give him a deposit for a steamship ticket," presently glimmered through his mind, as he adjusted his hold upon the two girls, snugly gathering them to his sides.

3

IN THE GRIP OF HIS PAST

Jake had never even vaguely abandoned the idea of supplying his wife and child with the means of coming to join him. He was more or less prompt in remitting her monthly allowance of ten rubles, and the visit to the draft and passage office had become part of the routine of his life. It had the invariable effect of arousing his dormant scruples, and he hardly ever left the office without ascertaining the price of a steerage voyage from Hamburg to New York. But no sooner did he emerge from the dingy basement into the noisy scenes of Essex Street, than he would consciously let his mind wander off to other topics.

Formerly, during the early part of his sojourn in Boston, his landing place, where some of his townsfolk resided and where he had passed his first two years in America, he used to mention his Gitl and his Yosselé so frequently and so enthusiastically, that some wags among the Hanover Street tailors would sing "Yekl and wife and the baby" to the tune of "Molly and I and the Baby." In the natural course of things, however, these retrospective effusions gradually became far between, and since he had shifted his abode to New York he carefully avoided all reference to his antecedents. The Jewish quarter of the metropolis, which is a vast and compact city within a city, offers its denizens incomparably fewer chances of contact with the English-speaking portion of the population than any of the three separate Ghettos of Boston. As a consequence, since Jake's advent to New York his passion for American sport had considerably cooled off. And, to make up for this, his enthusiastic nature before long found vent in dancing and in a general life of gallantry. His proved knack with the gentle sex had turned his head and now cost him all his leisure time. Still, he would occasionally attend some variety show in which boxing was the main drawing card, and somehow managed to keep track of the salient events of the sporting world generally. Judging from his unstaid habits and happy-go-lucky abandon to the pleasures of life, his present associates took it for granted that he was single, and instead of twitting him with the feigned assumption that he had deserted a family—a piece of burlesque as old as the Ghetto—they would quiz him as to which of his girls he was "dead struck" on and as to the day fixed for the wedding. On more than one such occasion he had on the top of his tongue the seemingly jocular question, "How do you know I am not married already?" But he never let the sentence cross his lips, and would, instead, observe facetiously that he was not "shtruck on nu goil," and that he was dead struck on all of them in "whulshale." "I hate retail beesnesh,

shee? Dot'sh a' kin' a man *I* am!" One day, in the
course of an intimate conversation with Joe, Jake,
dropping into a philosophical mood, remarked:

"It's something like a baker, *ain't it*? The more *cakes*
he has the less he likes them. You and I have a *lot* of
girls; they's why we don't *care* for any one of them."

But if his attachment for the girls of his acquaintance collectively was not coupled with a quivering of
his heart for any individual Mamie, or Fanny, or Sarah,
it did not, on the other hand, preclude a certain lingering tenderness for his wife. But then his wife had long
since ceased to be what she had been of yore. From a
reality she had gradually become transmuted into a
fancy. During the three years since he had set foot on
the soil, where a "shister* becomes a mister and a mister a shister," he had lived so much more than three
years—so much more, in fact, than in all the twenty-
two years of his previous life—that his Russian past
appeared to him a dream and his wife and child, together with his former self, fellow characters in a
charming tale, which he was neither willing to banish
from his memory nor able to reconcile with the actual-
ities of his American present. The question of how to
effect this reconciliation, and of causing Gitl and little
Yosselé to step out of the thickening haze of reminiscence and to take their stand by his side as living parts
of his daily life, was a fretful subject from the consid-
eration of which he cowardly shrank. He wished he
could both import his family and continue his present
mode of life. At the bottom of his soul he wondered
why this should not be feasible. But he knew that it
was not, and his heart would sink at the notion of for-
feiting the lion's share of attentions for which he came
in at the hands of those who lionized him. Moreover,
how will he look people in the face in view of the lie
he has been acting? He longed for an interminable respite. But as sooner or later the minds of his acquaint-
ances were bound to become disabused, and he would
have to face it all out anyway, he was many a time on

*Yiddish for shoemaker.

the point of making a clean breast of it, and failed to do so for a mere lack of nerve, each time letting himself off on the plea that a week or two before his wife's arrival would be a more auspicious occasion for the disclosure.

Neither Jake nor his wife nor his parents could write even Yiddish, although both he and his old father read fluently the punctuated Hebrew of the Old Testament or the Prayer Book. Their correspondence had therefore to be carried on by proxy, and, as a consequence, at longer intervals than would have been the case otherwise. The missives which he received differed materially in length, style, and degree of illiteracy as well as in point of penmanship; but they all agreed in containing glowing encomiums of little Yosselé, exhorting Yekl not to stray from the path of righteousness, and reproachfully asking whether he ever meant to send the ticket. The latter point had an exasperating effect on Jake. There were times, however, when it would touch his heart and elicit from him his threadbare vow to send the ticket at once. But then he never had money enough to redeem it. And, to tell the truth, at the bottom of his heart he was at such moments rather glad of his poverty. At all events, the man who wrote Jake's letters had a standing order to reply in the sharpest terms at his command that Yekl did not spend his money on drink; that America was not the land they took it for, where one could "scoop gold by the skirtful"; that Gitl need not fear lest he meant to desert her, and that as soon as he had saved enough to pay her way and to set up a decent establishment she would be sure to get the ticket.

Jake's scribe was an old Jew who kept a little stand on Pitt Street, which is one of the thoroughfares and market places of the Galician quarter of the Ghetto, and where Jake was unlikely to come upon any people of his acquaintance. The old man scraped together his livelihood by selling Yiddish newspapers and cigarettes, and writing letters for a charge varying, according to the length of the epistle, from five to ten cents. Each time Jake received a letter he would take it to the

Galician, who would first read it to him (for an extra remuneration of one cent) and then proceed to pen five cents' worth of rhetoric, which might have been printed and forwarded one copy at a time for all the additions or alterations Jake ever caused to be made in it.

"What else shall I write?" the old man would ask his patron, after having written and read aloud the first dozen lines, which Jake had come to know by heart.

"How do *I* know?" Jake would respond. "It is you who can write; so you ought to understand what else to write."

And the scribe would go on to write what he had written on almost every previous occasion. Jake would keep the letter in his pocket until he had spare United States money enough to convert into ten rubles, and then he would betake himself to the draft office and have the amount, together with the well-crumpled epistle, forwarded to Povodye.

And so it went month in and month out.

The first letter which reached Jake after the scene at Joe Peltner's dancing academy came so unusually close upon its predecessor that he received it from his landlady's hand with a throb of misgiving. He had always labored under the presentiment that some unknown enemies—for he had none that he could name—would some day discover his wife's address and anonymously represent him to her as contemplating another marriage, in order to bring Gitl down upon him unawares. His first thought accordingly was that this letter was the outcome of such a conspiracy. "Or maybe there is some death in the family?" he next reflected, half with terror and half with a feeling almost amounting to reassurance.

When the cigarette vender unfolded the letter he found it to be of such unusual length that he stipulated an additional cent for the reading of it.

"*Alla right,* hurry up now!" Jake said, grinding his teeth on a mumbled English oath.

"*Righd evay! Righd evay!*" the old fellow returned

jubilantly, as he hastily adjusted his spectacles and addressed himself to his task.

The letter had evidently been penned by some one laying claim to Hebrew scholarship and ambitious to impress the New World with it; for it was quite replete with poetic digressions, strained and twisted to suit some quotation from the Bible. And what with this unstinted verbosity, which was Greek to Jake, one or two interruptions by the old man's customers, and interpretations necessitated by difference of dialect, a quarter of an hour had elapsed before the scribe realized the trend of what he was reading.

Then he suddenly gave a start, as if shocked.

"Vot'sh a madder? Vot'sh a madder?"

"*Vot's der madder?* What should be the *madder*? Wait—a—I don't know what I can do"—he halted in perplexity.

"Any bad news?" Jake inquired, turning pale. "Speak out!"

"Speak out! It is all very well for you to say 'speak out.' You forget that one is a piece of Jew," he faltered, hinting at the orthodox custom which enjoins a child of Israel from being the messenger of sad tidings.

"Don't *bodder* a head!" Jake shouted savagely. "I have paid you, haven't I?"

"*Say,* young man, you need not be so angry," the other said, resentfully. "Half of the letter I have read, have I not? so I shall refund you one cent and leave me in peace." He took to fumbling in his pockets for the coin, with apparent reluctance.

"Tell me what is the matter," Jake entreated, with clenched fists. "Is anybody dead? Do tell me now."

"*Vell,* since you know it already, I may as well tell you," and the scribe cunningly, glad to retain the cent and Jake's patronage. "It is your father who has been freed; may he have a bright paradise."

"Ha?" Jake asked aghast, with a wide gape.

The Galician resumed the reading in solemn, doleful accents. The melancholy passage was followed by a jeremiade upon the penniless condition of the family and Jake's duty to send the ticket without further procrastination. As to his mother, she preferred the Povodye graveyard to a watery sepulcher, and hoped that her beloved and only son, the apple of her eye, whom she had been awake nights to bring up to manhood, and so forth, would not forget her.

"So now they will be here for sure, and there can be no more delay!" was Jake's first distinct thought. "Poor father!" he inwardly exclaimed the next moment, with deep anguish. His native home came back to him with a vividness which it had not had in his mind for a long time.

"Was he an old man?" the scribe queried sympathetically.

"About seventy," Jake answered, bursting into tears.

"Seventy? Then he had lived to a good old age. May no one depart younger," the old man observed, by way of "consoling the bereaved."

As Jake's tears instantly ran dry he fell to wringing his hands and moaning.

"Good-night!" he presently said, taking leave. "I'll see you tomorrow, if God be pleased."

"Good-night!" the scribe returned with heartfelt condolence.

As he was directing his steps to his lodgings Jake wondered why he did not weep. He felt that this was the proper thing for a man in his situation to do, and he endeavored to inspire himself with emotions befitting the occasion. But his thoughts teasingly gambolled about among the people and things of the street. By-and-by, however, he became sensible of his mental eye being fixed upon the big fleshy mole on his father's scantily bearded face. He recalled the old man's carriage, the melancholy nod of his head, his deep sigh upon taking snuff from the time-honored birch bark which Jake had known as long as himself; and his heart writhed with pity and with the acutest pangs of homesickness. "And it was evening and it was morning, the sixth day. And the heavens and the earth were finished." As the Hebrew words of the Sanctification of the Sabbath resounded in Jake's ears, in his father's senile treble, he could see his gaunt figure swaying over a pair of Sabbath loaves. It is Friday night. The little room, made tidy for the day of rest and faintly illuminated by the mysterious light of two tallow candles rising from freshly burnished candlesticks, is pervaded by a benign, reposeful warmth and a general air of peace and solemnity. There, seated by the side of the head of the little family and within easy reach of the huge brick oven, is his old mother, flushed with fatigue, and with an effort keeping her drowsy eyes open to attend, with a devout mien, her husband's prayer. Opposite to her, by the window, is Yekl, the present Jake, awaiting his turn to chant the same words in the holy tongue, and impatiently thinking of the repast to come after it. Besides the three of them there is no one else in the chamber, for Jake visioned the fascinating scene as he had known it for almost twenty years, and not as it had appeared during the short period since the family had been joined by Gitl and subsequently by Yosselé.

Suddenly he felt himself a child, the only and pampered son of a doting mother. He was overcome with a heart-wringing consciousness of being an orphan, and his soul was filled with a keen sense of desolation and self-pity. And thereupon everything around him—the rows of gigantic tenement houses, the hum and buzz of the scurrying pedestrians, the jingling horse cars—all suddenly grew alien and incomprehensible to Jake. Ah, if he could return to his old home and old days, and have his father recite Sanctification again, and sit by his side, opposite to mother, and receive from her hand a plate of reeking *tzimess,** as of yore! Poor mother! He *will* not forget her—But what is the Italian playing on that organ, anyhow? Ah, it is the new waltz! By the way, this is Monday and they are dancing at Joe's now and he is not there. "I shall not go there tonight, nor any other night," he commiserated himself, his reveries for the first time since he had left the Pitt Street cigarette stand passing to his wife and child. Her image now stood out in high relief with the multitudinous

---

*A kind of dessert made of carrots or turnips.

noisy scene at Joe's academy for a discordant, disquieting background, amid which there vaguely defined itself the reproachful saintlike visage of the deceased. "I will begin a new life!" he vowed to himself.

He strove to remember the child's features, but could only muster the faintest recollection—scarcely anything beyond a general symbol—a red little thing smiling, as he, Jake, tickles it under its tiny chin. Yet Jake's finger at this moment seemed to feel the soft touch of that little chin, and it sent through him a thrill of fatherly affection to which he had long been a stranger. Gitl, on the other hand, loomed up in all the individual sweetness of her rustic face. He beheld her kindly mouth opening wide—rather too wide, but all the lovelier for it—as she spoke; her prominent red gums, her little black eyes. He could distinctly hear her voice with her peculiar lisp, as one summer morning she had burst into the house and, clapping her hands in despair, she had cried, "A weeping to me! The yellow rooster is gone!" or, as coming into the smithy she would say: "Father-in-law, mother-in-law calls you to dinner. Hurry up, Yekl, dinner is ready." And although this was all he could recall her saying, Jake thought himself retentive of every word she had ever uttered in his presence. His heart went out to Gitl and her environment, and he was seized with a yearning tenderness that made him feel like crying. "I would not exchange her little finger for all the American *ladas,*" he soliloquized, comparing Gitl in his mind with the dancing-school girls of his circle. It now filled him with disgust to think of the morals of some of them, although it was from his own sinful experience that he knew them to be of a rather loose character.

He reached his lodgings in a devout mood, and before going to bed he was about to say his prayers. Not having said them for nearly three years, however, he found, to his dismay, that he could no longer do it by heart. His landlady had a prayer book, but, unfortunately, she kept it locked in the bureau, and she was now asleep, as was everybody else in the house. Jake reluctantly undressed and went to bed on the kitchen lounge, where he usually slept.

When a boy his mother had taught him to believe that to go to sleep at night without having recited the bed prayer rendered one liable to be visited and choked in bed by some ghost. Later, when he had grown up, and yet before he had left his birthplace, he had come to set down this earnest belief of his good old mother as a piece of womanish superstition, while since he had settled in America he had hardly ever had an occasion to so much as think of bed prayers. Nevertheless, as he now lay vaguely listening to the weird ticking of the clock on the mantelpiece over the stove, and at the same time desultorily brooding upon his father's death, the old belief suddenly uprose in his mind and filled him with mortal terror. He tried to persuade himself that it was a silly notion worthy of womenfolk, and even affected to laugh at it audibly. But all in vain."Cho-king! Cho-king! Cho-king!" went the clock, and the form of a man in white burial clothes never ceased gleaming in his face. He resolutely turned to the wall, and, pulling the blanket over his head, he huddled himself snugly up for instanteous sleep. But presently he felt the cold grip of a pair of hands about his throat, and he even mentally stuck out his tongue, as one does while being strangled.

With a fast-beating heart Jake finally jumped off the lounge, and gently knocked at the door of his landlady's bedroom.

"*Eshcoosh me, mishesh,* .be so kind as to lend me your prayer book. I want to say the night prayer," he addressed her imploringly.

The old woman took it for a cruel practical joke, and flew into a passion.

"Are you crazy or drunk? A nice time to make fun!"

And it was not until he had said with suppliant vehemence, "May I as surely be alive as my father is dead!" and she had subjected him to a cross-examination, that she expressed sympathy and went to produce the keys.

4

THE MEETING

A few weeks later, on a Saturday morning, Jake, with an unfolded telegram in his hand, stood in front of one of the desks at the Immigration Bureau of Ellis Island. He was freshly shaven and clipped, smartly dressed in his best clothes and ball shoes, and, in spite of the sickly expression of shamefacedness and anxiety which distorted his features, he looked younger than usual.

All the way to the island he had been in a flurry of joyous anticipation. The prospect of meeting his dear wife and child, and, incidentally, of showing off his swell attire to her, had thrown him into a fever of impatience. But on entering the big shed he had caught a distant glimpse of Gitl and Yousselé through the railing separating the detained immigrants from their visitors, and his heart had sunk at the sight of his wife's uncouth and un-American appearance. She was slovenly dressed in a brown jacket and skirt of grotesque cut, and her hair was concealed under a voluminous wig of a pitch-black hue. This she had put on just before leaving the steamer, both "in honor of the Sabbath" and by way of sprucing herself up for the great event. Since Yekl had left home she had gained considerably in the measurement of her waist. The wig, however, made her seem stouter and shorter than she would have appeared without it. It also added at least five years to her looks. But she was aware neither of this nor of the fact that in New York even a Jewess of her station and orthodox breeding is accustomed to blink at the wickedness of displaying her natural hair, and that none but an elderly matron may wear a wig without being the occasional target for snowballs or stones. She was naturally dark of complexion, and the nine or ten days spent at sea had covered her face with a deep bronze, which combined with her prominent cheek bones, inky little eyes, and, above all, the smooth black wig, to lend her resemblance to a squaw.

Jake had no sooner caught sight of her than he had
averted his face, as if loath to rest his eyes on her, in
the presence of the surging crowd around him, before
it was inevitable. He dared not even survey that crowd
to see whether it contained any acquaintance of his,
and he vaguely wished that her release were delayed
indefinitely.

Presently the officer behind the desk took the telegram from him, and in another little while Gitl, hugging Youssélé with one arm and a bulging parcel with
the other, emerged from a side door.

"Yekl!" she screamed out in a piteous high key, as if
crying for mercy.

"Dot'sh all right!" he returned in English, with a
wan smile and unconscious of what he was saying. His
wandering eyes and dazed mind were striving to fix
themselves upon the stern functionary and the questions he bethought himself of asking before finally releasing his prisoners. The contrast between Gitl and
Jake was so striking that the officer wanted to make
sure—partly as a matter of official duty and partly for
the fun of the thing—that the two were actually man
and wife.

"*Oi* a lamentation upon me! He shaves his beard!"
Gitl ejaculated to herself as she scrutinized her husband. "Yossélé, look! Here is *taté*!"

But Yossélé did not care to look at taté. Instead, he
turned his frightened little eyes—precise copies of
Jake's—and buried them in his mother's cheek.

When Gitl was finally discharged she made to fling
herself on Jake. But he checked her by seizing both
loads from her arms. He started for a distant and deserted corner of the room, bidding her follow. For a
moment the boy looked stunned, then he burst out crying and fell to kicking his father's chest with might
and main, his reddened little face appealingly turning
to Gitl. Jake continuing his way tried to kiss his son
into toleration, but the little fellow proved too nimble
for him. It was in vain that Gitl, scurrying behind, kept
expostulating with Yossélé: "Why, it is taté!" Taté was

forced to capitulate before the march was brought to its end.

At length, when the secluded corner had been reached, and Jake and Gitl had set down their burdens, husband and wife flew into mutual embrace and fell to kissing each other. The performance had an effect of something done to order, which, it must be owned, was far from being belied by the state of their minds at the moment. Their kisses imparted the taste of mutual estrangement to both. In Jake's case the sensation was quickened by the strong steerage odors which were emitted by Gitl's person, and he involuntarily recoiled.

"You look like a *poritz*,"* she said shyly.

"How are you? How is mother?"

"How should she be? So, so. She sends you her love," Gitl mumbled out.

"How long was father ill?"

"Maybe a month. He cost us health enough."

He proceeded to make advances to Yosselé, she appealing to the child in his behalf. For a moment the sight of her, as they were both crouching before the boy, precipitated a wave of thrilling memories on Jake and made him feel in his own environment. Presently, however, the illusion took wing and here he was, Jake the Yankee, with this bonnetless, wigged, dowdyish little greenhorn by his side! That she was his wife, nay, that he was a married man at all, seemed incredible to him. The sturdy, thriving urchin had at first inspired him with pride; but as he now cast another side glance at Gitl's wig he lost all interest in him, and began to regard him, together with his mother, as one great obstacle dropped from heaven, as it were, in his way.

Gitl on her part, was overcome with a feeling akin to awe. She, too, could not get herself to realize that this stylish young man—shaved and dressed as in Povodye is only some young nobleman—was Yekl, her own Yekl, who had all these three years never been absent from her mind. And while she was once more examining Jake's blue diagonal cutaway, glossy stand-up col-

*Yiddish for nobleman.

lar, the white four-in-hand necktie, coquettishly tucked away in the bosom of his starched shirt, and, above all, his patent leather shoes, she was at the same time mentally scanning the Yekl of three years before. The latter alone was hers, and she felt like crying to the image to come back to her and let her be *his* wife.

Presently, when they had got up and Jake was plying her with perfunctory questions, she chanced to recognize a certain movement of his upper lip—an old trick of his. It was as if she had suddenly discovered her own Yekl in an apparent stranger, and, with another pitiful outcry, she fell on his breast.

"Don't!" he said, with patient gentleness, pushing away her arms. "Here everything is so different."

She colored deeply.

"They don't wear wigs here," he ventured to add.

"What then?" she asked, perplexedly.

"You will see. It is quite another world."

"Shall I take it off, then? I have a nice Saturday kerchief," she faltered. "It is of silk—I bought it at Kalmen's for a bargain. It is still brand new."

"Here one does not wear even a kerchief."

"How then? Do they go about with their own hair?" she queried in ill-disguised bewilderment.

"*Vell, alla right,* put it on, quick!"

As she set about undoing her parcel, she bade him face about and screen her, so that neither he nor any stranger could see her bareheaded while she was replacing the wig by the kerchief. He obeyed. All the while the operation lasted he stood with his gaze on the floor, gnashing his teeth with disgust and shame, or hissing some Bowery oath.

"Is this better?" she asked bashfully, when her hair and part of her forehead were hidden under a kerchief of flaming blue and yellow, whose end dangled down her back.

The kerchief had a rejuvenating effect. But Jake thought that it made her look like an Italian woman of Mulberry Street on Sunday.

"*Alla, right,* leave it be for the present," he said in

despair, reflecting that the wig would have been the lesser evil of the two.

When they reached the city Gitl was shocked to see him lead the way to a horse car.

"*Oi* woe is me! Why, it is Sabbath!" she gasped.

He irately essayed to explain that a car, being an uncommon sort of vehicle, riding in it implied no violations of the holy day. But this she sturdily met by reference to railroads. Besides, she had seen horse cars while stopping in Hamburg, and knew that no orthodox Jew would use them on the seventh day. At length Jake, losing all self-control, fiercely commanded her not to make him the laughingstock of the people on the street and to get in without further ado. As to the sin of the matter he was willing to take it all upon himself. Completely dismayed by his stern manner, amid the strange, uproarious, forbidding surroundings, Gitl yielded.

As the horses started she uttered a groan of consternation and remained looking aghast and with a violently throbbing heart. If she had been a culprit on the way to the gallows she could not have been more terrified than she was now at this her first ride on the day of rest.

The conductor came up for their fares. Jake handed him a ten-cent piece, and raising two fingers, he roared out: "Two! He ain' no maur as tree years, de liddle feller!" And so great with the impression which his dashing manner and his English produced on Gitl, that for some time it relieved her mind and she even forgot to be shocked by the sight of her husband handling coin on the Sabbath.

Having thus paraded himself before his wife, Jake all at once grew kindly disposed toward her.

"You must be hungry?" he asked.

"Not at all! Where do you eat your *varimess*?"*

"Don't say varimess," he corrected her complaisantly; "Here it is called *dinner*."

*Yiddish for dinner.

"*Dinner?** And what if one becomes fatter?" she confusedly ventured an irresistible pun.

This was the way in which Gitl came to receive her first lesson in the five or six score English words and phrases which the omnivorous Jewish jargon has absorbed in the Ghettos of English-speaking countries.

5

A PATERFAMILIAS

It was early in the afternoon of Gitl's second Wednesday in the New World. Jake, Bernstein and Charley, their two boarders, were at work. Youssélé was sound asleep in the lodgers' double bed, in the smallest of the three tiny rooms which the family rented on the second floor of one of a row of brand-new tenement houses. Gitl was by herself in the little front room which served the quadruple purpose of kitchen, dining room, sitting room, and parlor. She wore a skirt and a loose jacket of white Russian calico, decorated with huge gay figures, and her dark hair was only half covered by a bandana of red and yellow. This was Gitl's compromise between her conscience and her husband. She panted to yield to Jake's demands completely, but could not nerve herself up going about "in her own hair, like a Gentile woman." Even the expostulations of Mrs. Kavarsky—the childless middle-aged woman who occupied with her husband the three rooms across the narrow hallway—failed to prevail upon her. Nevertheless Jake, succumbing to Mrs. Kavarsky's annoying solicitations, had bought his wife a cheap high-crowned hat, utterly unfit to be worn over her voluminous wig, and even a corset. Gitl could not be coaxed into accompanying them to the store; but the eloquent neighbor had persuaded Jake that her presence at the transaction was not indispensable after all.

"Leave it to me," she said; "I know what will become her and what won't. I'll get her a hat that will

*Yiddish for thinner.

make a Fifth Avenue lady of her, and you shall see if
she does not give in. If she is then not *satezfiet* to go
with her own hair, *vell*?" What then would take place
Mrs. Kavarsky left unsaid.

The hat and the corset had been lying in the house
now three days, and the neighbor's predictions had not
yet come true, save for Gitl's prying once or twice into
the pasteboard boxes in which those articles lay, otherwise unmolested, on the shelf over her bed.

The door was open. Gitl stood toying with the knob
of the electric bell, and deriving much delight from the
way the street door latch kept clicking under her magic
touch two flights above. Finally she wearied of her di-
version, and shutting the door she went to take a look
at Yosselé. She found him fast asleep, and, as she was
retracing her steps through her own and Jake's bedroom, her eye fell upon the paper boxes. She got up on
the edge of her bed and, lifting the cover from the hat-
box, she took a prolonged look at its contents. All at
once her face brightened up with temptation. She went
to fasten the hallway door of the kitchen on its latch,
and then regaining the bedroom shut herself in. After a
lapse of some ten or fifteen minutes she re-emerged,
attired in her brown holiday dress in which she had
first confronted Jake on Ellis Island, and with the tall
black straw hat on her bed. Walking on tiptoe, as
though about to commit a crime, she crossed over to
the looking glass. Then she paused, her eyes on the
door, to listen for possible footsteps. Hearing none she
faced the glass. "Quite a *panenke*!"* she thought to
herself, all aglow with excitement, a smile, at once
shamefaced and beatific, melting her features. She
turned to the right, then to the left, to view herself in
profile, as she had seen Mrs. Kavarsky do, and drew
back a step to ascertain the effect of the corset. To tell
the truth, the corset proved utterly impotent against the
baggy shapelessness of the Povodye garment. Yet Gitl
found it to work wonders, and readily pardoned it for
the very uncomfortable sensation which it caused her.

*A young noblewoman.

She viewed herself again and again, and was in a flutter both of ecstasy and alarm when there came a timid rap on the door. Trembling all over, she scampered on tiptoe back into the bedroom, and after a little she returned in her calico dress and bandana kerchief. The knock at the door had apparently been produced by some peddler or beggar, for it was not repeated. Yet so violent was Gitl's agitation that she had to sit down on the haircloth lounge for breath and to regain composure.

"What is it they call this?" she presently asked herself, gazing at the bare boards of the floor. "Floor!" she recalled, much to her self-satisfaction. "And that?" she further examined herself, as she fixed her glance on the ceiling. This time the answer was slow in coming, and her heart grew faint. "And what was it Yekl called that?"—transferring her eyes to the window. "Veen—neev-veenda," she at last uttered exultantly. The evening before she had happened to call it *fentzter,* in spite of Jake's repeated corrections.

"Can't you say *veenda?*" he had growled. "What a peasant head! Other *greenhorns* learn to speak American *shtyle* very fast; and she—one might tell her the same word eighty thousand times, and it is *nu used.*"

*"Es is of'n veenda mein ich,"** she hastened to set herself right.

She blushed as she said it, but at the moment she attached no importance to the matter and took no more notice of it. Now, however, Jake's tone of voice, as he had rebuked her backwardness in picking up American Yiddish, came back to her and she grew dejected.

She was getting used to her husband, in whom her own Yekl and Jake the stranger were by degrees merging themselves into one undivided being. When the hour of his coming from work drew near she would every little while consult the clock and become impatient with the slow progress of its hands; although mixed with this impatience there was a feeling of apprehension lest the supper, prepared as it was under culinary

---

*It is on the window, I meant to say.

conditions entirely new to her, should fail to please Jake and the boarders. She had even become accustomed to address her husband as Jake without reddening in the face; and, what is more, was getting to tolerate herself being called by him Goitie (Gertie)—a word phonetically akin to Yiddish for Gentile. For the rest she was too inexperienced and too simple-hearted naturally to comment upon his manner toward her. She had not altogether overcome her awe of him, but as he showed her occasional marks of kindness she was upon the whole rather content with her new situation. Now, however, as she thus sat in solitude, with his harsh voice ringing in her ears and his icy look before her, a feeling of suspicion darkened her soul. She recalled other scenes where he had looked and spoken as he had done the night before. "He must hate me! A pain upon me!" she concluded with a fallen heart. She wondered whether his demeanor toward her was like that of other people who hated their wives. She remembered a woman of her native village who was known to be thus afflicted, and she dropped her head in a fit of despair. At one moment she took a firm resolve to pluck up courage and cast away the kerchief and the wig; but at the next she reflected that God would be sure to punish her for the terrible sin, so that instead of winning Jake's love the change would increase his hatred for her. It flashed upon her mind to call upon some "good Jew" to pray for the return of his favor, or to seek some old Polish beggar woman who could prescribe a love potion. But then, alas! who knows whether there are in this terrible America any good Jews or beggar women with love potions at all! Better she had never known this "black year" of a country! Here everybody says she is green. What an ugly word to apply to people! She had never been green at home, and here she had suddenly become so. What do they mean by it, anyhow? Verily, one might turn green and yellow and gray while young in such a dreadful place. Her heart was wrung with the most excruciating pangs of homesickness. And as she thus sat brooding and listlessly surveying her new surroundings—the iron stove, the stationary washtubs, the window opening vertically, the fire escape, the yellowish broom with its painted handle—things which she had never dreamed of at her birthplace—these objects seemed to stare at her haughtily and inspired her with fright. Even the burnished cup of the electric bell knob looked contemptuously and seemed to call her "Greenhorn! greenhorn!" "Lord of the world! Where am I?" she whispered with tears in her voice.

The dreary solitude terrified her, and she instinctively rose to take refuge at Yosselé's bedside. As she got up, a vague doubt came over her whether she should find there her child at all. But Yosselé was found safe and sound enough. He was rubbing his eyes and announcing the advent of his famous appetite. She seized him in her arms and covered his warm cheeks with fervent kisses which did her aching heart good. And by-and-by, as she admiringly watched the boy making savage inroads into a generous slice of rye bread, she thought of Jake's affection for the child; whereupon things began to assume a brighter aspect, and she presently set about preparing supper with a lighter heart, although her countenance for some time retained its mournful woebegone expression.

Meanwhile Jake sat at his machine merrily pushing away at a cloak and singing to it some of the popular American songs of the day.

The sensation caused by the arrival of his wife and child had nearly blown over. Peltner's dancing school he had not visited since a week or two previous to Gitl's landing. As to the scene which had greeted him in the shop after the stirring news had first reached it, he had faced it out with much more courage and got over it with much less difficulty than he had anticipated.

"Did I ever tell you I was a *tzingle man*?" he laughingly defended himself, though blushing crimson, against his shopmate's taunts. "And am I obliged to give you a *report* whether my wife has come or not? You are not worth mentioning her name to, *anyhoy*."

The boss then suggested that Jake celebrate the event with two pints of beer, the motion being seconded by the presser, who volunteered to fetch the beverage. Jake obeyed with alacrity, and if there had still lingered any trace of awkwardness in his position it was soon washed away by the foaming liquid.

As a matter of fact, Fanny's embarrassment was much greater than Jake's. The stupefying news was broken to her on the very day of Gitl's arrival. After passing a sleepless night she felt that she could not bring herself to face Jake in the presence of her other shopmates, to whom her feelings for him were an open secret. As luck would have it, it was Sunday, the beginning of a new working week in the metropolitan Ghetto, and she went to look for a job in another place.

Jake at once congratulated himself upon her absence and missed her. But then he equally missed the company of Mamie and of all the other dancing-school girls, whose society and attentions now more than ever seemed to him necessities of his life. They haunted his mind day and night; he almost never beheld them in his imagination except as clustering together with his fellow-cavaliers and making merry over him and his wife; and the vision pierced his heart with shame and jealousy. All his achievements seemed wiped out by a sudden stroke of ill fate. He thought himself a martyr, an innocent exile from a world to which he belonged by right; and he frequently felt the sobs of self-pity mounting to his throat. For several minutes at a time, while kicking at his treadle, he would see, reddening before him, Gitl's bandana kerchief and her prominent gums, or hear an un-American piece of Yiddish pronounced with Gitl's peculiar lisp—that very lisp, which three years ago he used to mimic fondly, but which now grated on his nerves and was apt to make his face twitch with sheer disgust, insomuch that he often found a vicious relief in mocking that lisp of hers audibly over his work. But can it be that he is doomed for life? No! no! he would revolt, conscious at the same time that there was really no escape. "Ah, may she be killed, the horrid greenhorn!" he would gasp to himself in a paroxysm of despair. And then he would bewail his lost youth, and curse all Russia for his premature marriage. Presently, however, he would recall the plump, spunky face of his son who bore such close resemblance to himself, to whom he was growing more strongly attached every day, and who was getting to prefer his company to his mother's; and thereupon his heart would soften toward Gitl, and he would gradually feel the qualms of pity and remorse, and make a vow to treat her kindly. "Never min'," he would at such instances say in his heart, "she will *oyshgreen** herself and I shall get used to her. She is a—*shight* better than all the dancing-school girls." And he would inspire himself with respect for her spotless purity, and take comfort in the fact of her being a model housewife, undiverted from her duties by any thoughts of balls or picnics. And despite a deeper consciousness which exposed his readiness to sacrifice it all at any time, he would work himself into a dignified feeling as the head of a household and the father of a promising son, and soothe himself with the additional consolation that sooner or later the other fellows of Joe's academy would also be married.

On the Wednesday in question Jake and his shopmates had warded off a reduction of wages by threatening a strike, and were accordingly in high feather. And so Jake and Bernstein came home in unusually good spirits. Little Joey—for such was Yosselé's name now—with whom his father's plays were for the most part of an athletic character, welcomed Jake by a challenge for a pugilistic encounter, and the way he said "Coom a fight!" and held out his little fists so delighted Mr. Podkovnik, Sr., that upon ordering Gitl to serve supper he vouchsafed a fillip on the tip of her nose.

While she was hurriedly setting the table, Jake took to describing to Charley his employer's defeat. "You should have seen how he looked, the cockroach!" he

---

*A verb coined from the Yiddish *oys,* out, and the English *green,* and signifying to cease being green.

said. "He became as pale as the wall and his teeth were chattering as if he had been shaken up with fever, *'pon my void*. And how quiet he became all of a sudden, as if he could not count two! One might apply him to an ulcer, so soft was he—ha-ha-ha!" he laughed, looking to Bernstein, who smiled assent.

At last supper was announced. Bernstein donned his hat, and did not sit down to the repast before he had performed his ablutions and whispered a short prayer. As he did so Jake and Charley interchanged a wink. As to themselves, they dispensed with all devotional preliminaries, and took their seats with uncovered heads. Gitl also washed her fingers and said the prayer, and as she handed Yosselé his first slice of bread she did not release it before he had recited the benediction.

Bernstein, who, as a rule, looked daggers at his meal, this time received his plate of *borshtch**—his favorite dish—with a radiant face; and as he ate he pronounced it a masterpiece, and lavished compliments on the artist.

"It's a long time since I tasted such a borshtch! Simply a vivifier! It melts in every limb!" he kept rhapsodizing, between mouthfuls. "It ought to be sent to the Chicago Exposition. The *misses* would get a medal."

"A *regely* European borshtch!" Charley chimed in. "It is worth ten cents a spoonful, *'pon mine vort*!"

"Go away! You are only making fun of me," Gitl declared, beaming with pride. "What is there to be laughing at? I make it as well as I can," she added demurely.

"Let him who is laughing laugh with teeth," jested Charlie. "I tell you it is a —" The remainder of the sentence was submerged in a mouthful of the vivifying semi-liquid.

"Alla right!" Jake bethought himself. *"Charge* him ten *shent* for each spoonful. Mr. Bernstein, you shall be kind enough to be the *bookkeeper*. But if you don't pay, Chollie, I'll get out a *tzommesh* [summons] from *court*."

Whereat the little kitchen rang with laughter, in

*A sour soup of cabbage and beets.

which all participated except Bernstein. Even Joey, or Yosselé, joined in the general outburst of merriment. Otherwise he was busily engaged cramming borshtch into his mouth, and, in passing, also into his nose, with both his plump hands for a pair of spoons. From time to time he would interrupt operations to make a wry face and, blinking his eyes, to lisp out rapturously, "Sour!"

"Look—may you live long—do look; he is laughing, too!" Gitl called attention to Yosselé's bespattered face. "To think of such a crumb having as much sense as that!" She was positive that he appreciated his father's witticism, although she herself understood it but vaguely.

"May he know evil no better than he knows what he is laughing at," Jake objected, with a fatherly mien. "What makes you laugh, Joey?" The boy had no time to spare for an answer, being too busy licking his emptied plate. "Look at the soldier's appetite he has *de feller*! Joey, hoy you like de borshtch! Alla right?" Jake asked in English.

"Awrr-ra rr-right!" Joey pealed out his sturdy rustic r's, which he had mastered shortly before taking leave of his doting grandmother.

"See how well he speaks English?" Jake said, facetiously. "A —— *shight* better than his mamma, *anyvay*."

Gitl, who was in the meantime serving the meat, colored, but took the remark in good part.

"I *tell* you he is growing to be Presdent 'Nited States," Charlie interposed.

"*Greenhorn* that you are! A President must be American born," Jake explained, self-consciously. "Ain't it, Mr. Bernstein?"

"It's a pity, then, that he was not born in this country," Bernstein replied, his eye envyingly fixed now on Gitl, now at the child, on whose plate she was at this moment carving a piece of meat into tiny morsels. "*Vell*, if he cannot be a President of the United States, he may be one of a synagogue, so he is a president."

"Don't you worry for his sake," Gitl put in, delighted with the attention her son was absorbing. "He does not need to be a pesdent; he is growing to be a rabbi; don't be making fun of him." And she turned her head to kiss the future rabbi.

"Who is making fun?" Bernstein demurred. "I wish I had a boy like him."

"Get married and you will have one," said, Gitl, beamingly.

"*Shay,* Mr. Bernstein, how about your *shadchen?*"* Jake queried. He gave a laugh, but forthwith checked it, remaining with an embarrassed grin on his face, as though anxious to swallow the question. Bernstein blushed to the roots of his hair, and bent an irate glance on his plate, but held his peace.

His reserved manner, if not his superior education, held Bernstein's shopmates at a respectful distance from him, and, as a rule, rendered him proof against their badinage, although behind his back they would indulge an occasional joke on his inferiority as a work-man, and—while they were at it—on his dyspepsia, his books, and staid, methodical habits. Recently, how-ever, they had got wind of his clandestine visits to a marriage broker's, and the temptation to chaff him on the subject had proved resistless, all the more so be-cause Bernstein, whose leading foible was his well-controlled vanity, was quick to take offence in general, and on this matter in particular. As to Jake, he was by no means averse to having a laugh at somebody else's expense; but since Bernstein had become his boarder he felt that he could not afford to wound his pride. Hence his regret and anxiety at his allusion to the mat-rimonial agent.

After supper Charlie went out for the evening, while Bernstein retired to their little bedroom. Gitl busied herself with the dishes, and Jake took to romping about with Joey and had a hearty laugh with him. He was be-ginning to tire of the boy's company and to feel lone-some generally, when there was a knock at the door.

"Coom in!" Gitl hastened to say somewhat coquett-

*A matrimonial agent.

ishly, flourishing her proficiency in American manners, as she raised her head from the pot in her hands.

"Coom in!" repeated Joey.

The door flew open, and in came Mamie, preceded by a cloud of cologne odors. She was apparently dressed for some occasion of state, for she was powdered and straight-laced and resplendent in a waist of blazing red, gaudily trimmed, and with puff sleeves, each wider than the vast expanse of white straw, surmounted with a whole forest of ostrich feathers, which adorned her head. One of her gloved hands held the huge hoop-shaped yellowish handle of a blue parasol.

"Good-evenin', Jake!" she said, with ostentatious vivacity.

"Good-evenin', Mamie!" Jake returned, jumping to his feet and violently reddening, as if suddenly pricked. "Mish Fein, my vife! My vife, Mish Fein!"

Miss Fein made a stately bow, primly biting her lip as she did so. Gitl, with the pot in her hands, stood staring sheepishly, at a loss what to do.

"Say 'I'm glyad to meech you,'" Jake urged her, confusedly.

The English phrase was more than Gitl could venture to echo.

"She is still *green*," Jake apologized for her, in Yiddish.

"*Never min'*, she will soon *oysgreen* herself," Mamie remarked, with patronizing affability.

"The *lada* is an acquaintance of mine," Jake explained bashfully, his hand feeling the few days' growth of beard on his chin.

Gitl instinctively scented an enemy in the visitor, and eyed her with an uneasy gaze. Nevertheless she mustered a hospitable air, and drawing up the rocking chair, she said, with shamefaced cordiality: "Sit down; why should you be standing? You may be seated for the same money."

In the conversation which followed Mamie did most of the talking. With a nervous volubility often broken by an irrelevant giggle, and violently rocking with her chair, she expatiated on the charms of America, proph-

esying that her hostess would bless the day of her arrival on its soil, and went off in ecstasies over Joey.
She spoke with an overdone American accent in the dialect of the Polish Jews, affectedly Germanized and
profusely interspersed with English, so that Gitl, whose
mother tongue was Lithuanian Yiddish, could scarcely
catch the meaning of one half of her flood of garrulity.
And as she thus rattled on, she now examined the
room, now surveyed Gitl from head to foot, now fixed
her with a look of studied sarcasm, followed by a side
glance at Jake, which seemed to say, "Woe to you,
what a rag of a wife yours is!" Whenever Gitl ventured
a timid remark, Mamie would nod assent with dignified amiability, and thereupon imitate a smile, broad
yet fleeting, which she had seen performed by some
uptown ladies.

Jake stared at the lamp with a faint simper, scarcely
following the caller's words. His head swam with embarrassment. The consciousness of Gitl's unattractive
appearance made him sick with shame and vexation,
and his eyes carefully avoided her bandana, as a culprit
schoolboy does the evidence of his offence.

"You mush vant you twenty-fife dollars," he presently nerved himself up to say in English, breaking an
awkward pause.

"I should cough!" Mamie rejoined.

"In a coupel a veeksh, Mamie, as sure as my name
is Jake."

"In a couple o' veeks! No, sirree! I mus' have my
money at oncet. I don't know vere you vill get it,
dough. Vy, a married man!"—with a chuckle. "You got
a—of a lot o' t'ings to pay for. You took de foinitsha
by a custom peddler, ain' it? But what a—do *I* care? I
vant my money. I voiked hard enough for it."

"Don' shpeak English. She'll t'ink I don' knu vot ve
shpeakin'," he besought her, in accents which implied
intimacy between the two of them and a common
aloofness from Gitl.

"Vot d'I care vot she t'inks? She's your vife, ain' it?
Vell, she mus' know ev'ryt'ing. Dot's right! A husban'
dass'n't hide not'ink from his vife!"—with another

chuckle and another look of deadly sarcasm at Gitl. "I
can say de same in Jewish—"

"Shurr-r up, Mamie!" he interrupted her, gaspingly.

"Don'tch you like it, lump it! A vife mus'n't be
skinned like a strange lady, see?" she pursued inexora-
bly. "O'ly a strange goil a feller might bluff dot he ain'
married, and skin her out of twenty-five dollars." In
point of fact, he had never directly given himself out
for a single man to her. But it did not even occur to
him to defend himself on that score.

"Mamie! Ma-a-mie! Shtop! I'll pay you ev'ry shent.
Shpeak Jewesh, pleashe!" he implored, as if for life.

"You'r' afraid of her? Dot's right! Dot's right! Dot's
nice! All religious peoples is afraid of deir vifes. But
vy didn' you say you vas married from de sta't, an' dot
you vant money to send for dem?" she tortured him,
with a lingering arch leer.

"For Chrish' shake, Mamie!" he entreated her, winc-
ingly. "Shtop to shpeak English, an' shpeak shomet'ing
differench. I'll shee you—vere can I shee you?"

"You von't come by Joe no more?" she asked, with
sudden interest and even solicitude.

"You t'ink indeed I'm 'frait? If I vanted I can gu
dere more ash I ushed to gu dere. But vere can I findsh
you?"

"I guess you know vere I'm livin', don'ch you? So
kvick you forget? Vot a sho't mind you got! Vill you
come? Never min', I know you are only bluffin', an'
dot's all."

"I'll come, ash sure ash I leev."

"Vill you? All right. But if you don' come an' pay
me at least ten dollars for a sta't, you'll see!"

In the meanwhile Gitl, poor thing, sat pale and
horror-struck. Mamie's perfumes somehow terrified
her. She was racked with jealousy and all sorts of
suspicions, which she vainly struggled to disguise.
She could see that they were having a heated altercation, and that Jake was begging about something or
other, and was generally the under dog in the parley.
Ever and anon she strained her ears in the effort to fas-

ten some of the incomprehensible sounds in her memory, that she might subsequently parrot them over to
Mrs. Kavarsky, and ascertain their meaning. But, alas!
the attempt proved futile; "never min' " and "all right"
being all she could catch.

Mamie concluded her visit by presenting Joey with
the imposing sum of five cents.

"What do you say? Say 'danks, sir!' " Gitl prompted
the boy.

"Shay 't'ank you, ma'am!' " Jake overruled her.
" 'Shir' is said to a gentlemarn."

"Good-night!" Mamie sang out, as she majestically
opened the door.

"Good-night!" Jake returned, with a burning face.

"Goot-night!" Gitl and Joey chimed in duet.

"Say 'cull again!' "

"Cullye gain!"

"Good-night!" Mamie said once more, as she bowed
herself out of the door with what she considered an ex-
quisitely "tony" smile.

The guest's exit was succeeded by a momentary silence. Jake felt as if his face and ears were on fire.

"We used to work in the same shop," he presently
said.

"Is that the way a seamstress dresses in America?"
Gitl inquired. "It is not for nothing that it is called the
golden land," she added, with timid irony.

"She must be going to a ball," he explained, at the
same moment casting a glance at the looking glass.

The word "ball" had an imposing ring for Gitl's
ears. At home she had heard it used in connection with
the sumptuous life of the Russian or Polish nobility,
but had never formed a clear idea of its meaning.

"She looks a veritable *panenke*,"* she remarked,
with hidden sarcasm. "Was she born here?"

"*Nu,* but she has been very long here. She speaks
English like one American born. We are used to speak

*A young noblewoman.

in English when we talk *shop*. She came to ask me about a *job*."

Gitl reflected that with Bernstein Jake was in the habit of talking shop in Yiddish, although the boarder could even read English books, which her husband could not do so.

6

CIRCUMSTANCES ALTER CASES

Jake was left by Mamie in a state of unspeakable misery. He felt discomfited, crushed, the universal butt of ridicule. Her perfumes lingered in his nostrils, taking his breath away. Her venomous gaze stung his heart. She seemed to him elevated above the social plane upon which he had recently (though the interval appeared very long) stood by her side, nay, upon which he had had her at his beck and call; while he was degraded, as it were, wallowing in a mire, from which he yearningly looked up to his former equals, vainly begging for recognition. An uncontrollable desire took possession of him to run after her, to have an explanation, and to swear that he was the same Jake and as much of a Yankee and a gallant as ever. But here was his wife fixing him with a timid, piteous look, which at once exasperated and cowed him; and he dared not stir out of the house, as though nailed by that look of hers to the spot.

He lay down on the lounge, and shut his eyes. Gitl dutifully brought him a pillow. As she adjusted it under his head the touch of her hand on his face made him shrink, as if at the contact with a reptile. He was anxious to flee from his wretched self into oblivion, and his wish was soon gratified, the combined effort of a hard day's work and a plentiful and well-relished supper plunging him into a heavy sleep.

While his snores resounded in the little kitchen, Gitl put the child to bed, and then passed with noiseless step into the boarders' room. The door was ajar and she entered it without knocking, as was her wont. She found Bernstein bent over a book, with a ponderous dictionary by its side. A kerosene lamp with a red shade, occupying nearly all the remaining space on the table, spread a lurid mysterious light. Gitl asked the studious cloakmaker whether he knew a Polish girl named Mamie Fein.

"Mamie Fein? No. Why?" said Bernstein, with his index finger on the passage he had been reading, and his eyes on Gitl's plumpish cheek, bathed in the rose-ate light.

"Nothing. May not one ask?"

"What is the matter? Speak out! Are you afraid to tell me?" he insisted.

"What should be the matter? She was here. A nice *lada*."

"Your husband knows many nice *ladies*," he said, with a faint but significant smile. And immediately regretting the remark he went on to smooth it down by characterizing Jake as an honest and good-natured fellow.

"You ought to think yourself fortunate in having him for your husband," he added.

"Yes, but what did you mean by what you said first?" she demanded, with an anxious air.

"What did I mean? What should I have meant? I meant what I said. 'F cou'se he knows many girls. But who does not? You know there are always girls in the shops where we work. Never fear, Jake has nothing to do with them."

"Who says I fear! Did I say I did? Why should I?"

Encouraged by the cheering effect which his words were obviously having on the credulous, unsophisticated woman, he pursued: "May no Jewish daughter have a worse husband. Be easy, be easy. I tell you he is melting away for you. He never looked as happy as he does since you came."

"Go away! You must be making fun of me!" she said, beaming with delight.

"Don't you believe me? Why, are you not a pretty young woman?" he remarked, with an oily look in his eye.

The crimson came into her cheek, and she lowered her glance.

"Stop making fun of me, I beg you," she said softly. "Is it true?"

"Is what true? That you are a pretty young woman? Take a looking glass and see for yourself."

"Strange man that you are!" she returned, with confused deprecation. "I mean what you said before about Jake," she faltered.

"Oh, about Jake! Then say so," he jested. "Really he loves you as life."

"How do you know?" she queried, wistfully.

"How do I know!" he repeated, with an amused smile. "As if one could not see!"

"But he never told you himself!"

"How do you know he did not? You have guessed wrongly, see! He did, lots of times," he concluded gravely, touched by the anxiety of the poor woman.

She left Bernstein's room all thrilling with joy, and repentant for her excess of communicativeness. "A wife must not tell other people what happens to her husband," she lectured herself, in the best of humors. Still, the words "Your husband knows many nice *ladas*," kept echoing at the bottom of her soul, and in another few minutes she was at Mrs. Kavarsky's, confidentially describing Mamie's visit as well as her talk with the boarder, omitting nothing save the latter's compliments to her looks.

Mrs. Kavarsky was an eccentric, scraggy little woman, with a vehement manner and no end of words and gesticulations. Her dry face was full of warts and surmounted by a chaotic mass of ringlets and curls of a faded brown. None too tidy about her person, and rather slattern in general appearance, she zealously kept up the over-scrupulous cleanliness for which the fame of her apartments reached far and wide. Her neighbors and townsfolk pronounced her crazy but "with a heart of diamond," that is to say, the diametrical opposite of the precious stone in point of hardness, and resembling it in the general sense of excellence of quality. She was neighborly enough, and as she was the most prosperous and her establishment the best equipped in the whole tenement, many a woman would come to borrow some cooking utensil or other, or even a few dollars on rent day, which Mrs. Kavarsky always started by refusing in the most pointed terms, and almost always finished by granting.

She started to listen to Gitl's report with a fierce mien which gradually thawed into a sage smile. When the young neighbor had rested her case, she first nodded her head, as who should say, "What fools this young generation be!" and then burst out:

"Do you know what *I* have to tell you? Guess!"

Gitl thought Heaven knows what revelations awaited her.

"That you are a lump of horse and a greenhorn and nothing else!" (Gitl felt much relieved.) "That piece of ugliness should *try* and come to *my* house! Then she would know the price of a pound of evil. I should open the door and—*march* to eighty black years! Let her go to where she came from! America is not Russia, thanked be the Lord of the world. Here one must remember *'ladas foist'*—but then you do not even know what that means!" she exclaimed, with a despairing wave of her hand.

"What does it mean?" Gitl inquired, pensively.

"What does it mean? What should it mean? It means but too well, *never min'*. It means that when a husband does not *behabe* as he should, one does not stroke his cheeks for it. A prohibition upon me if one does. If the wife is no greenhorn she gets him shoved into the oven, over there, across the river."

"You mean they send him to prison?"

"Where else—to the theater?" Mrs. Kavarsky mocked her furiously.

"A weeping to me!" Gitl said, with horror. "May God save me from such things!"

In due course Mrs. Kavarsky arrived at the subject of headgear, and for the third or fourth time she elicited from her pupil a promise to discard the kerchief and to sell the wig.

"No wonder he does hate you, seeing you in that

horrid rag, which makes a grandma of you. Drop it, I
tell you! Drop it so that no survivor nor any refugee is
left of it. If you don't obey me this time, dare not cross
my threshold any more, do you hear?" she thundered.
"One might as well talk to the wall as to her!" she proceeded, actually addressing herself to the opposite wall
of her kitchen, and referring to her interlocutrice in the
third person. "I am working and working for her, and
here she appreciates it as much as the cat. Fie!" With
which the irate lady averted her face in disgust.

"I shall take it off; now for sure—as sure as this is
Wednesday," said Gitl, beseechingly.

Mrs. Kavarsky turned back to her pacified.

"Remember now! If you *deshepoitn* [disappoint] me
this time, well!—look at me! I should think I was no
Gentile woman, either. I am as pious as you *anyhull*,
and come from no mean family, either. You know I
hate to boast; *but* my father—peace be upon him!—
was fit to be a rabbi. *Vell,* and yet I am not afraid to go
with my own hair. May no greater sins be committed!
Then it would be *never min'* enough. Plenty of time for
putting on the patch [meaning the wig] when I get old;
but as long as I am young, I am young *an' dots ull*! It
can not be helped; when one lives in an *edzecate* country, one must live like *edzecate peoples*. As they play,
so one dances, as the saying is. But I think it is time
for you to be going. Go, my little kitten," Mrs.
Kavarsky said, suddenly lapsing into accents of the
most tender affection. "He may be up by this time and
wanting *tea*. Go, my little lamb, go and *try* to make
yourself agreeable to him and the Uppermost will help.
In America one must take care not to displease a husband. Here one is today in New York and tomorrow in
Chicago; do you understand? As if there were any
shame or decency here! A father is no father, a wife,
no wife—*not'ing*! Go now, my baby! Go and throw
away your rag and be a nice woman, and everything
will be *ull right.*" And so hurrying Gitl to go, she detained her with ever a fresh torrent of loquacity for another ten minutes, till the young woman, standing on
pins and needles and scarcely lending an ear, plucked

up courage to plead her household duties and take a hasty departure.

She found Jake fast asleep. It was after eleven when he slowly awoke. He got up with a heavy burden on his soul—a vague sense of having met with some horrible rebuff. In his semi-consciousness he was unaware, however, of his wife's and son's existence and of the change which their advent had produced in his life, feeling himself the same free bird that he had been a fortnight ago. He stared about the room, as if wondering where he was. Noticing Gitl, who at that moment came out of the bedroom, he instantly realized the situation, recalling Mamie, hat, perfumes, and all, and his heart sank within him. The atmosphere of the room became stifling to him. After sitting on the lounge for some time with a drooping head, he was tempted to fling himself on the pillow again, but instead of doing so he slipped on his hat and coat and went out.

Gitl was used to his goings and comings without explanation. Yet this time his slam of the door sent a sharp pang through her heart. She had no doubt but that he was bending his steps to another interview with the Polish witch, as she mentally branded Miss Fein.

Nor was she mistaken, for Jake did start, mechanically, in the direction of Chrystie Street, where Mamie lodged. He felt sure that she was away to some ball, but the very house in which she roomed seemed to draw him with magnetic force. Moreover, he had a lurking hope that he might, after all, find her about the building. Ah, if by a stroke of good luck he came upon her on the street! All he wished was to have a talk, and that for the whole purpose of amending her unfavorable impression of him. Then he would never so much as think of Mamie, for, indeed, she was hateful to him, he persuaded himself.

Arrived at his destination, and failing to find Mamie on the sidewalk, he was tempted to wait till she came from the ball, when he was seized with a sudden sense of the impropriety of his expedition, and he forthwith returned home, deciding in his mind, as he walked, to move with his wife and child to Chicago.

Meanwhile Mamie lay brooding in her cot-bed in the parlor, which she shared with her landlady's two daughters. She was in the most wretched frame of mind, ineffectually struggling to fall asleep. She had made her way down the stairs leading from the Podkovniks with a violently palpitating heart. She had been bound for no more imposing a place than Joe's academy, and before repairing thither she had had to betake herself home to change her stately toilet for a humbler attire. For, as a matter of fact, it was expressly for her visit to the Podkovniks that she had thus pranked herself out, and that would have been much too gorgeous an appearance to make at Joe's establishment on one of its regular dancing evenings. Having changed her toilet she did call at Joe's; but so full was her mind of Jake and his wife and, accordingly, she was so irritable, that in the middle of a quadrille she picked a quarrel with the dancing master, and abruptly left the hall.

The next day Jake's work fared badly. When it was at last over he did not go direct home as usual, but first repaired to Mamie's. He found her with her landlady in the kitchen. She looked careworn and was in a white blouse which lent her face a convalescent, touching effect.

"Good-eveni'g, Mrs. Bunetzky! Good-eveni'g, Mamie!" he fairly roared, as he playfully fillipped his hat backward. And after addressing a pleasantry or two to the mistress of the house, he boldly proposed to her boarder to go out with him for a talk. For a moment Mamie hesitated, fearing lest her landlady had become aware of the existence of a Mrs. Podkovnik; but instantly flinging all considerations to the wind, she followed him out into the street.

"You'sh afraid I vouldn't pay you, Mamie?" he began, with bravado, in spite of his intention to start on a different line, he knew not exactly which.

Mamie was no less disappointed by the opening of

the conversation than he. "I ain't afraid a bit," she answered, sullenly.

"Do you think my *kshpenshesh* are larger now?" he resumed in Yiddish. "May I lose as much through sickness. On the countrary, I *shpend* even much less than I used to. We have two nice boarders—I keep them only for company's sake—and I have a *shteada job—a puddin' of a job*. I shall have still more money to *shpend outshite*," he added, falteringly.

"Outside?"—and she burst into an artificial laugh which sent the blood to Jake's face.

"Why, do you think I sha'n't go to Joe's, nor to the theater, nor anywhere any more? Still oftener than before! *Hoy much vill you bet?*"

"*Rats!* A married man, a papa go to a dancing school! Not unless your wife drags along with you and never lets go of your skirts," she said sneeringly, adding the declaration that Jake's "bluffs" gave her a "regula' pain in de neck."

Jake, writhing under her lashes, protested his freedom as emphatically as he could; but it only served to whet Mamie's spite, and against her will she went on twitting him as a henpecked husband and an old-fashioned Jew. Finally she reverted to the subject of his debt, whereupon he took fire, and after an interchange of threats and some quite forcible language they parted company.

From that evening the specter of Mamie dressed in her white blouse almost unremittingly preyed on Jake's mind. The mournful sneer which had lit her pale, invalid-looking face on their last interview, when she wore that blouse, relentlessly stared down into his heart; gnawed at it with tantalizing deliberation; "drew out his soul," as he once put it to himself, dropping his arms and head in despair. "Is this what they call love?" he wondered, thinking of the strange, hitherto unexperienced kind of malady, which seemed to be gradually consuming his whole being. He felt as if Mamie had breathed a delicious poison into his veins, which was now taking effect, spreading a devouring fire through his soul, and kindling him with a frantic thirst for more of the same virus. His features became distended, as it were, and acquired a feverish effect; his eyes had a pitiable, beseeching look, like those of a child in the period of teething.

He grew more irritable with Gitl every day, the energy failing him to dissemble his hatred for her. There were moments when, in his hopeless craving for the presence of Mamie, he would consciously seek refuge in a feeling of compunction and of pity for his wife; and on several such occasions he made an effort to take an affectionate tone with her. But the unnatural sound of his voice each time only accentuated to himself the depth of his repugnance, while the hysterical promptness of her answers, the servile gratitude which trembled in her voice and shone out of her radiant face would, at such instances, make him breathless with rage. Poor Gitl! she strained every effort to please him; she tried to charm him by all the simple-minded little coquetries she knew, by every art which her artless brain could invent; and only succeeded in making herself more offensive than ever.

As to Jake's feelings for Joey, they now alternated between periods of indifference and gusts of exaggerated affection; while in some instances, when the boy let himself be fondled by his mother or returned her caresses in his childish way, he would appear to Jake as siding with his enemy, and share with Gitl his father's odium.

One afternoon, shortly after Jake's interview with Mamie in front of the Chrystie Street tenement house, Fanny called on Gitl.

"Are you Mrs. Podkovnik?" she inquired, with an embarrassed air.

"Yes; why?" Mrs. Podkovnik replied, turning pale. "She is come to tell me that Jake has eloped with that Polish girl," flashed upon her overwrought mind. At the same moment Fanny, sizing her up, exclaimed inwardly, "So this is the kind of woman she is, poor thing!"

"Nothing. I *just* want to speak to you," the visitor uttered, mysteriously.

"What is it?"

"As I say, nothing at all. Is there nobody else in the house?" Fanny demanded, looking about.

"May I not live till tomorrow if there is a living soul except my boy, and he is asleep. You may speak; never fear. But first tell me who you are; do not take ill my question. Be seated."

The girl's appearance and manner began to inspire Gitl with confidence.

"My name is Rosy—Rosy Blank," said Fanny, as she took a seat on the further end of the lounge. " *'F cou'se,* you don't know me, how should you? But I know you well enough, never mind that we have never seen each other before. I used to work with your husband in one shop. I have come to tell you such an important thing! You must know it. It makes no difference that you don't know who I am. May God grant me as good a year as my friendship is for you."

"Something about Jake?" Gitl blurted out, all anxiety, and instantly regretted the question.

"How did you guess? About Jake it is! About him and somebody else. But see how you did guess! Swear that you won't tell anybody that I have been here."

"May I be left speechless, may my arms and legs be paralyzed, if I ever say a word!" Gitl recited vehemently, thrilling with anxiety and impatience. "So it is! they have eloped!" she added in her heart, seating herself close to her caller. "A darkness upon my years! What will become of me and Yosselé now?"

"Remember, now, not a word, either to Jake or to anybody else in the world. I had a mountain of *trouble* before I found out where you lived, and I *stopped* work on purpose to come and speak to you. As true as you see me alive. I wanted to call when I was sure to find you alone, you understand. Is there really nobody about?" And after a preliminary glance at the door and exacting another oath of discretion from Mrs. Podkovnik, Fanny began in an undertone:

"There is a girl; well, her name is Mamie; well, she

and your husband used to go to the same dancing
school—that is a place where *fellers* and *ladies* learn to
dance," she explained. "I go there, too; but I know
your husband from the shop."

"But that *lada* has also worked in the same shop
with him, hasn't she?" Gitl broke in, with a desolate
look in her eye.

"Why, did Jake tell you she had?" Fanny asked in
surprise.

"No, not at all, not at all! I am just asking. May I be
sick if I know anything."

"The idea! How could they work together, seeing
that she is a shirtmaker and he a cloakmaker. Ah, if
you knew what a witch she is! She has set her mind
on your husband, and is bound to take him away from
you. She hitched on to him long ago. But since you
came I thought she would have God in her heart, and
be ashamed of people. Not she! She be ashamed! You
may sling a cat into her face and she won't mind it.
The black year knows where she grew up. I tell you
there is not a girl in the whole dancing school but can
not bear the sight of that Polish lizard!"

"Why, do they meet and kiss?" Gitl moaned out.
"Tell me, do tell me all, my little crown, keep nothing
from me, tell me my whole dark lot."

"*Ull right,* but be sure not to speak to anybody. I'll
tell you the truth: My name is not Rosy Blank at all. It
is Fanny Scutelsky. You see, I am telling you the whole
truth. The other evening they stood near the house
where she *boards,* on Chrystie Street; so they were
looking into each other's eyes and talking like a pair of
little doves. A *lady* who is a *particla* friend of mine
saw them; so she says a child could have guessed that
she was making love to him and *trying* to get him
away from you. 'F *cou'se* it is none of my *business.* Is
it my *business,* then? What do I *care*? It is only *becuss*
I pity you. It is like the nature I have; I can not bear
to see anybody in trouble. Other people would not
care, but I do. Such is my nature. So I thought to myself I must go and tell Mrs. Podkovnik all about it, in
order that she might know what to do."

For several moments Gitl sat speechless, her head hung down, and her bosom heaving rapidly. Then she fell to swaying her frame sidewise, and vehemently wringing her hands.

"*Oi! Oi!* Little mother! A pain to me!" she moaned. "What is to be done? Lord of the world, what is to be done? Come to the rescue! People, do take pity, come to the rescue!" She broke into a fit of low sobbing, which shook her whole form and was followed by a torrent of tears.

Whereupon Fanny also burst out crying, and falling upon Gitl's shoulder she murmured: "My little heart! you don't know what a friend I am to you! Oh, if you knew what a serpent that Polish thief is!"

7

MRS. KAVARSKY'S COUP D'ÉTAT

It was not until after supper time that Gitl could see Mrs. Kavarsky; for the neighbor's husband was in the installment business, and she generally spent all day in helping him with his collections as well as canvassing for new customers. When Gitl came in to unburden herself of Fanny's revelations, she found her confidant out of sorts. Something had gone wrong in Mrs. Kavarsky's affairs, and, while she was perfectly aware that she had only herself to blame, she had laid it all to her husband and had nagged him out of the house before he had quite finished his supper.

She listened to her neighbor's story with a bored and impatient air, and when Gitl had concluded and paused for her opinion, she remarked languidly: "It serves you right! It is all *becuss* you will not throw away that ugly kerchief of yours. What is the use of your asking my advice?"

"*Oi!* I think even that wouldn't help it now," Gitl rejoined, forlornly. "The Uppermost knows what drug she has charmed him with. A cholera into her, Lord of the world!" she added, fiercely.

Mrs. Kavarsky lost her temper.

"*Say,* will you stop talking nonsense?" she shouted savagely. "No wonder your husband does not *care* for you, seeing these stupid greenhornlike notions of yours."

"How then could she have bewitched him, the witch that she is? Tell me, little heart, little crown, do tell me! Take pity and be a mother to me. I am so lonely and——" Heartrending sobs choked her voice.

"What shall I tell you? that you are a blockhead? *Oi! Oi! Oi!*" she mocked her. "Will the crying help you? *Ull right,* cry away!"

"But what shall I do?" Gitl pleaded, wiping her tears. "It may drive me mad. I won't wear the kerchief any more. I swear this is the last day," she added, propitiatingly.

"*Dot's right!* When you talk like a man I like you. And now sit still and listen to what an older person and a business woman has to tell you. In the first place, who knows what that girl—Jennie, Fannie, Shmennie, Yomtzedemennie—whatever you may call her—is after?" The last two names Mrs. Kavarsky invented by poetical license to complete the rhyme and for the greater emphasis of her contempt. "In the second place, *asposel* [supposing] he did talk to that Polish piece of disturbance. *Vell,* what of it? It is all over with the world, isn't it? The mourner's prayer is to be said after it, I declare! A married man stood talking to a girl! Just think of it! May no greater evil befall any Yiddish daughter. This is not Europe where one dares not say a word to a strange woman! *Nu, sir!*"

"What, then, is the matter with him? At home he would hardly ever leave my side, and never ceased looking into my eyes. Woe is me, what America has brought me to!" And again her grief broke out into a flood of tears.

This time Mrs. Kavarsky was moved.

"Don't be crying, my child; he may come in for you," she said, affectionately. "Believe me you are making a mountain out of a fly—you are imagining too much."

"*Oi,* as my ill luck would have it, it is all but too

true. Have I no eyes, then? He mocks at everything I say or do; he can not bear the touch of my hand. America *has* made a mountain of ashes out of me. Really, a curse upon Columbus!" she ejaculated mournfully, quoting in all earnestness a current joke of the Ghetto.

Mrs. Kavarsky was too deeply touched to laugh. She proceeded to examine her pupil, in whispers, upon certain details, and thereupon her interest in Gitl's answers gradually superseded her commiseration for the unhappy woman.

"And how does he behave toward the boy?" she absently inquired, after a melancholy pause.

"Would he were as kind to me!"

"Then it is *ull right*! Such things will happen between man and wife. It is all *humbuk*. It will all come right, and you will some day be the happiest woman in the world. You shall see. Remember that Mrs. Kavarsky has told you so. And in the meantime stop crying. A husband hates a sniveller for a wife. You know the story of Jacob and Leah, as it stands written in the Holy Five Books, don't you? Her eyes became red with weeping, and Jacob, our father, did not *care* for her on that account. Do you understand?"

All at once Mrs. Kavarsky bit her lip, her countenance brightening up with a sudden inspiration. At the next instant she made a lunge at Gitl's head, and off went the kerchief. Gitl started with a cry, at the same moment covering her head with both hands.

"Take off your hands! Take them off at once, I say!" the other shrieked, her eyes flashing fire and her feet performing an Irish jig.

Gitl obeyed for sheer terror. Then, pushing her toward the sink, Mrs. Kavarsky said peremptorily: "You shall wash off your silly tears and I'll arrange your hair, and from this day on there shall be no kerchief, do you hear?"

Gitl offered but feeble resistance, just enough to set herself right before her own conscience. She washed herself quietly, and when her friend set about combing her hair, she submitted to the operation without a murmur, save for uttering a painful hiss each time there came a particularly violent tug at the comb; for, indeed, Mrs. Kavarsky plied her weapon rather energetically and with a bloodthirsty air, as if inflicting punishment. And while she was thus attacking Gitl's luxurious raven locks she kept growling, as glibly as the progress of the comb would allow, and modulating her voice to its movements: "Believe me you are a lump of hunchback, *sure;* you may—may depend up-upon it! Tell me, now, do you ever comb yourself? You have raised quite a plica, the black year take it! Another woman would thank God for such beau-beautiful hair, and here she keeps it hidden and makes a bu-bugbear of herself—a *regele monkey!*" she concluded, gnashing her teeth at the stout resistance with which her implement was at that moment grappling.

Gitl's heart swelled with delight, but she modestly kept silent.

Suddenly Mrs. Kavarsky paused thoughtfully, as if conceiving a new idea. In another moment a pair of scissors and curling irons appeared on the scene. At the sight of this Gitl's blood ran chill, and when the scissors gave their first click in her hair she felt as though her heart snapped. Nevertheless she endured it all without a protest, blindly trusting that these instruments of torture would help reinstall her in Jake's good graces.

At last, when all was ready and she found herself adorned with a pair of rich side bangs, she was taken in front of the mirror, and ordered to hail the transformation with joy. She viewed herself with an unsteady glance, as if her own face struck her as unfamiliar and forbidding. However, the change pleased her as much as it startled her.

"Do you really think he will like it?" she inquired with piteous eagerness, in a fever of conflicting emotions.

"If he does not, I shall refund your money!" her guardian snarled, in high glee.

For a moment or so Mrs. Kavarsky paused to admire the effect of her art. Then, in a sudden transport of enthusiasm, she sprang upon her ward, and with an "*Oi,* a health to you!" she smacked a hearty kiss on her burning cheek.

"And now come, piece of wretch!" So saying, Mrs. Kavarsky grasped Gitl by the wrist, and forcibly convoyed her into her husband's presence.

The two boarders were out, Jake being alone with Joey. He was seated at the table, facing the door, with the boy on his knees.

"*Goot-evenik,* Mr. Podkovnik! Look what I have brought you: a brand new wife!" Mrs. Kavarsky said, pointing at her charge, who stood faintly struggling to disengage her hand from her escort's tight grip, her eyes looking to the ground and her cheeks a vivid crimson.

Gitl's unwonted appearance impressed Jake as something unseemly and meretricious. The sight of her revolted him.

"It becomes her like a—a—a wet cat," he faltered out with a venomous smile, choking down a much stronger simile which would have conveyed his impression with much more precision, but which he dared not apply to his own wife.

The boy's first impulse upon the entrance of his mother had been to run up to her side and to greet her merrily; but he, too, was shocked by the change in her aspect, and he remained where he was, looking from her to Jake in blank surprise.

"Go away, you don't mean it!" Mrs. Kavarsky remonstrated distressedly, at the same moment releasing her prisoner, who forthwith dived into the bedroom to bury her face in a pillow, and to give way to a stream of tears. Then she made a few steps toward Jake, and speaking in an undertone she proceeded to take him to task. "Another man would consider himself happy to have such a wife," she said. "Such a quiet, honest woman! And such a housewife! Why, look at the way she keeps everything—like a fiddle. It is simply a treat to come into your house. I do declare you sin!"

"What do I do to her?" he protested morosely, cursing the intruder in his heart.

"Who says you do? Mercy and peace! Only—you understand—how shall I say it?—she is only a young woman; *vell*, so she imagines that you do not *care* for her as much as you used to. Come, Mr. Podkovnik, you know you are a sensible man! I have always thought you one—you may ask my husband. Really you ought to be ashamed of yourself. A prohibition upon me if I could ever have believed it of you. Do you think a stylish girl would make you a better wife? If you do, you are grievously mistaken. What are they good for, the hussies? To darken the life of a husband? That, I admit, they are really great hands at. They only know how to squander his money for a new hat or rag every Monday and Thursday, and to tramp around with other men, fie upon the abominations! May no good Jew know them!"

Her innuendo struck Mrs. Kavarsky as extremely ingenious, and, egged on by the dogged silence of her auditor, she ventured a step further.

"Do you mean to tell me," she went on, emphasizing each word, and shaking her whole body with melodramatic defiance, "that you would be better off with a *dantzin'-school* girl?"

"A *danshin'-shchool* girl?" Jake repeated, turning ashen pale, and fixing his inquisitress with a distant gaze. "Who says I care for a danshin'-shchool girl?" he bellowed, as he let down the boy and started to his feet red as a cockscomb. "It was she who told you that, was it?"

Joey had tripped up to the lounge where he now stood watching his father with a stare in which there was more curiosity than fright.

The little woman lowered her crest. "Not at all! God be with you!" she said quickly, in a tone of abject cowardice, and involuntarily shrinking before the ferocious attitude of Jake's strapping figure. "Who? What? When? I did not mean anything at all, *sure*. Gitl *never* said a word to me. A prohibition if she did. Come, Mr. Podkovnik, why should you get *ektzited*?" she pursued, beginning to recover her presence of mind. "By-the-by—I came near forgetting—how about the boarder you promised to get me; do you remember, Mr. Podkovnik?"

"Talk away a toothache for your grandma, not for me. Who told her about *danshin'* girls?" he thundered again, re-enforcing the ejaculation with an English oath, and bringing down a violent fist on the table as he did so.

At this Gitl's sobs made themselves heard from the bedroom. They lashed Jake into a still greater fury.

"What is she whimpering about, the piece of stench! *Alla right,* I do hate her; I can not bear the sight of her; and let her do what she likes. *I don' care!"*

"Mr. Podkovnik! To think of a *sma't* man like you talking in this way!"

"Dot'sh alla right!" he said, somewhat relenting. "I don't *care* for any *danshin'* girls. It is a ——— lie! It was that scabby *greenhorn* who must have taken it into her head. I don't *care* for anybody; not for her certainly"—pointing to the bedroom. "I am an *American feller,* a *Yankee*—that's what I am. What punishment is due to me, then, if I can not stand a *shnooza* like her? It is *nu ushed;* I can not live with her, even if she stand one foot on heaven and one on earth. Let her take everything"—with a wave at the household effects— "and I shall pay her as much *cash* as she asks—I am willing to break stones to pay her— provided she agrees to a divorce."

The word had no sooner left his lips than Gitl burst out of the darkness of her retreat, her bangs dishevelled, her face stained and flushed with weeping and rage, and her eyes, still suffused with tears, flashing fire.

"May you and your Polish harlot be jumping out of your skins and chafing with wounds as long as you will have to wait for a divorce!" she exploded. "He thinks I don't know how they stand together near her house making love to each other!"

Her unprecedented show of pugnacity took him aback.

"Look at the Cossack of straw!" he said quietly, with a forced smile. "Such a piece of cholera!" he added, as if speaking to himself, as he resumed his seat. "I wonder who tells her all these fibs?"

Gitl broke into a fresh flood of tears.

"*Vell,* what do you want now?" Mrs. Kavarsky said, addressing herself to her. "He says it is a lie. I told you you take all sorts of silly notions into your head."

"*Ach,* would it were a lie!" Gitl answered between her sobs.

At this juncture the boy stepped up to his mother's side, and nestled against her skirt. She clasped his head with both her hands, as though gratefully accepting an offer of succor against an assailant. And then, for the vague purpose of wounding Jake's feelings, she took the child in her arms, and huddling him close to her bosom, she half turned from her husband, as much as to say, "We two are making common cause against you." Jake was cut to the quick. He kept his glance fixed on the reddened, tear-stained profile of her nose, and, choking with hate, he was going to say, "For my part, hang yourself together with him!" But he had self-mastery enough to repress the exclamation, confining himself to a disdainful smile.

"Children, children! Woe, how you do sin!" Mrs. Kavarsky sermonized. "Come now, obey an older person. Whoever takes notice of such trifles? You have had a quarrel? *ull right!* And now make peace. Have an embrace and a good kiss and *dot's ull! Hurry yup,* Mr. Podkovnik! Don't be ashamed!" she beckoned to him, her countenance wreathed in voluptuous smiles in anticipation of the love scene about to enact itself before her eyes. Mr. Podkovnik failing to hurry up, however, she went on disappointedly: "Why, Mr. Podkovnik! Look at the boy the Uppermost has given you. Would he might send me one like him. Really, you ought to be ashamed of yourself."

"Vot you kickin' aboyt, anyhoy?" Jake suddenly fired out, in English. "Min' jou on businesh an' dot'sh ull," he added indignantly, averting his head.

Mrs. Kavarsky grew as red as a boiled lobster.

"Vo—vo—vot *you* keeck aboyt?" she panted, drawing herself up and putting her arms akimbo. "He must think I, too, can be scared by his English. I declare my shirt has turned linen for fright! I was in America while you were hauling away at the bellows in Povodye; do you know it?"

"Are you going out of my house or not?" roared Jake, jumping to his feet.

"And if I am not, what will you do? Will you call a *politzman*? Ull right, do. That is just what I want. I shall tell him I can not leave her alone with a murderer like you, for fear you might kill her and the boy, so that you might dawdle around with that Polish wench of yours. Here you have it!" Saying which, she put her thumb between her index and third finger—the Russian version of the well-known gesture of contempt—presenting it to her adversary together with a generous portion of her tongue.

Jake's first impulse was to strike the meddlesome woman. As he started toward her, however, he changed his mind. "*Alla right,* you may remain with her!" he said, rushing up to the clothes rack, and slipping on his coat and hat. "*Alla right,*" he repeated with broken breath, "we shall see!" And with a frantic bang of the door he disappeared.

The fresh autumn air of the street at once produced its salutary effect on his over-excited nerves. As he grew more collected he felt himself in a most awkward muddle. He cursed his outbreak of temper, and wished the next few days were over and the breach healed. In his abject misery he thought of suicide, of fleeing to Chicago or St. Louis, all of which passed through his mind in a stream of the most irrelevant and the most frivolous reminiscences. He was burning to go back, but the nerve failing him to face Mrs. Kavarsky, he wondered where he was going to pass the night. It was too cold to be tramping about till it was time to go to work, and he had not change enough to pay for a night's rest in a lodging house; so in his despair he fulminated against Gitl and, above all, against her tutoress. Having passed as far as the limits of the Ghetto he took a homeward course by a parallel street, knowing all the while that he would lack the courage to enter his house. When he came within sight of it he again turned back, yearningly thinking of the cozy little home behind him, and invoking maledictions upon Gitl for enjoying it now while he was exposed to the chill air without the prospect of shelter for the night. As he thus sauntered reluctantly about he meditated upon the scenes coming in his way, and upon the thousand and one things which they brought to his mind. At the same time his heart was thirsting for Mamie, and he felt himself a wretched outcast, the target of ridi-cule—a martyr paying the penalty of sins, which he failed to recognize as sins, or of which, at any rate, he could not hold himself culpable.

Yes, he will go to Chicago, or to Baltimore, or, bet-ter still, to England. He pictured to himself the sensa-tion it would produce and Gitl's despair. "It will serve her right. What does she want of me?" he said to him-self, revelling in a sense of revenge. But then it was such a pity to part with Joey! Whereupon, in his rev-erie, Jake beheld himself stealing into his house in the dead of night, and kidnapping the boy. And what would Mamie say? Would she not be sorry to have him disappear? Can it be that she does not care for him any longer? She seemed to. But that was before she knew him to be a married man. And again his heart uttered curses against Gitl. Ah, if Mamie did still care for him, and fainted upon hearing of his flight, and then could not sleep, and ran around wringing her hands and rav-ing like mad! It would serve *her* right, too! She should have come to tell him she loved him instead of making that scene at his house and taking a derisive tone with him upon the occasion of his visit to her. Still, should she come to join him in London, he would receive her, he decided magnanimously. They speak English in London, and have cloak shops like here. So he would be no greenhorn there, and wouldn't they be hap-py—he, Mamie, and little Joey! Or, supposing his wife suddenly died, so that he could legally marry Mamie and remain in New York——

A mad desire took hold of him to see the Polish girl,

and he involuntarily took the way to her lodging. What is he going to say to her? Well, he will beg her not to be angry for his failure to pay his debt, take her into his confidence on the subject of his proposed flight, and promise to send her every cent from London. And while he was perfectly aware that he had neither the money to take him across the Atlantic nor the heart to forsake Gitl and Joey, and that Mamie would never let him leave New York without paying her twenty-five dollars, he started out on a run in the direction of Chrystie Street. Would she might offer to join him in his flight! She must have money enough for two passage tickets, the rogue. Wouldn't it be nice to be with her on the steamer! he thought, as he wrathfully brushed apart a group of street urchins impeding his way.

8

A HOUSETOP IDYL

Jake found Mamie on the sidewalk in front of the tenement house where she lodged. As he came rushing up to her side, she was pensively rehearsing a waltz step.

"Mamie, come shomeversh! I got to shpeak to you a lot," he gasped out.

"Vot's de madder?" she demanded, startled by his excited manner.

"This is not the place for speaking," he rejoined vehemently, in Yiddish. "Let us go to the Grand Street dock or to Seventh Street park. These we can speak so that nobody overhears us."

"I bet you he is going to ask me to run away with him," she prophesied to herself; and in her feverish impatience to hear him out she proposed to go on the roof, which, the evening being cool, she knew to be deserted.

When they reached the top of the house they found it overhung with rows of half-dried linen, held together with wooden clothespins and trembling to the fresh au-

tumn breeze. Overhead, fleecy clouds were floating
across a starry blue sky, now concealing and now exposing to view a pallid crescent of new moon. Coming
from the street below there was a muffled, mysterious
hum ever and anon drowned in the clatter and jingle of
a passing horse car. A lurid, exceedingly uncanny sort
of idyl it was; and in the midst of it there was something extremely weird and gruesome in those stretches
of wavering, fitfully silvered white, to Jake's overtaxed
mind vaguely suggesting the burial clothes of the inmates of a Jewish graveyard.

After picking and diving their way beneath the trembling lines of underwear, pillowcases, sheets, and what
not, they paused in front of a tall chimney pot. Jake, in
a medley of superstitious terror, infatuation, and bashfulness, was at a loss how to begin and, indeed, what
to say. Feeling that it would be easy for him to break
into tears he instinctively chose this as the only way
out of his predicament.

"*Vot's de madder*, Jake? Speak out!" she said, with
motherly harshness.

He now wished to say something, although he still
knew not what; but his sobs once called into play were
past his control.

"She must give you *trouble*," the girl added softly,
after a slight pause, her excitement growing with every
moment.

"Ach, Mamielé!" he at length exclaimed, resolutely
wiping his tears with his handkerchief. "My life has
become so dark and bitter to me, I might as well put a
rope around my neck."

"Does she eat you?"

"Let her go to all lamentations! Somebody told her
I go around with you."

"But you know it is a lie! Some one must have seen
us the other evening when we were standing downstairs. You had better not come here, then. When you
have some money, you will send it to me," she concluded, between genuine sympathy and an intention to
draw him out.

"*Ach*, don't say that, Mamie. What is the good of my

life without you? I don't sleep nights. Since she came I began to understand how dear you are to me. I can not tell it so well," he said, pointing to his heart.

"*Yes, but* before she came you didn't *care* for me!" she declared, laboring to disguise the exultation which made her heart dance.

"I always did, Mamie. May I drop from this roof and break hand and foot if I did not."

A flood of wan light struck Mamie full in her swarthy face, suffusing it with ivory effulgence, out of which her deep dark eyes gleamed with a kind of unearthly luster. Jake stood enravished. He took her by the hand, but she instantly withdrew it, edging away a step. His touch somehow restored her to calm self-possession, and even kindled a certain thirst for revenge in her heart.

"It is not what it used to be, Jake," she said in tones of complaisant earnestness. "Now that I know you are a married man it is all gone. *Yes*, Jake, it is all gone! You should have cared for me when she was still there. Then you could have gone to a rabbi and sent her a writ of divorce. It is too late now, Jake."

"It is not too late!" he protested, tremulously. "I will get a divorce, *anyhoy*. And if you don't take me I will hang myself," he added, imploringly.

"On a burned straw?" she retorted, with a cruel chuckle.

"It is all very well for you to laugh. But if you could enter my heart and see how I *shuffer*!"

"Woe is me! I don't see how you will stand it," she mocked him. And abruptly assuming a grave tone, she pursued vehemently: "But I don't understand; since you sent her tickets and money, you must like her."

Jake explained that he had all along intended to send her rabbinical divorce papers instead of a passage ticket, and that it had been his old mother who had pestered him, with her tear-stained letters, into acting contrary to his will.

"*All right,*" Mamie resumed, with a dubious smile; "but why don't you go to Fanny, or Beckie, or Beilké the 'Black Cat'? You used to care for them more than for me. Why should you just come to me?"

Jake answered by characterizing the girls she had mentioned in terms rather too high-scented for print, protesting his loathing for them. Whereupon she subjected him to a rigid cross-examination as to his past conduct toward herself and her rivals; and although he managed to explain matters to her inward satisfaction, owing, chiefly, to a predisposition on her own part to credit his assertions on the subject, she could not help continuing obdurate and in a spiteful, vindictive mood.

"All you say is not worth a penny, and it is too late, *anyvay*," was her verdict. "You have a wife and a child; better go home and be a father to your *boy*." Her last words were uttered with some approach to sincerity, and she was mentally beginning to give herself credit for magnanimity and pious self-denial. She would have regretted her exhortation, however, had she been aware of its effect on her listener; for her mention of the boy and appeal to Jake as a father aroused in him a lively sense of the wrong he was doing. Moreover, while she was speaking his attention had been attracted to a loosened pillowcase ominously fluttering and flapping a yard or two off. The figure of his dead father, attired in burial linen, uprose to his mind.

"You don' vanted? Alla right, you be shorry," he said half-heartedly, turning to go.

"Hol' on!" she checked him, irritatedly. "How are you going to *fix* it? Are you *sure* she will take a divorce?"

"Will she have a choice then? She will have to take it. I won't live with her *anyhoy*," he replied, his passion once more welling up in his soul. "Mamie, my treasure, my glory!" he exclaimed, in tremulous accents. "Say that you are *shatichfied;* my heart will become lighter." Saying which, he strained her to his bosom, and fell to raining fervent kisses on her face. At first she made a faint attempt at freeing herself, and then suddenly clasping him with mad force she pressed her lips to his in a fury of passion.

The pillowcase flapped aloud, ever more sternly, warningly, portentously.

Jake cast an involuntary side glance at it. His spell of passion was broken and supplanted by a spell of benumbing terror. He had an impulse to withdraw his arms from the girl; but, instead, he clung to her all the faster, as if for shelter from the ghostlike thing.

With a last frantic hug Mamie relaxed her hold. "Remember now, Jake!" she then said, in a queer hollow voice. "Now it is all *settled*. Maybe you are making fun of me? If you are, you are playing with fire. Death to me—death to you!" she added, menacingly.

He wished to say something to reassure her, but his tongue seemed grown fast to his palate.

"Am I to blame?" she continued with ghastly vehemence, sobs ringing in her voice. "Who asked you to come? Did I lure you from her, then? I should sooner have thrown myself into the river than taken away somebody else's husband. You say yourself that you would not live with her, *anyvay*. But now it is all gone. Just try to leave me now!" And giving vent to her tears, she added, "Do you think my heart is no heart?"

A thrill of joyous pity shot through his frame. Once again he caught her to his heart, and in a voice quivering with tenderness he murmured: "Don't be uneasy, my dear, my gold, my pearl, my consolation! I will let my throat be cut, into fire or water will I go, for your sake."

"Dot's all right," she returned, musingly. "But how are you going to get rid of her? You von't go back on me, vill you?" she asked in English.

"*Me?* May I not be able to get away from this spot. Can it be that you still distrust me?"

"Swear!"

"How else shall I swear?"

"By your father, peace upon him."

"May my father as surely have a bright paradise," he said, with a show of alacrity, his mind fixed on the loosened pillowcase. "*Vell*, are you *shatichfied* now?"

"All right," she answered, in a matter-of-fact way,

and as if only half satisfied. "But do you think she will take money?"

"But I have none."

"Nobody asks you if you have. But would she take it, if you had?"

"If I had! I am sure she would take it; she would have to, for what would she gain if she did not?"

"Are you *sure*?"

" *'F caush!*"

"*Ach,* but, after all, why did you not tell me you liked me before she came?" she said testily, stamping her foot.

"Again!" he exclaimed, wincing.

"*All right;* wait."

She turned to go somewhere, but checked herself, and facing about, she exacted an additional oath of allegiance. After which she went to the other side of the chimney. When she returned she held one of her arms behind her.

"You will not let yourself be talked away from me?"

He swore.

"Not even if your father came to you from the other world—if he came to you in a dream, I mean—and told you to drop me?"

Again he swore.

"And you really don't care for Fanny?"

And again he swore.

"Nor for Beckie?"

The ordeal was too much, and he begged her to desist. But she wouldn't, and so, chafing under inexorable cross-examination, he had to swear again and again that he had never cared for any of Joe's female pupils or assistants except Mamie.

At last she relented.

"Look, piece of loafer you!" she then said, holding out an open bank book to his eyes. "But what is the *use*? It is not light enough, and you can not read, *anyvay*. You can eat, *dot's all. Vell,* you could make out figures, couldn't you? There are three hundred and forty dollars," she proceeded, pointing to the balance line, which represented the savings, for a marriage portion, of five years' hard toil. "It should be three hundred and sixty-five, but then for the twenty-five dollars you owe me I may as well light a mourner's candle, *ain' it?*"

When she had started to produce the bank book from her bosom he had surmised her intent, and while she was gone he was making guesses as to the magnitude of the sum to her credit. His most liberal estimate, however, had been a hundred and fifty dollars; so that the revelation of the actual figure completely overwhelmed him. He listened to her with a broad grin, and when she paused he burst out:

"Mamielé, you know what? Let us run away!"

"You are a fool!" she overruled him, as she tucked the bank book under her jacket. "I have a better plan. But tell me the truth, did you not guess I had money? Now you need not fear to tell me all."

He swore that he had not even dreamt that she possessed a bank account. How could he? And was it not because he had suspected the existence of such an account that he had come to declare his love to her and not to Fanny, or Beckie, or the "Black Cat"? No, may he be thunderstruck if it was. What does she take him for? On his part she is free to give the money away or throw it into the river. He will become a boss, and take her penniless, for he can not live without her; she is lodged in his heart; she is the only woman he ever cared for.

"Oh, but why did you not tell me all this long ago?" With which, speaking like the complete mistress of the situation that she was, she proceeded to expound a project, which had shaped itself in her lovelorn mind, hypothetically, during the previous few days, when she had been writhing in despair of ever having an occasion to put it into practice. Jake was to take refuge with her married sister in Philadelphia until Gitl was brought to terms. In the meantime some chum of his, nominated by Mamie and acting under her orders, would carry on negotiations. The State divorce, as she had already taken pains to ascertain, would cost fifty dollars; the rabbinical divorce would take five or eight

dollars more. Two hundred dollars would be deposited
with some Canal Street banker, to be paid to Gitl when
the whole procedure was brought to a successful termination. If she can be got to accept less, so much the
better; if not, Jake and Mamie will get along, anyhow.
When they are married they will open a dancing
school.

To all of which Jake kept nodding approval, once or
twice interrupting her with a demonstration of enthusiasm. As to the fate of his boy, Mamie deliberately cir-
cumvented all reference to the subject. Several times
Jake was tempted to declare his ardent desire to have
the child with them, and that Mamie should like him
and be a mother to him; for had she not herself found
him a bright and nice fellow? His heart bled at the
thought of having to part with Joey. But somehow the
courage failed him to touch upon the question. He saw
himself helplessly entangled in something foreboding
no good. He felt between the devil and the deep sea, as
the phrase goes; and unnerved by the whole situation
and completely in the shop girl's power, he was glad to
be relieved from all initiative—whether forward or
backward—to shut his eyes, as it were, and leaning
upon Mamie's strong arm, let himself be led by her in
whatever direction she chose.

"Do you know, Jake?—now I may as well tell you,"
the girl pursued, *à propos* of the prospective dancing
school; "do you know that Joe has been *bodering* me
to marry him? And he did not know I had a cent, either."

"An' you didn' vanted?" Jake asked, joyfully.

"Sure! I knew all along Jakie was my predestined
match," she replied, drawing his bulky head to her lips.
And following the operation by a sound twirl of his
ear, she added: "Only he is a great lump of hog, Jakie
is. But a heart is a clock: it told me I would have you
some day. I could have got *lots* of suitors—may the
two of us have as many thousands of dollars—and
business people, too. Do you see what I am doing for
you? Do you deserve it, *monkey you*?"

"Never min', you shall see what a *danshin' shchool*

I *shta't*. If I don't take away every *shcholar* from Jaw, my name won't be Jake. Won't he squirm!" he exclaimed, with childish ardor.

"Dot's all right; but foist min' dot you don't go back on me!"

An hour or two later Mamie with Jake by her side stood in front of the little window in the ferryhouse of the Pennsylvania Railroad, buying one ticket for the midnight train for Philadelphia.

"Min' je, Jake," she said anxiously a little after, as she handed him the ticket. "This is as good as a marriage certificate, do you understand?" And the two hurried off to the boat in a meager stream of other passengers.

9

THE PARTING

It was on a bright frosty morning in the following January, in the kitchen of Rabbi Aaronovitz, on the third floor of a rickety old tenement house, that Jake and Gitl, for the first time since his flight, came face to face. It was also to be their last meeting as husband and wife.

The low-ceiled room was fairly crowded with men and women. Besides the principal actors in the scene, the rabbi, the scribe, and the witnesses, and, as a matter of course, Mrs. Kavarsky, there was the rabbi's wife, their two children, and an envoy from Mamie, charged to look after the fortitude of Jake's nerve. Gitl, extremely careworn and haggard, was "in her own hair," thatched with a broad-brimmed winter hat of a brown colour, and in a jacket of black beaver. The rustic, "greenhornlike" expression was completely gone from her face and manner, and, although she now looked bewildered and as if terror-stricken, there was noticeable about her a suggestion of that peculiar air of self-confidence with which a few months' life in America is sure to stamp the looks and bearing of every immigrant. Jake, flushed and plainly nervous and fidgety, made repeated attempts to conceal his state of mind now by screwing up a grim face, now by giving his enormous head a haughty posture, now by talking aloud to his escort.

The tedious preliminaries were as trying to the rabbi as they were to Jake and Gitl. However, the venerable old man discharged his duty of dissuading the young couple from their contemplated step as scrupulously as he dared in view of his wife's signals to desist and not to risk the fee. Gitl, prompted by Mrs. Kavarsky, responded to all questions with an air of dazed resignation, while Jake, ever conscious of his guard's glance, gave his answers with bravado. At last the scribe, a gaunt middle-aged man, with an expression of countenance at once devout and businesslike, set about his task. Whereupon Mrs. Aaronovitz heaved a sigh of relief, and forthwith banished her two boys into the parlor.

An imposing stillness fell over the room. Little by little, however, it was broken, at first by whispers and then by an unrestrained hum. The rabbi, in a velvet skullcap, faded and besprinkled with down, presided with pious dignity, though apparently ill at ease, at the head of the table. Alternately stroking his yellowish-gray beard and curling his scanty sidelocks, he kept his eyes on the open book before him, now and then stealing a glance at the other end of the table, where the scribe was rapturously drawing the square characters of the holy tongue.

Gitl carefully looked away from Jake. But he invincibly haunted her mind, rendering her deaf to Mrs. Kavarsky's incessant buzz. His presence terrified her, and at the same time it melted her soul in a fire, torturing yet sweet, which impelled her at one moment to throw herself upon him and scratch out his eyes, and at another to prostrate herself at his feet and kiss them in a flood of tears.

Jake, on the other hand, eyed Gitl quite frequently, with a kind of malicious curiosity. Her general Americanized makeup, and, above all, that broad-brimmed, rather fussy, hat of hers, nettled him. It seemed to defy him, and as if devised for that express purpose. Every time she and her adviser caught his eye, a feeling of devouring hate for both would rise in his heart. He was panting to see his son; and, while he was thoroughly alive to the impossibility of making a child the witness of a divorce scene between father and mother, yet, in his fury, he interpreted their failure to bring Joey with them as another piece of malice.

"Ready!" the scribe at length called out, getting up with the document in his hand, and turning it over to the rabbi.

The rest of the assemblage also rose from their seats, and clustered round Jake and Gitl, who had taken places on either side of the old man. A beam of hard, cold sunlight, filtering in through a grimy windowpane and falling lurid upon the rabbi's wrinkled brow, enhanced the impressiveness of the spectacle. A momentary pause ensued, stern, weird, and casting a spell of awe over most of the bystanders, not excluding the rabbi. Mrs. Kavarsky even gave a shudder and gulped down a sob.

"Young woman!" Rabbi Aaronovitz began, with bashful serenity, "here is the writ of divorce all ready. Now thou mayst still change thy mind."

Mrs. Aaronovitz anxiously watched Gitl, who answered by a shake of her head.

"Mind thee, I tell thee once again," the old man pursued, gently. "Thou must accept this divorce with the same free will and readiness with which thou hast married thy husband. Should there be the slightest objection hidden in thy heart, the divorce is null and void. Dost thou understand?"

"Say that you are *saresfied,*" whispered Mrs. Kavarsky.

"*Ull ride,* I am *salesfiet,*" murmured Gitl, looking down on the table.

"Witnesses, hear ye what this young woman says? That she accepts the divorce of her own free will," the rabbi exclaimed solemnly, as if reading the Talmud.

"Then I must also tell you once more," he then addressed himself to Jake as well as to Gitl, "that this divorce is good only upon condition that you are also divorced by the Government of the land—by the court—do you understand? So it stands written in the separate paper which you get. Do you understand what I say?"

"Dot'sh alla right," Jake said, with ostentatious ease of manner. "I have already told you that the *dvosh* of the *court* is already *fikshed,* haven't I?" he added, even angrily.

Now came the culminating act of the drama. Gitl was affectionately urged to hold out her hands, bringing them together at an angle, so as to form a receptacle for the fateful piece of paper. She obeyed mechanically, her cheeks turning ghastly pale. Jake, also pale to his lips, his brows contracted, received the paper, and obeying directions, approached the woman who in the eye of the Law of Moses was still his wife. And then, repeating word for word after the rabbi, he said:

"Here is thy divorce. Take thy divorce. And by this divorce thou art separated from me and free for all other men!"

Gitl scarcely understood the meaning of the formula, though each Hebrew word was followed by its Yiddish translation. Her arms shook so that they had to be supported by Mrs. Kavarsky and by one of the witnesses.

At last Jake deposited the writ and instantly drew back.

Gitl closed her hands upon the paper as she had been instructed; but at the same moment she gave a violent tremble, and with a heartrending groan fell on the witness in a fainting swoon.

In the ensuing commotion Jake slipped out of the room, presently followed by Mamie's ambassador, who had remained behind to pay the bill.

Gitl was soon brought to by Mrs. Kavarsky and the mistress of the house. For a moment or so she sat staring about her, when, suddenly awakening to the meaning of the ordeal she had just been through, and finding

Jake gone, she clapped her hands and burst into a fit of sobbing.

Meanwhile the rabbi had once again perused the writ, and having caused the witnesses to do likewise, he made two diagonal slits in the paper.

"You must not forget, my daughter," he said to the young woman, who was at the moment crying as if her heart would break, "that you dare not marry again before ninety-one days, counting from today, go by; while you—where is he, the young man? Gone?" he asked with a frustrated smile and growing pale.

"You want him badly, don't you?" growled Mrs. Kavarsky. "Let him go I know where, the every-evil-in-him that he is!"

Mrs. Aaronovitz telegraphing to her husband that the money was safe in her pocket, he remarked sheepishly: "*He* may wed even today." Whereupon Gitl's sobs became still more violent, and she fell to nodding her head and wringing her hands.

"What are you crying about, foolish face that you are!" Mrs. Kavarsky fired out. "Another woman would thank God for having at last got rid of the lump of leavened bread. What say you, rabbi? A rowdy, a sinner of Israel, a *regely loifer,* may no good Jew know him! *Never min',* the Name, be It blessed, will send you your destined one, and a fine, learned, respectable man, too," she added significantly.

Her words had an instantaneous effect. Gitl at once composed herself, and fell to drying her eyes.

Quick to catch Mrs. Kavarsky's hint, the rabbi's wife took her aside and asked eagerly:

"Why, has she got a suitor?"

"What is the *differentz*? You need not fear; when there is a wedding canopy I shall employ no other man than your husband," was Mrs. Kavarsky's self-important but good-natured reply.

10

A DEFEATED VICTOR

When Gitl, accompanied by her friend, reached home, they were followed into the former's apartments by a batch of neighbors, one of them with Joey in tow. The moment the young woman found herself in her kitchen she collapsed, sinking down on the lounge. The room seemed to have assumed a novel aspect, which brought home to her afresh that the bond between her and Jake was now at last broken forever and beyond repair. The appalling fact was still further accentuated in her consciousness when she caught sight of the boy.

"Joeyelé! Joeyinké! Birdie! Little kitten!"—with which she seized him in her arms, and, kissing him all over, burst into tears, Then shaking with the child backward and forward, and intoning her words as Jewish women do over a grave, she went on: "Ai, you have no papa any more, Joeyelé! Yoselé, little crown, you will never see him again! He is dead, taté is!" Whereupon Yoselé, following his mother's example, let loose his stentorian voice.

"*Shurr-r up!*" Mrs. Kavarsky whispered, stamping her foot. "You want Mr. Bernstein to leave you, too, do you? No more is wanted than that he should get wind of your crying."

"Nobody will tell him," one of the neighbors put in, resentfully. "But, *anyhull,* what is the *used* crying?"

"Ask her, the piece of hunchback!" said Mrs. Kavarsky. "Another woman would dance for joy, and here she is whining, the cudgel. What is it you are snivelling about? That you have got rid of an unclean bone and a dunce, and that you are going to marry a young man of silk who is fit to be a rabbi, and is as *smart* and *ejecate* as a lawyer? You would have got a match like that in Povodye, would you? I dare say a man like Mr. Bernstein would not have spoken to you there. You ought to say Psalms for your coming to America. It is only here that it is possible for a blacksmith's wife to marry a learned man, who is a blessing both for God and people. And yet you are not *saresfied*! Cry away! If Bernstein refuses to go under the wedding canopy, Mrs. Kavarsky will no more *bodder* her head about you, depend upon it. It is not enough for her that I neglect *business* on her account," she appealed to the bystanders.

"Really, what are you crying about, Mrs. Podkovnik?" one of the neighbors interposed. "You ought to bless the hour when you became free."

All of which haranguing only served to stimulate Gitl's demonstration of grief. Having let down the boy, she went on clapping her hands, swaying in all directions, and wailing.

The truth must be told, however, that she was now continuing her lamentations by the mere force of inertia, and as if enjoying the very process of the thing. For, indeed, at the bottom of her heart she felt herself far from desolate, being conscious of the existence of a man who was to take care of her and her child, and even relishing the prospect of the new life in store for her. Already on her way from the rabbi's house, while her soul was full of Jake and the Polish girl, there had fluttered through her imagination a picture of the grocery business which she and Bernstein were to start with the money paid to her by Jake.

While Gitl thus sat swaying and wringing her hands, Jake, Mamie, her emissary at the divorce proceeding, and another mutual friend, were passengers on a Third Avenue cable car, all bound for the mayor's office. While Gitl was indulging herself in an exhibition of grief, her recent husband was flaunting a hilarious mood. He did feel a great burden to have rolled off his heart, and the proximity of Mamie, on the other hand, caressed his soul. He was tempted to catch her in his arms, and cover her glowing cheeks with kisses. But in his inmost heart he was the reverse of eager to reach the City Hall. He was painfully reluctant to part with his long-coveted freedom so soon after it had at last been attained, and before he had had time to relish it. Still worse than this thirst for a taste of liberty was a feeling which was now gaining upon him, that, instead of a conqueror, he had emerged from the rabbi's house the victim of an ignominious defeat. If he could now have seen Gitl in her paroxysm of anguish, his heart would perhaps have swelled with a sense of his triumph, and Mamie would have appeared to him the embodiment of his future happiness. Instead of this he beheld her, Bernstein, Yoselé, and Mrs. Kavarsky celebrating their victory and bandying jokes at his expense. Their future seemed bright with joy, while his own loomed dark and impenetrable. What if he should now dash into Gitl's apartments and, declaring his authority as husband, father, and lord of the house, fiercely eject the strangers, take Yoselé in his arms, and sternly command Gitl to mind her household duties?

But the distance between him and the mayor's office was dwindling fast. Each time the car came to a halt he wished the pause could be prolonged indefinitely; and when it resumed its progress, the violent lurch it gave was accompanied by a corresponding sensation in his heart.

BRITISH CLASSICS

☐ **LORD JIM by Joseph Conrad.**   (522346—$3.95)

☐ **HEART OF DARKNESS and THE SECRET SHARER by Joseph Conrad. Introduction by Albert J. Guerard.**   (523210—$3.95)

☐ **FAR FROM THE MADDING CROWD by Thomas Hardy. Afterword by James Wright Macalester.**   (523601—$4.95)

☐ **JUDE THE OBSCURE by Thomas Hardy. Foreword by A. Alvarez.**

(523709—$4.95)

☐ **THE MAYOR OF CASTERBRIDGE by Thomas Hardy. Afterword by Walter Allen.**   (525191—$4.95)

☐ **THE RETURN OF THE NATIVE by Thomas Hardy.**   (524713—$4.95)

☐ **KIM by Rudyard Kipling. Afterword by Raymond Carney.**   (525493—$3.95)

☐ **CAPTAINS COURAGEOUS by Rudyard Kipling. Afterword by C.A. Bodelsen.**   (523814—$3.95)

☐ **THE JUNGLE BOOKS by Rudyard Kipling. Afterword by Marcus Cunliffe.**   (523407—$4.95)

☐ **JUST SO STORIES by Rudyard Kipling.**   (524330—$3.95)

Prices slightly higher in Canada.
